ARTHUR KOESTLER

Born in Budapest in 1905, educated in Vienna, Arthur
Koestler early immersed himself in the major ideological
and social conflicts of his time. A Communist during the
1930's, and visitor for a time in the Soviet Union, he became disillusioned with the Party and left it in 1938.
Later that year in Spain, he was captured by the Fascist
forces under Franco, and sentenced to death. Released
through the last-minute intervention of the British government, he went to France where, the following year, he
again was arrested for his political views. Released again
in 1940, he went to England, where he has since made his
home. His novels, reportage, autobiographical works, and
political and cultural writings have established his world-
wide eminence as a commentator on the dilemmas of our
troubled century. Of his works, none demonstrates more
vividly his narrative power and uncompromising clarity of
vision than the remarkable

DARKNESS AT NOON

Arthur Koestler
Darkness at Noon

Translated by DAPHNE HARDY

BANTAM BOOKS
TORONTO • NEW YORK • LONDON • SYDNEY • AUCKLAND

🏳

DARKNESS AT NOON

*A Bantam Book / published by arrangement with
The Macmillan Company*

PRINTING HISTORY
Macmillan edition published May 1941

2nd printing	1944	5th printing	1949
3rd printing	1945	6th printing	1953
4th printing	1946	7th printing	1959

Modern Library edition published June 1946

Time, Inc. edition published March 1962

Bantam edition / April 1966

2nd printing	May 1966	3rd printing	August 1967

Bantam Modern Classic edition / February 1968

5th printing	September 1968	12th printing	November 1972
6th printing	February 1969	13th printing	February 1974
7th printing	August 1969	14th printing	May 1975
8th printing	August 1970	15th printing	July 1976
9th printing	October 1970	16th printing	November 1977
10th printing	April 1971	17th printing	June 1979
11th printing	February 1972	18th printing	March 1980
		19th printing	April 1981

ISBN 0-553-20135-2

Bantam Books are published by Bantam Books, Inc. Its trademark, consisting of the words "Bantam Books" and the portrayal of a bantam, is Registered in U.S. Patent and Trademark Office and in other countries. Marca Registrada. Bantam Books, Inc., 666 Fifth Avenue, New York, New York 10103.

PRINTED IN THE UNITED STATES OF AMERICA

28 27 26 25 24 23

He who establishes a dictatorship and does
not kill Brutus, or he who founds a republic
and does not kill the sons of Brutus, will
only reign a short time.

MACHIAVELLI:
Discorsi

Man, man, one cannot live quite without
pity.

DOSTOEVSKY:
Crime and Punishment

The characters in this book are fictitious. The historical circumstances which determined their actions are real. The life of the man N. S. Rubashov is a synthesis of the lives of a number of men who were victims of the so-called Moscow Trials. Several of them were personally known to the author. This book is dedicated to their memory.

PARIS.
October, 1938–April, 1940.

Contents

The First Hearing

Nobody can rule guiltlessly.
SAINT–JUST

1

THE CELL DOOR SLAMMED BEHIND RUBASHOV.

He remained leaning against the door for a few seconds, and lit a cigarette. On the bed to his right lay two fairly clean blankets, and the straw mattress looked newly filled. The wash-basin to his left had no plug, but the tap functioned. The can next to it had been freshly disinfected, it did not smell. The walls on both sides were of solid brick, which would stifle the sound of tapping, but where the heating and drain pipe penetrated it, it had been plastered and resounded quite well; besides, the heating pipe itself seemed to be noise-conducting. The window started at eye-level; one could see down into the courtyard without having to pull oneself up by the bars. So far everything was in order.

He yawned, took his coat off, rolled it up and put it on the mattress as a pillow. He looked out into the yard. The snow shimmered yellow in the double light of the moon and the electric lanterns. All round the yard, along the walls, a narrow track had been cleared for the daily exercise. Dawn had not yet appeared; the stars still shone clear and frostily, in spite of the lanterns. On the rampart of the outside wall, which lay opposite Rubashov's cell, a soldier with slanted rifle was marching the hundred steps up and down; he stamped at every step as if on parade. From time to time the yellow light of the lanterns flashed on his bayonet.

Rubashov took his shoes off, still standing at the window. He put out his cigarette, laid the stump on the floor at the end of his bedstead, and remained sitting on the mattress for a few minutes. He went back to the window once more. The courtyard was still; the sentry was just turning; above the machine-gun tower he saw a streak of the Milky Way.

Rubashov stretched himself on the bunk and wrapped himself in the top blanket. It was five o'clock and it was unlikely that one had to get up here before seven in winter. He was very sleepy and, thinking it over, decided that he would hardly be brought up for examination for another three or four days. He took his pince-nez off, laid it on the stone-paved floor next the cigarette stump, smiled and shut his eyes. He was warmly wrapped up in the blanket, and felt protected; for the first time in months he was not afraid of his dreams.

When a few minutes later the warder turned the light off from outside, and looked through the spy-hole into his cell, Rubashov, ex-Commissar of the People, slept, his back turned to the wall, with his head on his outstretched left arm, which stuck stiffly out of the bed; only the hand on the end of it hung loosely and twitched in his sleep.

2

An hour earlier, when the two officials of the People's Commissariat of the Interior were hammering on Rubashov's door, in order to arrest him, Rubashov was just dreaming that he was being arrested.

The knocking had grown louder and Rubashov strained to wake up. He was practised in tearing himself out of nightmares, as the dream of his first arrest had for years returned periodically and ran its course with the regularity of clockwork. Sometimes, by a strong effort of will, he managed to stop the clockwork, to pull himself out of the dream by his own effort, but this time he did not succeed; the last weeks had exhausted him, he sweated and panted in his sleep; the clockwork hummed, the dream went on.

He dreamed, as always, that there was a hammering on his door, and that three men stood outside, waiting to arrest him. He could see them through the closed door, standing outside, banging against its framework. They had on brand-new uniforms, the becoming costume of the Prætorian guards of the German Dictatorship; on their caps and sleeves they wore their insignia: the aggressively barbed cross; in their free hand they carried grotesquely big pistols; their straps and trappings smelled of fresh leather. Now they were in his room, at his bedside. Two were overgrown peasant lads with thick lips and fish-eyes; the third was short and fat. They stood by his bed, holding their pistols in their hands, and breathing heavily at him. It was quite still save for the asthmatic panting of the short, fat one. Then someone in an upper story pulled a plug and the water rushed down evenly through the pipes in the walls.

The clockwork was running down. The hammering on Rubashov's door became louder; the two men outside, who had come to arrest him, hammered alternatively and blew on their frozen hands. But Rubashov could not wake up, although he knew that now would follow a particularly painful scene: the three still stand by his bed and he tries to put on his dressing-gown. But the sleeve is turned inside out; he cannot manage to put his arm into it. He strives vainly until a kind of paralysis descends on him: he cannot move, although everything depends on his getting the sleeve on in time. This tormenting helplessness lasts a number of seconds, during which Rubashov moans and feels the cold wetness on his temples and the hammering on his door penetrates his sleep like a distant roll of drums; his arm under the pillow twitches in the feverish effort to find the sleeve of his dressing-gown; then at last he is released by the first smashing blow over the ear with the butt of the pistol. . . .

With the familiar sensation, repeated and lived through again a hundred times, of this first blow—from which his deafness dated—he usually woke up. For a while he would still shiver and his hand, jammed under the pillow, would continue to strain for the dressing-gown sleeve; for, as a rule, before he was fully awake, he still had the last and worst stage to go through. It consisted of a dizzy, shapeless feeling that this awakening was the real dream and that in fact he was still lying on the damp stone floor of the dark cell, at his feet the can, next to his head the jug of water and a few crumbs of bread. . . .

This time also, for a few seconds, the bemused condition held, the uncertainty whether his groping hand would touch the can or the switch of his bedside lamp. Then the light blazed on and the mist parted. Rubashov breathed deeply several times and, like a convalescent, his hands folded on his breast, enjoyed the delicious feeling of freedom and safety. He dried his forehead and the bald patch on the back of his head with the sheet, and blinked up with already returning irony at the colour-print of No. 1, leader of the Party, which hung over his bed on the wall of his room—and on the walls of all the rooms next to, above or under his; on all the walls of the house, of the town, and of the enormous country for which he had fought and suffered, and which now had taken him up again in its enormous, protecting lap. He was now fully awake; but the hammering on his door went on.

3

The two men who had come to arrest Rubashov stood outside on the dark landing and consulted each other. The porter Vassilij, who had shown them the way up-stairs, stood in the open lift doorway and panted with fear. He was a thin old man; above the torn collar of the military overcoat he had thrown over his nightshirt appeared a broad red scar which gave him a scrofulous look. It was the result of a neck wound received in the Civil War, throughout which he had fought in Rubashov's Partisan regiment. Later Rubashov had been ordered abroad and Vassilij had heard of him only occasionally, from the newspaper which his daughter read to him in the evenings. She had read to him the speeches which Rubashov made to the Congresses; they were long and difficult to understand, and Vassilij could never quite manage to find in them the tone of voice of the little bearded Partisan commander who had known such beautiful oaths that even the Holy Madonna of Kasan must have smiled at them. Usually Vassilij fell asleep in the middle of these speeches, but always woke up when his daughter came to the final sentences and the applause, solemnly raising her voice. To every one of the ceremonial endings, "Long live the International! Long live the Revolution! Long live No. 1", Vassilij added a heartfelt "Amen" under his breath, so that the daughter should not hear it; then took his jacket off, crossed himself secretly and with a bad conscience and went to bed. Above his bed also hung a portrait of No. 1, and next to it a photograph of Rubashov as Partisan commander. If that photograph were found, he would probably also be taken away.

It was cold, dark and very quiet on the staircase. The younger of the two men from the Commissariat of the Interior proposed to shoot the lock of the door to pieces. Vassilij leant against the lift door; he had not had the time to put on his boots properly, and his hands trembled so much that he could not tie the laces. The elder of the two men was against shooting; the arrest had to be carried out discreetly. They both blew on their stiff hands and began again to hammer against the door; the younger banged on it with the butt of his revolver. A few floors below them a woman screamed in a piercing voice. "Tell her to shut up," said the young man to Vassilij. "Be quiet," shouted Vassilij. "Here is Authority." The woman became quiet at once. The young man changed over to belabouring the door with his boots. The noise filled the whole staircase; at last the door fell open.

The three of them stood by Rubashov's bed, the young man with his pistol in his hand, the old man holding himself stiffly as though standing to attention; Vassilij stood a few steps behind them, leaning against the wall. Rubashov was still drying the sweat from the back of his head; he looked at them shortsightedly with sleepy eyes. "Citizen Rubashov, Nicolas Salmanovitch, we arrest you in the name of the law," said the young man. Rubashov felt for his glasses under the pillow and propped himself up a bit. Now that he had his glasses on, his eyes had the expression which Vassilij and the elder official knew from old photographs and colour-prints. The elder official stood more stiffly to attention; the young one, who had grown up under new heroes, went a step closer to the bed; all three saw that he was about to say or do something brutal to hide his awkwardness.

"Put that gun away, comrade," said Rubashov to him. "What do you want with me, anyhow?"

"You hear you are arrested," said the boy. "Put your clothes on and don't make a fuss."

"Have you got a warrant?" asked Rubashov.

The elder official pulled a paper out of his pocket, passed it to Rubashov and stood again to attention.

Rubashov read it attentively. "Well, good," he said. "One never is any the wiser from those things; the devil take you."

"Put your clothes on and hurry up," said the boy. One saw that his brutality was no longer put on, but was natural to him. A fine generation have we produced, thought Rubashov. He recalled the propaganda posters on which youth was always represented with a laughing face. He felt very tired. "Pass me my dressing-gown, instead of fumbling about with your revolver," he said to the boy. The boy reddened, but remained silent. The elder official passed the dressing-gown to Rubashov. Rubashov worked his arm into the sleeve. "This time it goes at least," he said with a strained smile. The three others did not understand and said nothing. They watched him as he got slowly out of bed and collected his crumpled clothes together.

The house was silent after the one shrill woman's cry, but they had the feeling that all the inhabitants were awake in their beds, holding their breath.

Then they heard someone in an upper story pull the plug and the water rushing down evenly through the pipes.

4

At the front door stood the car in which the officials had come, a new American make. It was still dark; the chauffeur had put on the headlights, the street was asleep or pretended to be. They got in, first the lad, then Rubashov, then the elder official. The chauffeur, who was also in uniform, started the car. Beyond the corner the asphalt surface stopped; they were still in the centre of the town; all around them were big modern buildings of nine and ten stories, but the roads were country cart-tracks of frozen mud, with a thin powdering of snow in the cracks. The chauffeur drove at a walking pace and the superbly sprung motor car creaked and groaned like an oxen wagon.

"Drive faster," said the lad, who could not bear the silence in the car.

The chauffeur shrugged his shoulders without looking round. He had given Rubashov an indifferent and unfriendly look as he got into the car. Rubashov had once had an accident; the man at the wheel of the ambulance-car had looked at him in the same way. The slow, jolting drive through the dead streets, with the wavering light of the head lamps before them, was difficult to stand. "How far is it?" asked Rubashov, without looking at his companions. He nearly added: to the hospital. "A good half-hour," said the older man in uniform. Rubashov dug cigarettes out of his pocket, put one in his mouth and passed the packet round automatically. The young man refused abruptly, the elder one took two and passed one on to the chauffeur. The chauffeur touched his cap and gave everybody a light, holding the steering-wheel with one hand. Rubashov's heart became lighter; at the same time he was annoyed with himself for it. Just the time to get sentimental, he thought. But he could not resist the temptation to speak and to awaken a little human warmth around him. "A pity for the car," he said. "Foreign cars cost quite a bit of gold, and after half a year on our roads they are finished."

"There you are quite right. Our roads are very backward," said the old official. By his tone Rubashov realized that he had understood his helplessness. He felt like a dog to whom one had just thrown a bone; he decided not to speak again. But suddenly the boy said aggressively:

"Are they any better in the capitalist states?"

Rubashov had to grin. "Were you ever outside?" he asked.

"I know all the same what it is like there," said the boy. "You need not try to tell me stories about it."

"Whom do you take me for, exactly?" asked Rubashov very quietly. But he could not prevent himself from adding: "You really ought to study the Party history a bit."

The boy was silent and looked fixedly at the driver's back. Nobody spoke. For the third time the driver choked off the panting engine and let it in again, cursing. They jolted through the suburbs; in the appearance of the miserable wooden houses nothing was changed. Above their crooked silhouettes hung the moon, pale and cold.

5

In every corridor of the new model prison electric light was burning. It lay bleakly on the iron galleries, on the bare whitewashed walls, on the cell doors with the name cards and the black holes of the judas-eyes. This colourless light, and the shrill echoless sound of their steps on the tiled paving were so familiar to Rubashov that for a few seconds he played with the illusion that he was dreaming again. He tried to make himself believe that the whole thing was not real. If I succeed in believing that I am dreaming, then it will really be a dream, he thought.

He tried so intensely that he nearly became dizzy; then immediately a choking shame rose in him. This has to be gone through, he thought. Right through to the end. They reached cell No. 404. Above the spy-hole was a card with his name on it, Nicolas Salmanovitch Rubashov. They have prepared everything nicely, he thought; the sight of his name on the card made an uncanny impression on him. He wanted to ask the warder for an extra blanket, but the door had already slammed behind him.

6

At regular intervals the warder had peeped through the judas into Rubashov's cell. Rubashov had been lying tranquilly on the bunk; only his hand had twitched from time

to time in his sleep. Beside the bunk lay his pince-nez and
a cigarette stump on the tiles.

At seven o'clock in the morning—two hours after he
had been brought to cell 404—Rubashov was woken
by a bugle call. He had slept dreamlessly, and his head
was clear. The bugle repeated three times the same blar-
ing sequence. The trembling tones re-echoed and died out;
a malevolent silence remained.

It was not yet quite day; the contours of the can and of
the wash-basin were softened by the dim light. The window grate was a black pattern silhouetted against the
dingy glass; top left a broken pane had a piece of newspaper stuck over it. Rubashov sat up, reached for the pince-
nez and the cigarette stump at the end of his bed and lay
back again. He put on the pince-nez and managed to
make the stump glow. The silence lasted. In all the whitewashed cells of this honeycomb in concrete, men were
simultaneously arising from their bunks, cursing and groping about on the tiles, yet in the isolation cells one heard
nothing—except from time to time retreating footsteps in
the corridor. Rubashov knew that he was in an isolation
cell and that he was to stay there until he was shot. He
drew his fingers through his short, pointed beard, smoked
his cigarette-end and lay still.

So I shall be shot, thought Rubashov. Blinking, he
watched the movement of his big toe, which stuck up
vertically at the end of the bed. He felt warm, secure
and very tired; he had no objection to dozing straight off
into death, there and then, if only one let him remain
lying under the warm blanket. "So they are going to shoot
you," he told himself. He slowly moved his toes in the
sock and a verse occurred to him which compared the
feet of Christ to a white roebuck in a thornbush. He
rubbed his pince-nez on his sleeve with the gesture familiar to all his followers. He felt in the warmth of the
blanket almost perfectly happy and feared only one
thing, to have to get up and move. "So you are going to
be destroyed," he said to himself half-aloud and lit another cigarette, although only three were left. The first

cigarettes on an empty stomach caused him sometimes
a slight feeling of drunkenness; and he was already in
that peculiar state of excitement familiar to him from former experiences of the nearness of death. He knew at the
same time that this condition was reprehensible and, from
a certain point of view, unpermissible, but at the moment
he felt no inclination to take that point of view. Instead,
he observed the play of his stockinged toes. He smiled. A
warm wave of sympathy for his own body, for which usually he had no liking, played over him and its imminent
destruction filled him with a self-pitying delight. "The old
guard is dead," he said to himself. "We are the last."
"We are going to be destroyed." "For golden lads and
girls all must, as chimney-sweepers, come to dust. . . ."
He tried to recall the tune of "come to dust . . .", but only
the words came to him. "The old guard is dead," he repeated and tried to remember their faces. He could only
recall a few. Of the first Chairman of the International,
who had been executed as a traitor, he could only conjure up a piece of a check waistcoat over the slightly
rotund belly. He had never worn braces, always leather
belts. The second Prime Minister of the Revolutionary
State, also executed, had bitten his nails in moments of
danger. . . . History will rehabilitate you, thought Rubashov, without particular conviction. What does history
know of nail-biting? He smoked and thought of the dead,
and of the humiliation which had preceded their death.
Nevertheless, he could not bring himself to hate No. 1
as he ought to. He had often looked at the colour-print
of No. 1 hanging over his bed and tried to hate it. They
had, between themselves, given him many names, but in
the end it was No. 1 that stuck. The horror which No. 1
emanated, above all consisted in the possibility that he
was in the right, and that all those whom he killed had
to admit, even with the bullet in the back of their necks,
that he conceivably might be in the right. There was no
certainty; only the appeal to that mocking oracle they
called History, who gave her sentence only when the
jaws of the appealer had long since fallen to dust.
    Rubashov had the feeling that he was being watched

through the spy-hole. Without looking, he knew that a pupil pressed to the hole was staring into the cell; a moment later the key did actually grind in the heavy lock. It took some time before the door opened. The warder, a little old man in slippers, remained at the door:

"Why didn't you get up?" he asked.

"I am ill," said Rubashov.

"What is the matter with you? You cannot be taken to the doctor before to-morrow."

"Toothache," said Rubashov.

"Toothache, is it?" said the warder, shuffled out and banged the door.

Now I can at least remain lying here quietly, thought Rubashov, but it gave him no more pleasure. The stale warmth of the blanket became a nuisance to him, and he threw it off. He again tried to watch the movements of his toes, but it bored him. In the heel of each sock there was a hole. He wanted to darn them, but the thought of having to knock on the door and request needle and thread from the warder prevented him; the needle would probably be refused him in any case. He had a sudden wild craving for a newspaper. It was so strong that he could smell the printer's ink and hear the crackling and rustling of the pages. Perhaps a revolution had broken out last night, or the head of a state had been murdered, or an American had discovered the means to counteract the force of gravity. His arrest could not be in it yet; inside the country, it would be kept secret for a while, but abroad the sensation would soon leak through, they would print ten-year-old photographs dug out of the newspaper archives and publish a lot of nonsense about him and No. 1. He now no longer wanted a newspaper, but with the same greed desired to know what was going on in the brain of No. 1. He saw him sitting at his desk, elbows propped, heavy and gloomy, slowly dictating to a stenographer. Other people walked up and down while dictating, blew smoke-rings or played with a ruler. No. 1 did not move, did not play, did not blow rings. . . . Rubashov noticed suddenly that he himself had been walking up and down for the last five minutes; he had risen from the bed without realizing it. He was caught again by his old ritual of never walking on the edges of the paving stones, and he already knew the pattern by heart. But his thoughts had not left No. 1 for a second, No. 1, who, sitting at his desk and dictating immovably, had gradually turned into his own portrait, into that well-known colour-print, which hung over every bed or sideboard in the country and stared at people with its frozen eyes.

Rubashov walked up and down in the cell, from the door to the window and back, between bunk, wash-basin and bucket, six and a half steps there, six and a half steps back. At the door he turned to the right, at the window to the left: it was an old prison habit; if one did not change the direction of the turn one rapidly became dizzy. What went on in No. 1's brain? He pictured to himself a cross-section through that brain, painted neatly with grey water-colour on a sheet of paper stretched on a drawing-board with drawing-pins. The whorls of grey matter swelled to entrails, they curled round one another like muscular snakes, became vague and misty like the spiral nebulæ on astronomical charts. . . . What went on in the inflated grey whorls? One knew everything about the far-away nebulæ, but nothing about the whorls. That was probably the reason that history was more of an oracle than a science. Perhaps later, much later, it would be taught by means of tables of statistics, supplemented by such anatomical sections. The teacher would draw on the blackboard an algebraic formula representing the conditions of life of the masses of a particular nation at a particular period: "Here, citizens, you see the objective factors which conditioned this historical process." And, pointing with his ruler to a grey foggy landscape between the second and third lobe of No. 1's brain: "Now here you see the subjective reflection of these factors. It was this which in the second quarter of the twentieth century led to the triumph of the totalitarian principle in the East of Europe." Until this stage was reached, politics would remain bloody dilettantism, mere superstition and black magic. . . .

Rubashov heard the sound of several people marching

down the corridor in step. His first thought was: now the
beating-up will start. He stopped in the middle of
the cell, listening, his chin pushed forward. The marching
steps came to a halt before one of the neighboring cells,
a low command was heard, the keys jangled. Then there
was silence.

Rubashov stood stiffly between the bed and the bucket,
held his breath, and waited for the first scream. He remembered that the first scream, in which terror still pre-
dominated over physical pain, was usually the worst;
what followed was already more bearable, one got used
to it and after a time one could even draw conclusions on
the method of torture from the tone and rhythm of the
screams. Towards the end, most people behaved in the
same way, however different they were in temperament and
voice: the screams became weaker, changed over into
whining and choking. Usually the door would slam soon
after. The keys would jangle again; and the first scream
of the next victim often came even before they had
touched him, at the mere sight of the men in the doorway.

Rubashov stood in the middle of his cell and waited for
the first scream. He rubbed his glasses on his sleeve
and said to himself that he would not scream this time
either, whatever happened to him. He repeated this sentence as if praying with a rosary. He stood and waited;
the scream still did not come. Then he heard a faint
clanging, a voice murmured something, the cell-door
slammed. The footsteps moved to the next cell.

Rubashov went to the spy-hole and looked into the corridor. The men stopped nearly opposite his cell, at No.
407. There was the old warder with two orderlies dragging a tub of tea, a third carrying a basket with slices of
black bread, and two uniformed officials with pistols.
There was no beating-up; they were bringing breakfast. . . .

No. 407 was just being given bread. Rubashov could
not see him. No. 407 was presumably standing in the reg-
ulation position, a step behind the door; Rubashov could
only see his forearms and hands. The arms were bare
and very thin; like two parallel sticks, they stuck out of

the doorway into the corridor. The palms of the invisible
No. 407 were turned upwards, curved in the shape of
a bowl. When he had taken the bread, he clasped his
hands and withdrew into the darkness of his cell. The
door slammed.

Rubashov abandoned the spy-hole and resumed his
marching up and down. He ceased rubbing his spectacles on his sleeve, put them in place, breathed deeply
and with relief. He whistled a tune and waited for his
breakfast. He remembered with a slight feeling of uneasiness those thin arms and the curved hands; they reminded him vaguely of something he could not define.
The outlines of those stretched-out hands and even the
shadows on them were familiar to him—familiar and
yet gone from his memory like an old tune or the smell
of a narrow street in a harbour.

7

The procession had unlocked and slammed a row of
doors, but not yet his. Rubashov went back to the judas,
to see whether they were coming at last; he was looking
forward to the hot tea. The tub had been steaming, and
thin slices of lemon had floated on its surface. He took
off his pince-nez and pressed his eye to the spy-hole. His
range of sight held four of the cells opposite: Nos. 401
to 407. Above the cells ran a narrow iron gallery; behind
it were more cells, those on the second floor. The procession was just coming back along the corridor from
the right; evidently they first did the odd numbers, then
the even. Now they stood at No. 408; Rubashov only saw
the backs of the two uniformed men with the revolver
belts; the rest of the procession stood outside his view-
range. The door slammed; now they all came to No. 406.
Rubashov saw again the steaming tub and the orderly
with the bread basket in which only a few slices were
left. The door of No. 406 slammed instantly; the cell was
uninhabited. The procession approached, passed his door
and stopped at No. 402.

Rubashov began to drum on the door with his fists. He
saw that the two orderlies with the tub looked at each

other and glanced at his door. The warder busied himself with the lock on the door of No. 402 and pretended not to hear. The two men in uniform stood with their backs to Rubashov's spy-hole. Now the bread was being passed in through the door of No. 402; the procession started to move on. Rubashov drummed more loudly. He took a shoe off and banged on the door with it.

The bigger of the two men in uniform turned round, stared expressionlessly at Rubashov's door and turned away again. The warder slammed the door of No. 402. The orderlies with the tub of tea stood about hesitantly. The man in uniform who had turned round said something to the older warder, who shrugged his shoulders and with jangling keys shuffled to Rubashov's door. The orderlies with the tub followed him; the orderly with the bread said something through the spy-hole to No. 402.

Rubashov drew back a step from his door and waited for it to open. The tension inside him gave way suddenly; he did not care any more whether he was given tea or not. The tea in the tub had no longer steamed on the way back and the slices of lemon on the rest of the pale yellow liquid had looked limp and shrunken.

The key was turned in his door, then a staring pupil appeared in the spy-hole and disappeared again. The door flew open. Rubashov had seated himself on the bed and was putting his shoe on again. The warder held the door open for the big man in uniform who entered the cell. He had a round, clean-shaven skull and expressionless eyes. His stiff uniform creaked; so did his boots; Rubashov thought he could smell the leather of his revolver belt. He stopped next to the bucket and looked round the cell, which seemed to have become smaller through his presence.

"You have not cleaned up your cell," he said to Rubashov. "You know the regulations, surely."

"Why was I omitted at breakfast?" said Rubashov, examining the officer through his pince-nez.

"If you want to argue with me, you will have to stand up," said the officer.

"I haven't got the slightest desire to argue or even to

speak to you," said Rubashov, and laced up his shoe.

"Then don't bang on the door next time, else the usual disciplinary measures will have to be applied to you," said the officer. He looked round the cell again. "The prisoner has no mop to clean the floor," he said to the warder.

The warder said something to the bread-orderly, who vanished down the corridor at a trot. The two other orderlies stood in the open doorway and gazed into the cell with curiosity. The second officer had his back turned; he stood in the corridor with his legs straddled and his hands behind his back.

"The prisoner has no eating bowl either," said Rubashov, still busied with the lacing of his shoe. "I suppose you want to save me the trouble of a hunger-strike. I admire your new methods."

"You are mistaken," said the officer, looking at him expressionlessly. He had a broad scar on his shaven skull and wore the ribbon of the Revolutionary Order in his buttonhole. So he was in the Civil War, after all, thought Rubashov. But that is long ago and makes no difference now. . . .

"You are mistaken. You were left out at breakfast because you had reported yourself sick."

"Toothache," said the old warder, who stood leaning against the door. He still wore slippers, his uniform was crumpled and spotted with grease.

"As you like," said Rubashov. It was on the tip of his tongue to ask whether it was the latest achievement of the régime to treat invalids by compulsory fasting, but he controlled himself. He was sick of the whole scene.

The bread-orderly came running, panting and flapping a dirty rag. The warder took the rag out of his hand and threw it in a corner next to the bucket.

"Have you any more requests?" asked the officer without irony.

"Leave me alone and stop this comedy," said Rubashov. The officer turned to go, the warder jangled his bunch of keys. Rubashov went to the window, turning his back on them. When the door had slammed he remem-

bered that he had forgotten the chief thing and with a
bound he was back at the door.

"Paper and pencil," he shouted through the spy-hole.
He took off his pince-nez and stuck his eye to the hole to
see whether they turned round. He had shouted very
loudly, but the procession moved down the corridor
as if it had heard nothing. The last he saw of it was the
back of the officer with the shaven skull and the broad
leather belt with the revolver-case attached to it.

8

Rubashov resumed walking up and down his cell, six
and a half steps to the window, six and a half steps back.
The scene had stirred him; he recapitulated it in minute detail while rubbing his pince-nez on his sleeve. He
tried to hold on to the hatred he had for a few minutes
felt for the officer with the scar; he thought it might
stiffen him for the coming struggle. Instead, he fell once
more under the familiar and fatal constraint to put himself in the position of his opponent, and to see the scene
through the other's eyes. There he had sat, this man Rubashov, on the bunk—small, bearded, arrogant—and in an
obviously provocative manner, had put his shoe on over
the sweaty sock. Of course, this man Rubashov had his
merits and a great past; but it was one thing to see
him on the platform at a congress and another, on a palliasse in a cell. So that is the legendary Rubashov,
thought Rubashov in the name of the officer with the expressionless eyes. Screams for his breakfast like a school-
boy and isn't even ashamed. Cell not cleaned up. Holes
in his sock. Querulous intellectual. Conspired against law
and order: whether for money or on principle makes no
difference. We did not make the revolution for cranks.
True, he helped to make it; at that time he was a man;
but now he is old and self-righteous, ripe for liquidation.
Perhaps he was so even at that time; there were many
soap bubbles in the revolution which burst afterwards.
If he still had a vestige of self-respect, he would clean
his cell.

For a few seconds Rubashov wondered whether he should really scrub the tiles. He stood hesitantly in the middle of the cell, then put his pince-nez on again and propped himself at the window.

The yard was now in daylight, a greyish light tinged with yellow, not unfriendly, promising more snow. It was about eight—only three hours had passed since he first entered the cell. The walls surrounding the yard looked like those of barracks; iron gates were in front of all the windows, the cells behind them were too dark for one to see into them. It was impossible even to see whether anyone stood directly behind his window, looking down, like him, at the snow in the yard. It was nice snow, slightly frozen; it would crackle if one walked on it. On both sides of the path which ran round the yard at a distance of ten paces from the walls, a hilly parapet of snow had been shovelled up. On the rampart opposite the sentinel was pacing up and down. Once, when turning, he spat in a wide arc into the snow; then leant over the ramp to see where it had fallen and frozen.

The old disease, thought Rubashov. Revolutionaries should not think through other people's minds.

Or, perhaps they should? Or even ought to?

How can one change the world if one identifies oneself with everybody?

How else can one change it?

He who understands and forgives—where would he find a motive to act?

Where would he not?

They will shoot me, thought Rubashov. My motives will be of no interest to them. He leaned his forehead on the window pane. The yard lay white and still.

So he stood a while, without thinking, feeling the cool glass on his forehead. Gradually, he became conscious of a small but persistent ticking sound in his cell.

He turned round listening. The knocking was so quiet that at first he could not distinguish from which wall it came. While he was listening, it stopped. He started tapping himself, first on the wall over the bucket, in the direction of No. 406, but got no answer. He tried the other wall, which separated him from No. 402, next to his bed. Here he got an answer. Rubashov sat down comfortably on the bunk, from where he could keep an eye on the spy-hole, his heart beating. The first contact was always very exciting.

No. 402 was now tapping regularly; three times with short intervals, then a pause, then again three times, then again a pause, then again three times. Rubashov repeated the same series to indicate that he heard. He was anxious to find out whether the other knew the "quadratic alphabet"—otherwise there would be a lot of fumbling until he had taught it to him. The wall was thick, with poor resonance; he had to put his head close to it to hear clearly and at the same time he had to watch the spy-hole. No. 402 had obviously had a lot of practice; he tapped distinctly and unhurriedly, probably with some hard object such as a pencil. While Rubashov was memorizing the numbers, he tried, being out of practice, to visualize the square of letters with the 25 compartments—five horizontal rows with five letters in each. No. 402 first tapped five times—accordingly the fifth row: V to Z; then twice; so it was the second letter of the row: W. Then a pause; then two taps—the second row, F—J; then three taps— the third letter of the row: H. Then three times and then five times; so fifth letter of the third row: O. He stopped.

WHO?

A practical person, thought Rubashov; he wants to know at once whom he has to deal with. According to the revolutionary etiquette, he should have started with a political tag; then given the news; then talked of food and tobacco; much later only, days later, if at all, did one introduce oneself. However, Rubashov's experience had been so far confined to countries in which the Party was persecuted, not persecutor, and the members of the Party, for conspiratorial reasons, knew each other only by their Christian names—and changed even these so often that a name lost all meaning. Here, evidently, it was different. Rubashov hesitated as to whether he should give his name. No. 402 became impatient; he knocked again: WHO?

Well, why not? thought Rubashov. He tapped out his full name: NICOLAS SALMANOVITCH RUBASHOV, and waited for the result.

For a long time there was no answer. Rubashov smiled; he could appreciate the shock it had given his neighbour. He waited a full minute and then another; finally, he shrugged his shoulders and stood up from the bunk. He resumed his walk through the cell, but at every turn he stopped, listening to the wall. The wall remained mute. He rubbed his pince-nez on his sleeve, went slowly, with tired steps, to the door and looked through the spy-hole into the corridor.

The corridor was empty; the electric lamps spread their stale, faded light; one did not hear the slightest sound. Why had No. 402 become dumb?

Probably from fear; he was afraid of compromising himself through Rubashov. Perhaps No. 402 was an unpolitical doctor or engineer who trembled at the thought of his dangerous neighbour. Certainly without political experience, else he would not have asked for the name as a start. Presumably mixed up in some affair of sabotage. Has obviously been in prison quite a time already, has perfected his tapping and is devoured by the wish to prove his innocence. Still in the simple belief that his subjective guilt or innocence makes a difference, and with no idea of the higher interests which are really at stake. In all probability he was now sitting on his bunk, writing his hundredth protest to the authorities, who will never read it, or the hundredth letter to his wife, who will never receive it; has in despair grown a beard—a black Pushkin beard—has given up washing and fallen into the habit of biting his nails and of erotic day-dreams. Nothing is worse in prison than the consciousness of one's innocence; it prevents acclimatization and undermines one's morale. . . . Suddenly the ticking started again.

Rubashov sat down quickly on the bunk; but he had already missed the first two letters. No. 402 was now tapping quickly and less clearly, he was obviously very excited:

... RVES YOU RIGHT.

"Serves you right."

That was unexpected. No. 402 was a conformist. He hated the oppositional heretics, as one should, believed that history ran on rails according to an infallible plan and an infallible pointsman, No. 1. He believed that his own arrest was merely the result of a misunderstanding, and that all the catastrophes of the last years—from China to Spain, from the famine to the extermination of the old guard—were either regrettable accidents or caused by the devilish tricks of Rubashov and his oppositional friends. No. 402's Pushkin beard vanished; he now had a clean-shaven, fanatical face; he kept his cell painfully tidy and conformed strictly to the regulations. There was no sense in arguing with him; this kind was unteachable. But neither was there any sense in cutting off the only and perhaps the last contact with the world.

WHO? knocked Rubashov very clearly and slowly. The answer came in agitated fits and starts:

NONE OF YOUR BUSINESS.

AS YOU LIKE, tapped Rubashov, and stood up to resume his wandering through the cell, taking the conversation to be ended. But the tapping started again, this time very loudly and ringingly—No. 402 had obviously taken off a shoe in order to give more weight to his words:

LONG LIVE H.M. THE EMPEROR!

So that's it, thought Rubashov. There still exist genuine and authentic counter-revolutionaries—and we thought that nowadays they only occurred in the speeches of No. 1, as scapegoats for his failures. But there sits a real one, an alibi for No. 1 in flesh and blood, roaring, just as he should: long live the Monarch. ...

AMEN, tapped out Rubashov, grinning. The answer came immediately, still louder if possible.

SWINE!

Rubashov was amusing himself. He took off his pince-nez and tapped with the metal edge, in order to change the tone, with a drawling and distinguished intonation:

DIDN'T QUITE UNDERSTAND.

No. 402 seemed to go into a frenzy. He hammered out HOUN'—, but the D did not come. Instead, his fury suddenly flown, he tapped:

WHY HAVE YOU BEEN LOCKED UP?

What touching simplicity. . . . The face of No. 402 underwent a new transformation. It became that of a young Guards officer, handsome and stupid. Perhaps he even wore a monocle. Rubashov tapped with his pince-nez:

POLITICAL DIVERGENCIES.

A short pause. No. 402 was obviously searching his brain for a sarcastic answer. It came at last:

BRAVO! THE WOLVES DEVOUR EACH OTHER.

Rubashov gave no answer. He had enough of this sort of entertainment and started on his wanderings again. But the officer in 402 had become conversational. He tapped:

RUBASHOV . . .

Well, this was just about verging on familiarity.

YES? answered Rubashov.

No. 402 seemed to hesitate; then came quite a long sentence:

WHEN DID YOU LAST SLEEP WITH A WOMAN?

Certainly No. 402 wore an eye-glass; probably he was tapping with it and the bared eye was twitching nervously. Rubashov did not feel repelled. The man at least showed himself as he was; which was pleasanter than if he had tapped out monarchist manifestos. Rubashov thought it over for a bit, and then tapped:

THREE WEEKS AGO.

The answer came at once:

TELL ME ALL ABOUT IT.

Well, really, that was going a bit far. Rubashov's first impulse was to break off the conversation; but he remembered the man might later become very useful as a connecting link to No. 400 and the cells beyond. The cell to the left was obviously uninhabited; there the chain broke off. Rubashov racked his brain. An old pre-war song came to his memory, which he had heard as a student, in some cabaret where black-stockinged ladies danced the French can-can. He sighed resignedly and tapped with his pince-nez:

SNOWY BREASTS FITTING INTO CHAMPAGNE
GLASSES ...

He hoped that was the right tone. It was apparently,
for No. 402 urged:

GO ON. DETAILS.

By this time he was doubtless plucking nervously at
his moustache. He certainly had a little moustache with
twirled-up ends. The devil take the man; he was the only
connecting link; one had to keep up with him. What did
officers talk about in the mess? Women and horses.
Rubashov rubbed his pince-nez on his sleeve and tapped
conscientiously:

THIGHS LIKE A WILD MARE.

He stopped, exhausted. With the best will in the world
he could not do more. But No. 402 was highly satisfied.

GOOD CHAP! he tapped enthusiastically. He was
doubtless laughing boisterously, but one heard nothing;
he slapped his thighs and twirled his moustache, but one
saw nothing. The abstract obscenity of the dumb wall
was embarrassing to Rubashov.

GO ON, urged No. 402.

He couldn't. THAT'S ALL—tapped Rubashov and re-
gretted it immediately. No. 402 must not be offended.
But fortunately No. 402 did not let himself be offended. He
tapped on obstinately with his monocle:

GO ON—PLEASE, PLEASE. ...

Rubashov was now again practised to the extent of no
longer having to count the signs; he transformed them
automatically into acoustic perception. It seemed to him
that he actually heard the tone of voice in which No. 402
begged for more erotic material. The begging was repeated:

PLEASE—PLEASE. ...

No. 402 was obviously still young—probably grown
up in exile, sprung from an old Army family, sent back
into his country with a false passport—and he was obviously tormenting himself badly. He was doubtless plucking at his little moustache, had stuck his monocle to his

eye again and was staring hopelessly at the whitewashed
wall.

MORE—PLEASE, PLEASE.

. . . Hopelessly staring at the dumb, whitewashed wall,
staring at the stains caused by the damp, which gradually began to assume the outlines of the woman with
the champagne-cup breasts and the thighs of a wild mare.

TELL ME MORE—PLEASE.

Perhaps he was kneeling on the bunk with his hands
folded—like the prisoner in No. 407 had folded them to
receive his piece of bread.

And now at last Rubashov knew of what experience
this gesture had reminded him—the imploring gesture of
the meagre, stretched-out hands. *Pietà* . . .

9

Pietà. . . . The picture gallery of a town in southern
Germany on a Monday afternoon. There was not a soul in
the place, save for Rubashov and the young man whom
he had come to meet; their conversation took place on a
round plush sofa in the middle of an empty room, the
walls of which were hung with tons of heavy female flesh
by the Flemish masters. It was in the year 1933, during
the first months of terror, shortly before Rubashov's arrest. The movement had been defeated, its members were
outlawed and hunted and beaten to death. The Party was
no longer a political organization; it was nothing but a
thousand-armed and thousand-headed mass of bleeding
flesh. As a man's hair and nails continue to grow after his
death, so movement still occurred in individual cells,
muscles and limbs of the dead Party. All over the country
existed small groups of people who had survived the
catastrophe and continued to conspire underground.
They met in cellars, woods, railway stations, museums
and sport clubs. They continuously changed their sleeping quarters, also their names and their habits. They
knew each other only by their Christian names and did
not ask for each other's addresses. Each gave his life
into the other's hands, and neither trusted the other
an inch. They printed pamphlets in which they tried to

convince themselves and others that they were still alive.
They stole at night through narrow suburban streets and
wrote on the walls the old slogans, to prove that they
were still alive. They climbed at dawn on factory chimneys and hoisted the old flag, to prove that they were
still alive. Only a few people ever saw the pamphlets and
they threw them away quickly, for they shuddered at the
message of the dead; the slogans on the walls were gone
by cock's crow and the flags were pulled down from the
chimneys; but they always appeared again. For all over
the country there were small groups of people who called
themselves "dead men on holiday", and who devoted
their lives to proving that they still possessed life.

They had no communication with each other; the nerve
fibres of the Party were torn and each group stood for
itself. But, gradually, they started to put out feelers
again. Respectable commercial travellers came from
abroad, with false passports and with double-bottomed
trunks; they were the Couriers. Usually they were caught,
tortured and beheaded; others took their place. The
Party remained dead, it could neither move nor breathe,
but its hair and nails continued to grow; the leaders abroad
sent galvanizing currents through its rigid body, which
caused spasmodic jerks in the limbs.

Pietà. . . . Rubashov forgot No. 402 and went on
doing his six and a half steps up and down; he found
himself again on the round plush sofa in the picture
gallery, which smelled of dust and floor polish. He had
driven straight from the station to the appointed meeting place and had arrived a few minutes too soon. He
was fairly sure that he had not been observed. His suit-
case, which contained samples of a Dutch firm's latest
novelties in dentists' equipment, lay in the cloakroom.
He sat on the round plush sofa, looking through his
pince-nez at the masses of flabby flesh on the walls,
and waited.

The young man, who was known by the name of
Richard, and was at this time leader of the Party group
in this town, came a few minutes too late. He had
never seen Rubashov and Rubashov had never seen him,

either. He had already gone through two empty galleries when he saw Rubashov on the round sofa. On Rubashov's knee lay a book: Goethe's *Faust* in Reclam's Universal Edition. The young man noticed the book, gave a hurried look round and sat down beside Rubashov. He was rather shy and sat on the edge of the sofa, about two feet away from Rubashov, his cap on his knees. He was a locksmith by trade and wore a black Sunday suit; he knew that a man in overalls would be conspicuous in a museum.

"Well?" he said. "You must please excuse my being late."

"Good," said Rubashov. "Let us first go through your people. Have you got a list?"

The young man called Richard shook his head. "I don't carry lists," he said. "I've got it all in my head— addresses and all."

"Good," said Rubashov. "But what if they get you?"

"As for that," said Richard, "I have given a list to Anny. Anny is my wife, you know."

He stopped and swallowed and his Adam's apple moved up and down; then for the first time he looked Rubashov full in the face. Rubashov saw that he had inflamed eyes; the slightly prominent eyeballs were covered by a net of red veins; his chin and cheeks were stubbly over the black collar of the Sunday suit. "Anny was arrested last night, you know," he said and looked at Rubashov; and Rubashov read in his eyes the dull, childish hope that he, the Courier of the Central Committee, would work a miracle and help him.

"Really?" said Rubashov and rubbed his pince-nez on his sleeve. "So the police have got the whole list."

"No," said Richard, "for my sister-in-law was in the flat when they came to fetch her, you know, and she managed to pass it to her. It is quite safe with my sister-in-law, you know; she is married to a police constable, but she is with us."

"Good," said Rubashov. "Where were you when your wife was arrested?"

"This is how it was," said Richard. "I haven't slept in

my flat for three months, you know. I have a pal who is
a cinema operator; I can go to him, and when the per-
formance is over I can sleep in his cabin. One gets in
straight from the street by the fire escape. And cinema
for nothing. . . ." He paused and swallowed. "Anny was
always given free tickets by my pal, you know, and when
it was dark she would look up to the projecting room.
She couldn't see me, but sometimes I could see her face
quite well when there was a lot of light on the
screen. . . ."

He stopped. Just opposite him hung a "Last Judgment": curly-headed cherubs with rotund behinds flying
up into a thunderstorm, blowing trumpets. To Richard's
left hung a pen drawing by a German master; Rubashov could only see a part of it—the rest was hidden
by the plush back of the sofa and by Richard's head:
the Madonna's thin hands, curved upwards, hollowed
to the shape of a bowl, and a bit of empty sky covered
with horizontal pen-lines. More was not to be seen as,
while speaking, Richard's head persisted immovably in
the same position on his slightly bowed, reddish neck.

"Really?" said Rubashov. "How old is your wife?"

"She is seventeen," said Richard.

"Really? And how old are you?"

"Nineteen," said Richard.

"Any children?" asked Rubashov and stretched his
head out a little, but he could not see more of the
drawing.

"The first one is on the way," said Richard. He sat
motionlessly, as if cast in lead.

There was an interval and then Rubashov let him re-
cite the list of the Party's members. It consisted of about
thirty names. He asked a few questions and wrote down
several addresses in his order book for the Dutch firm's
dental instruments. He wrote them in the spaces he had
left in a long list of local dentists and respectable citizens
copied out of the telephone directory. When they had
finished, Richard said:

"Now I would like to give you a short report on our
work, comrade."

"Good," said Rubashov. "I'm listening."

Richard made his report. He sat slightly bent forward, a couple of feet away from Rubashov, on the narrow plush sofa, his big red hands on the knees of his Sunday suit; he did not change his position once while speaking. He spoke of the flags on the chimney stacks, the inscriptions on the walls and the pamphlets which were left in the factory latrines, stiffly and matter-of-factly as a book-keeper. Opposite him the trumpet-blowing angels flew into the thunderstorm, at the back of his head an invisible Virgin Mary stretched out her thin hands; from all around the walls colossal breasts, thighs and hips stared at them.

Breasts fitting to champagne glasses came into Rubashov's head. He stood still on the third black tile from the cell-window, to hear whether No. 402 was still tapping. There was no sound. Rubashov went to the spy-hole and looked over to No. 407, who had stretched out his hands for the bread. He saw the grey steel door of cell 407 with the small black judas. Electric light was burning in the corridor as always; it was bleak and silent; one could hardly believe that human beings lived behind those doors.

While the young man called Richard was giving his report, Rubashov did not interrupt him. Of the thirty men and women whom Richard had grouped together after the catastrophe, only seventeen remained. Two, a factory hand and his girl, had thrown themselves out of the window when they came to fetch them. One had deserted—had left the town, vanished. Two were suspected of being spies for the police, but this was not certain. Three had left the Party as a protest against the policy of the Central Committee; two of them had founded a new oppositional group, the third had joined the Moderates. Five had been arrested last night, among them Anny; it was known that at least two of these five were no longer alive. So there remained seventeen, who continued to distribute pamphlets and scribble on walls.

Richard told him all this in minute detail, so that

Rubashov should understand all the personal connections and causes which were particularly important; he did not know that the Central Committee had their own man in the group, who had long ago given Rubashov most of the facts. He did not know either that this man was his pal, the cinema operator, in whose cabin he slept; neither that this person had been for a long time on intimate terms with his wife Anny, arrested last night. None of this did Richard know; but Rubashov knew it. The movement lay in ruins, but its Intelligence and Control Department still functioned; it was perhaps the only part of it which did function, and at that time Rubashov stood at the head of it. The bull-necked young man in the Sunday suit did not know that either; he only knew that Anny had been taken away and that one had to go on distributing pamphlets and scribbling on walls; and that Rubashov, who was a comrade from the Central Committee of the Party, was to be trusted like a father; but that one must not show this feeling nor betray any weakness. For he who was soft and sentimental was no good for the task and had to be pushed aside—pushed out of the movement, into solitude and the outer darkness.

Outside in the corridor steps were approaching. Rubashov went to the door, took his pince-nez off and put his eye to the judas. Two officials with leather revolver-belts were conducting a young peasant along the corridor; behind them came the old warder with the bunch of keys. The peasant had a swollen eye and dry blood on his upper lip; as he passed he wiped his sleeve over his bleeding nose; his face was flat and expressionless. Further down the corridor, outside Rubashov's range, a cell door was unlocked and slammed. Then the officials and the warder came back alone.

Rubashov walked up and down in his cell. He saw himself, sitting on the round plush sofa next to Richard; he heard again the silence which had fallen when the boy had finished his report. Richard did not move; sat with his hands on his knees and waited. He sat as one

who had confessed and was waiting for the father-con-
fessor's sentence. For a long while Rubashov said nothing.
Then he said:

"Good. Is that all?"

The boy nodded; his Adam's apple moved up and
down.

"Several things are not clear in your report," said
Rubashov. "You spoke repeatedly of the leaflets and
pamphlets which you made yourselves. They are known
to us and their content was criticized sharply. There
are several phrases which the Party cannot accept."

Richard looked at him frightenedly: he reddened.
Rubashov saw the skin over his cheek-bones becoming
hot and the net of red veins in his inflamed eyes become denser.

"On the other hand," continued Rubashov, "we have
repeatedly sent you our printed material for distribution,
amongst which was the special small-size edition of the
official Party organ. You received these consignments."

Richard nodded. The heat did not leave his face.

"But you did not distribute our material; it is not even
mentioned in your report. Instead, you circulated the
material made by yourselves—without the control or
approval of the Party."

"B-but we had to," Richard brought out with a great
effort. Rubashov looked at him attentively through his
pince-nez; he had not noticed before that the boy stammered. "Curious," he thought, "this is the third case
in a fortnight. We have a surprising number of defectives
in the Party. Either it is because of the circumstances under which we work—or the movement itself promotes a
selection of defectives. . . ."

"You m-must understand, c-comrade," said Richard
in growing distress. "The t-tone of your propaganda material was wrong, b-because———"

"Speak quietly," said Rubashov suddenly in a sharp
tone, "and don't turn your head to the door."

A tall young man in the uniform of the black body-
guard of the régime had entered the room with his
girl. The girl was a buxom blonde; he held her round

her broad hip, her arm lay on his shoulder. They paid no attention to Rubashov and his companion and stopped in front of the trumpeting angels, with their backs to the sofa.

"Go on talking," said Rubashov in a calm, low voice and automatically took his cigarette case out of his pocket. Then he remembered that one may not smoke in museums and put the case back. The boy sat as if paralysed by an electric shock, and stared at the two. "Go on talking," said Rubashov quietly. "Did you stammer as a child? Answer and don't look over there."

"S-sometimes," Richard managed to bring out with a great effort.

The couple moved along the row of pictures. They stopped in front of a nude of a very fat woman, who lay on a satin couch and looked at the spectator. The man murmured something presumably funny, for the girl giggled and glanced fleetingly at the two figures on the sofa. They moved on a bit, to a still-life of dead pheasants and fruit.

"Sh-shouldn't we go?" asked Richard.

"No," said Rubashov. He was afraid that when they stood up the boy in his agitation would behave conspicuously. "They will soon go. We have our backs to the light; they cannot see us clearly. Breathe slowly and deeply several times. It helps."

The girl went on giggling and the pair moved slowly towards the way out. In passing, they both turned their heads towards Rubashov and Richard. They were just about to leave the room, when the girl pointed her finger at the pen drawing on the *Pietà;* they stopped to look at it. "Is it very di-disturbing when I s-stammer?" asked Richard in a low voice, staring down at the floor.

"One must control oneself," said Rubashov shortly. He could not now let any feeling of intimacy creep into the conversation.

"It will b-be b-better in a minute," said Richard, and his Adam's apple moved convulsively up and down. "Anny always laughed at me about it, you kn-now."

As long as the couple remained in the room, Rubashov could not steer the conversation. The back of the man in uniform nailed him down next to Richard. The common danger helped the boy over his shyness; he even slid a bit closer to Rubashov.

"She was fond of me all the s-same," he continued, whispering in another, quieter kind of agitation. "I n-never knew quite how to take her. She did not want to have the child, b-but she could not get rid of it. P-per-haps they won't do anything to her as she is p-pregnant. You c-can see it quite clearly, you know. Do you think that they beat pregnant women, t-too?"

With his chin, he indicated the young man in uniform. In the same instant the young man suddenly turned his head towards Richard. For a second they looked at each other. The young man in uniform said something to the girl in a low voice; she too turned her head. Rubashov again grasped his cigarette case, but this time let it go while still in his pocket. The girl said something and pulled the young man away with her. The pair of them left the gallery slowly, the man rather hesitatingly. One heard the girl giggling again outside and their footsteps receding.

Richard turned his head and followed them with his eyes. As he moved, Rubashov gained a better view of the drawing; he could now see the Virgin's thin arms up to the elbow. They were meagre, little girl's arms, raised weightlessly towards the invisible shaft of the cross.

Rubashov looked at his watch. The boy moved a bit further away from him on the sofa.

"We must come to a conclusion," said Rubashov. "If I understand you rightly, you said that you purposely did not distribute our material because you did not agree with its contents. But neither did we agree with the contents of your leaflets. You will understand, comrade, that certain consequences must come of that."

Richard turned his reddened eyes towards him. Then he lowered his head. "You know yourself that the material you sent was full of nonsense," he said in a flat voice. He had suddenly stopped stammering.

"Of that I know nothing," said Rubashov drily.

"You wrote as if nothing had happened," said Richard in the same tired voice. "They beat the Party to shambles, and you just wrote phrases about our unbroken will to victory—the same kind of lies as the communiqué in the Great War. Whoever we showed it to would just spit. You must know all that yourself."

Rubashov looked at the boy, who now sat leaning forward, elbows on his knees, his chin on his red fists. He answered drily:

"For the second time you ascribe to me an opinion which I do not hold. I must ask you to stop doing so."

Richard looked at him unbelievingly out of his inflamed eyes. Rubashov went on.

"The Party is going through a severe trial. Other revolutionary parties have been through even more difficult ones. The decisive factor is our unbroken will. Whoever now goes soft and weak does not belong in our ranks. Whoever spreads an atmosphere of panic plays into our enemy's hands. What his motives are in doing so does not make any difference. By his attitude he becomes a danger to our movement, and will be treated accordingly."

Richard still sat with his chin in his hands, his face turned to Rubashov.

"So I am a danger to the movement," he said. "I play into the enemy's hands. Probably I am paid for doing so. And Anny, too. . . ."

"In your pamphlets," continued Rubashov in the same dry tone of voice, "of which you admit to be the author, there frequently appear phrases such as this: that we have suffered a defeat, that a catastrophe has befallen the Party, and that we must start afresh and change our policy fundamentally. That is defeatism. It is demoralizing and it lames the Party's fighting spirit."

"I only know," said Richard, "that one must tell people the truth, as they know it already, in any case. It is ridiculous to pretend to them."

"The last congress of the Party," Rubashov went on, "stated in a resolution that the Party has not suffered a defeat and has merely carried out a strategic retreat; and that there is no reason whatever for changing its previous policy."

"But that's rubbish," said Richard.

"If you go on in this style," said Rubashov, "I am afraid we will have to break off the conversation."

Richard was silent for a while. The room began to darken, the contours of the angels and women on the walls became still softer and more nebulous.

"I am sorry," said Richard. "I mean: the Party leadership is mistaken. You talk of a 'strategic retreat' while half of our people are killed, and those which are left are so pleased to be still alive that they go over to the other side in shoals. These hair-splitting resolutions which you people outside fabricate are not understood here. . . ."

Richard's features began to become hazy in the growing dusk. He paused, then added:

"I suppose Anny also made a 'strategic retreat' last night. Please, you must understand. Here we are all living in the jungle. . . ."

Rubashov waited to see whether he still had anything to say, but Richard said nothing. Dusk was falling rapidly now. Rubashov took his pince-nez off and rubbed it on his sleeve.

"The Party can never be mistaken," said Rubashov. "You and I can make a mistake. Not the Party. The Party, comrade, is more than you and I and a thousand others like you and I. The Party is the embodiment of the revolutionary idea in history. History knows no scruples and no hesitation. Inert and unerring, she flows towards her goal. At every bend in her course she leaves the mud which she carries and the corpses of the drowned. History knows her way. She makes no mistakes. He who has not absolute faith in History does not belong in the Party's ranks."

Richard said nothing; head on his fists, he kept his immovable face turned to Rubashov. As he remained silent, Rubashov went on:

"You have prevented the distribution of our material;

you have suppressed the Party's voice. You have distributed pamphlets in which every word was harmful and false. You wrote: 'The remains of the revolutionary movement must be gathered together and all powers hostile to tyranny must unite; we must stop our old internal struggles and start the common fight afresh.' That is wrong. The Party must not join the Moderates. It is they who in all good faith have countless times betrayed the movement, and they will do it again next time, and the time after next. He who compromises with them buries the revolution. You wrote: 'When the house is on fire, all must help to quench it; if we go on quarrelling about doctrines, we will all be burnt to ashes.' That is wrong. We fight against the fire with water; the others do with oil. Therefore we must first decide which is the right method, water or oil, before uniting the fire-brigades. One cannot conduct politics that way. It is impossible to form a policy with passion and despair. The Party's course is sharply defined, like a narrow path in the mountains. The slightest false step, right or left, takes one down the precipice. The air is thin; he who becomes dizzy is lost."

Dusk had now progressed so far that Rubashov could no longer see the hands on the drawing. A bell rang twice, shrill and penetratingly; in a quarter of an hour the museum would be closed. Rubashov looked at his watch; he still had the decisive word to say, then it would be over. Richard sat motionless next to him, elbows on knees.

"Yes, to that I have no answer," he said finally, and again his voice was flat and very tired. "What you say is doubtless true. And what you said about that mountain path is very fine. But all I know is that we are beaten. Those who are still left desert us. Perhaps, because it is too cold up on our mountain path. The others—they have music and bright banners and they all sit round a nice warm fire. Perhaps that is why they have won. And why we are breaking our necks."

Rubashov listened in silence. He wanted to hear whether the young man had any more to say, before he himself pronounced the decisive sentence. Whatever Richard said, it could not now change that sentence in any way; but yet he waited.

Richard's heavy form was more and more obscured by the dusk. He had moved still further away on the round sofa; he sat with bent shoulders and his face nearly buried in his hands. Rubashov sat straight up on the sofa and waited. He felt a slight drawing pain in his upper jaw; probably the defective eye-tooth. After a while he heard Richard's voice:

"What will happen to me now?"

Rubashov felt for the aching tooth with his tongue. He felt the need to touch it with his finger before pronouncing the decisive word, but forbade himself. He said quietly:

"I have to inform you, in accordance with the Central Committee's decision, that you are no longer a member of the Party, Richard."

Richard did not stir. Again Rubashov waited for a while, before standing up. Richard remained sitting. He merely lifted his head, looked up at him and asked:

"Is that what you came here for?"

"Chiefly," said Rubashov. He wanted to go, but still stood there in front of Richard and waited.

"What will now become of me?" asked Richard. Rubashov said nothing. After a while, Richard said:

"Now I suppose I cannot live at my friend's cabin either?"

After a short hesitation Rubashov said:

"Better not."

He was at once annoyed with himself for having said it, and he was not certain whether Richard had understood the meaning of the phrase. He looked down on the seated figure:

"It will be better for us to leave the building separately. Good-bye."

Richard straightened himself, but remained sitting. In the twilight Rubashov could only guess the expression of the inflamed, slightly prominent eyes; yet it was just this blurred image of the clumsy, seated figure which stamped itself in his memory for ever.

He left the room and crossed the next one, which was equally empty and dark. His steps creaked on the parquet floor. Only when he had reached the way out did he remember that he had forgotten to look at the picture of the *Pietà;* now he would only know the detail of the folded hands and part of the thin arms, up to the elbow.

On the steps which led down from the entrance he stopped. His tooth was hurting him a bit more; it was cold outside. He wrapped the faded grey woollen scarf more tightly round his neck. The street lamps were already lit in the big quiet square in front of the gallery; at this hour there were few people about; a narrow tram ringing its bell clanged up the elm-bordered avenue. He wondered whether he would find a taxi here.

On the bottom step Richard caught him up, panting breathlessly. Rubashov went straight on, neither hastening nor slacking his pace and without turning his head. Richard was half a head bigger than he and much broader, but he held his shoulders hunched, making himself small beside Rubashov and shortening his steps. After a few paces he said:

"Was that meant to be a warning, when I asked you if I could go on living with my friend and you said 'Better not'?"

Rubashov saw a taxi with bright lights coming up the avenue. He stopped on the curb and waited for it to come closer. Richard was standing beside him. "I have no more to say to you, Richard," Rubashov said, and hailed the taxi.

"Comrade—b-but you couldn't d-denounce me, comrade . . ." said Richard. The taxi slowed down, it was no more than twenty paces from them. Richard stood hunched in front of Rubashov; he had caught the sleeve of Rubashov's overcoat and was talking straight down into his face; Rubashov felt his breath and a slight dampness sprayed on to his forehead.

"I am not an enemy of the Party," said Richard. "You c-can't throw me to the wolves, c-comrade. . . ."

The taxi stopped at the curb; the driver must certainly have heard the last word. Rubashov calculated rapidly that it was no use sending Richard away; there was a policeman posted a hundred yards further up. The driver, a little old man in a leather jacket, looked at them expressionlessly.

"To the station," said Rubashov and got in. The taxi driver reached back with his right arm and slammed the door behind him. Richard stood on the edge of the pavement, cap in hand; his Adam's apple moved rapidly up and down. The taxi started; it drove off towards the policeman; it passed the policeman. Rubashov preferred not to look back, but he knew that Richard was still standing on the edge of the pavement, staring at the taxi's red rear-light.

For a few minutes, they drove through busy streets; the taxi driver turned his head round several times, as if he wanted to make sure that his passenger was still inside. Rubashov knew the town too little to make out whether they were really going to the station. The streets became quieter; at the end of an avenue appeared a massive building with a large illuminated clock, they stopped at the station.

Rubashov got out; the taxis in this town had no meters yet. "How much is it?" he asked.

"Nothing," said the driver. His face was old and creased; he pulled a dirty red rag out of the pocket of his leather coat and blew his nose with ceremony.

Rubashov looked at him attentively through his pince-nez. He was certain he had not seen that face before. The driver put his handkerchief away. "For people like yourself, sir, it's always free," he said and busied himself with the handbrake. Suddenly he held his hand out. It was an old man's hand with thickened veins and black nails. "Good luck, sir," he said, smiling rather sheepishly at Rubashov. "If your young friend ever wants anything—my stand is in front of the museum. You can send him my number, sir."

Rubashov saw to his right a porter leaning against a
a post and looking at them. He did not take the driver's
outstretched hand; he put a coin into it and went into
the station, without a word.

He had to wait an hour for the departure of the train.
He drank bad coffee in the buffet; his tooth tormented
him. In the train he fell into a doze and dreamed he had
to run in front of the engine. Richard and the taxi-
driver were standing in it; they wanted to run him
over because he had cheated them of the fare. The
wheels came rattling closer and closer and his feet refused to move. He woke up with nausea and felt the
cold perspiration on his forehead; the other people in
the compartment looked at him in slight astonishment.
Outside was night; the train was rushing through a dark
enemy country, the affair with Richard had to be concluded, his tooth was aching. A week later he was
arrested.

10

Rubashov leant his forehead against the window
and looked down into the yard. He was tired in the legs
and dizzy in the head from walking up and down. He
looked at his watch; a quarter to twelve; he had been
walking to and fro in his cell for nearly four hours on
end, since first the *Pietà* had occurred to him. It did
not surprise him; he was well enough acquainted with
the day-dreams of imprisonment, with the intoxication
which emanates from the whitewashed walls. He remembered a younger comrade, by profession a hair-
dresser's assistant, telling him how, in his second and
worst year of solitary confinement, he had dreamed for
seven hours on end with his eyes open; in doing so he
had walked twenty-eight kilometres, in a cell five paces
long, and had blistered his feet without noticing it.

This time, however, it had come rather quickly; already, the first day the voice had befallen him, whereas
during his previous experiences it had started only after
several weeks. Another strange thing was that he had
thought of the past; chronic prison day-dreamers

dreamed nearly always of the future—and of the past only as it might have been, never as it actually *had* been. Rubashov wondered what other surprises his mental apparatus held in store for him. He knew from experience that confrontation with death always altered the mechanism of thought and caused the most surprising reactions—like the movements of a compass brought close to the magnetic pole.

The sky was still heavy with an imminent fall of snow; in the courtyard two men were doing their daily walk on the shovelled path. One of the two repeatedly looked up at Rubashov's window—apparently the news of his arrest had already spread. He was an emaciated man with a yellow skin and a hare-lip, wearing a thin waterproof which he clutched round his shoulders as if freezing. The other man was older and had wrapped a blanket round himself. They did not speak to each other during their round, and after ten minutes they were fetched back into the building by an official in uniform with a rubber truncheon and a revolver. The door in which the official waited for them lay exactly opposite Rubashov's window; before it closed behind the man with the hare-lip, he once more looked up towards Rubashov. He certainly could not see Rubashov, whose window must have appeared quite dark from the courtyard; yet his eyes lingered on the window searchingly. I see you and do not know you; you cannot see me and yet obviously you know me, thought Rubashov. He sat down on the bed and tapped to No. 402:

WHO ARE THEY?

He thought that No. 402 was probably offended and would not answer. But the officer did not seem to bear grudges; he answered immediately:

POLITICAL.

Rubashov was surprised; he had held the thin man with the hare-lip for a criminal.

OF YOUR SORT? he asked.

NO—OF YOURS, tapped No. 402, in all probability grinning with a certain satisfaction. The next sentence was louder—tapped with the monocle, perhaps.

HARE-LIP, MY NEIGHBOUR, NO. 400, WAS TORTURED YESTERDAY.

Rubashov remained silent a minute and rubbed his pince-nez on his sleeve, although he was only using it to tap with. He first wanted to ask "WHY?" but tapped instead:

HOW?

402 tapped back drily:

STEAMBATH.

Rubashov had been beaten up repeatedly during his last imprisonment, but of this method he only knew by hearsay. He had learned that every *known* physical pain was bearable; if one knew beforehand exactly what was going to happen to one, one stood it as a surgical operation—for instance, the extraction of a tooth. Really bad was only the unknown, which gave one no chance to foresee one's reactions and no scale to calculate one's capacity of resistance. And the worst was the fear that one would then do or say something which could not be recalled.

WHY? asked Rubashov.

POLITICAL DIVERGENCIES, tapped No. 402 ironically.

Rubashov put his pince-nez on again and felt in his pocket for his cigarette case. He had only two cigarettes left. Then he tapped:

AND HOW ARE THINGS WITH YOU?

THANKS, VERY WELL . . . tapped No. 402 and dropped the conversation.

Rubashov shrugged his shoulders; he lit his last cigarette but one and resumed his walking up and down. Strangely enough, what was in store for him made him nearly glad. He felt his stale melancholia leave him, his head become clearer, his nerves tauten. He washed face, arms and chest in cold water over the wash-basin, rinsed his mouth and dried himself with his handkerchief. He whistled a few bars and smiled—he was always hopelessly out of tune, and only a few days ago somebody had said to him: "If No. 1 were musical, he would long ago have found a pretext to have you shot."

"He will anyhow," he had answered, without seriously believing it.

He lit his last cigarette and with a clear head began to work out the line to take when he would be brought up for cross-examination. He was filled by the same quiet and serene self-confidence as he had felt as a student before a particularly difficult examination. He called to memory every particular he knew about the subject "steambath." He imagined the situation in detail and tried to analyse the physical sensations to be expected, in order to rid them of their uncanniness. The important thing was not to let oneself be caught unprepared. He now knew for certain that they would not succeed in doing so, any more than had the others over there; he knew he would not say anything he did not want to say. He only wished they would start soon.

His dream came to his mind: Richard and the old taxi-driver pursuing him, because they felt themselves cheated and betrayed by him.

I will pay my fare, he thought with an awkward smile.

His last cigarette was nearly at an end; it was burning his finger-tips; he let it drop. He was about to stamp it out, but thought better of it; he bent down, picked it up and stubbed out the glowing stump slowly on the back of his hand, between the blue snaky veins. He drew out this procedure for exactly half a minute, checking it by the second hand of his watch. He was pleased with himself: his hand had not twitched once during the thirty seconds. Then he continued his walk.

The eye which had been observing him for several minutes through the spy-hole withdrew.

11

The lunch procession went past in the corridor; Rubashov's cell was again left out. He wanted to spare himself the humiliation of looking through the spy-hole, so he did not discover what there was for lunch; but the smell of it filled his cell, and it smelled good.

He felt a strong desire for a cigarette. He would have to procure himself cigarettes somehow, in order to be able to concentrate; they were more important than food. He waited for half an hour after the doling out of food, then he began to hammer on the door. It took another quarter of an hour before the old warder shuffled up. "What do you want?" he asked, in his usual surly tone.

"Cigarettes to be fetched for me from the canteen," said Rubashov.

"Have you got prison vouchers?"

"My money was taken from me on my arrival," said Rubashov.

"Then you must wait until it has been changed for vouchers."

"How long will that take in this model establishment of yours?" asked Rubashov.

"You can write a letter of complaint," said the old man.

"You know quite well that I have neither paper nor pencil," said Rubashov.

"To buy writing materials you have to have vouchers," said the warder.

Rubashov could feel his temper rising, the familiar pressure in the chest and the choking feeling in the throat; but he controlled it. The old man saw Rubashov's pupils glitter sharply through his pince-nez; it reminded him of the colour prints of Rubashov in uniform, which in the old days one used to see everywhere; he smiled with senile spite and stepped back a pace.

"You little heap of dung," said Rubashov slowly, turned his back on him and went back to his window.

"I will report that you used insulting language," said the voice of the old man at his back; then the door slammed.

Rubashov rubbed his pince-nez on his sleeve and waited until he breathed more calmly. He had to have cigarettes, else he would not be able to hold out. He made himself wait ten minutes. Then he tapped through to No. 402:

HAVE YOU ANY TOBACCO?

He had to wait a bit for the answer. Then it came, clearly and well spaced:

NOT FOR YOU.

Rubashov went slowly back to the window. He saw the young officer with the small moustache, the monocle stuck in, staring with a stupid grin at the wall which separated them; the eye behind the lens was glassy, the reddish eyelid turned up. What went on in his head? Probably he was thinking: I gave it to you all right. Probably also: Canaille, how many of my people have you had shot? Rubashov looked at the whitewashed wall; he felt that the other was standing behind it with his face turned towards him; he thought he heard his panting breath. Yes, how many of yours have I had shot, I wonder? He really could not remember; it was long, long ago, during the Civil War, there must have been something between seventy and a hundred. What of it? That was all right; it lay on a different plane to a case like Richard's, and he would do it again to-day. Even if he knew beforehand that the revolution would in the end put No. 1 in the saddle? Even then.

With you, thought Rubashov and looked at the white-washed wall behind which the other stood—in the mean-time he had probably lit a cigarette and was blowing the smoke against the wall—with you I have no accounts to settle. To you I owe no fare. Between you and us there is no common currency and no common language. . . . Well, what do you want now?

For No. 402 had started to tap again. Rubashov went back to the wall. . . . SENDING YOU TOBACCO, he heard. Then, more faintly, he heard No. 402 hammering on his door in order to attract the warder's attention.

Rubashov held his breath; after a few minutes he heard the old man's shuffling footsteps approaching. The warder did not unlock No. 402's door, but asked through the spy-hole:

"What do you want?"

Rubashov could not hear the answer, although he would have liked to hear No. 402's voice. Then the old man said loudly, so that Rubashov should hear it:

"It is not allowed; against the regulations."

Again Rubashov could not hear the reply. Then the warder said:

"I will report you for using insulting language." His steps trailed over the tiles and were lost in the corridor.

For a time there was silence. Then No. 402 tapped: A BAD LOOK-OUT FOR YOU.

Rubashov gave no answer. He walked up and down, feeling the thirst for tobacco itching in the dry membranes of his throat. He thought of No. 402. "Yet I would do it again," he said to himself. "It was necessary and right. But do I perhaps owe you the fare all the same? Must one also pay for deeds which were right and necessary?"

The dryness in his throat increased. He felt a pressure in his forehead; he went restlessly back and forth, and while he thought his lips began to move.

Must one also pay for righteous acts? Was there another measure besides that of reason?

Did the righteous man perhaps carry the heaviest debt when weighed by this other measure? Was his debt, perhaps, counted double—for the others knew not what they did? . . .

Rubashov stood still on the third black tile from the window.

What was this? A breath of religious madness? He became conscious that he had for several minutes been talking half aloud to himself. And even as he was watching himself, his lips, independently of his will, moved and said:

"I shall pay."

For the first time since his arrest Rubashov was scared. He felt for his cigarettes. But he had none.

Then again he heard the delicate tappings on the wall over the bedstead. No. 402 had a message for him:

HARE-LIP SENDS YOU GREETINGS.

He saw in his mind's eye the yellow, upturned face of
the man: the message made him feel uncomfortable. He
tapped:

WHAT IS HIS NAME?

No. 402 answered:

HE WON'T SAY. BUT HE SENDS YOU GREET-
INGS.

12

During the afternoon Rubashov felt even worse. He
was seized by periodic fits of shivering. His tooth also
had started to ache again—the right eye-tooth which
was connected to the eye-nerve orbitalis. He had had
nothing to eat since his arrest, yet did not feel hungry.
He tried to collect his wits, but the cold shudders which
ran over him and itching and tickling in his throat prevented him. His thoughts circled alternatively round
two poles: the desperate thirst for a cigarette and the
sentence: I shall pay.

Memories overwhelmed him; they hummed and
buzzed subduedly in his ears. Faces and voices came up
and vanished; wherever he tried to hold them they hurt
him; his whole past was sore and festered at every
touch. His past was the movement, the Party; present
and future, too, belonged to the Party, were inseparably
bound up with its fate; but his past was identical with
it. And it was this past that was suddenly put in question. The Party's warm, breathing body appeared to
him to be covered with sores—festering sores, bleeding
stigmata. When and where in history had there ever been
such defective saints? Whenever had a good cause been
worse represented? If the Party embodied the will of
history, then history itself was defective.

Rubashov gazed at the damp patches on the walls of
his cell. He tore the blanket off the bunk and wrapped
it round his shoulders; he quickened his pace and
marched to and fro with short, quick steps, making
sudden turns at door and window; but shivers continued to run down his back. The buzzing in his ears
went on, mixed with vague, soft voices; he could not

make out whether they came from the corridor or whether he was suffering from hallucinations. It is the orbitalis, he said to himself; it comes from the broken-off root of the eye-tooth. I will tell the doctor about it tomorrow, but in the meantime there is still a lot to do. The cause of the Party's defectiveness must be found. All our principles were right, but our results were wrong. This is a diseased century. We diagnosed the disease and its causes with microscopic exactness, but wherever we applied the healing knife a new sore appeared. Our will was hard and pure, we should have been loved by the people. But they hate us. Why are we so odious and detested?

We brought you truth, and in our mouth it sounded a lie. We brought you freedom, and it looks in our hands like a whip. We brought you the living life, and where our voice is heard the trees wither and there is a rustling of dry leaves. We brought you the promise of the future, but our tongue stammered and barked. . . .

He shivered. A picture appeared in his mind's eye, a big photograph in a wooden frame: the delegates to the first congress of the Party. They sat at a long wooden table, some with their elbows propped on it, others with their hands on their knees; bearded and earnest, they gazed into the photographer's lens. Above each head was a small circle, enclosing a number corresponding to a name printed underneath. All were solemn, only the old man who was presiding had a sly and amused look in his slit Tartar eyes. Rubashov sat second to his right, with his pince-nez on his nose. No. 1 sat somewhere at the lower end of the table, four square and heavy. They looked like the meeting of a provincial town council, and were preparing the greatest revolution in human history. They were at that time a handful of men of an entirely new species: militant philosophers. They were as familiar with the prisons in the towns of Europe as commercial travellers with the hotels. They dreamed of power with the object of abolishing power; of ruling over the people to wean them from the habit of being ruled. All their thoughts became deeds and all their dreams were fulfilled. Where were they? Their brains, which had changed the course of the world, had each received a charge of lead. Some in the forehead, some in the back of the neck. Only two or three of them were left over, scattered throughout the world, worn out. And himself; and No. 1.

He was frozen, and he longed for a cigarette. He saw himself again in the old Belgian port, escorted by merry Little Loewy, who was slightly hunchbacked and smoked a sailor's pipe. He smelled again the smell of the harbour, a mixture of rotting seaweed and petrol; he heard the musical clock on the tower of the old guildhall, and saw the narrow streets with overhanging bays, from the lattices of which the harbour prostitutes hung their washing during the day. It was two years after the affair with Richard. They had not succeeded in proving anything against himself. He had kept silent when they beat him up, kept silent when they knocked the teeth out of his head, injured his hearing and broke his glasses. He had kept silent, and had gone on denying everything and lying coldly and circumspectly. He had marched up and down his cell, and crawled over the flagstones of the dark punishment cell, he had been afraid and he had gone on working at his defence; and when cold water woke him from unconsciousness, he had groped for a cigarette and gone on lying. In those days he felt no surprise at the hatred of those who tortured him, and did not wonder why he was so detestable to them. The whole legal machinery of the dictatorship ground its teeth, but they could prove nothing against him. After his release he was taken by aeroplane to his country— to the home of the Revolution. There were receptions and jubilant mass-meetings and military parades. Even No. 1 appeared repeatedly in public with him.

He had not been in his native country for years and found that much was changed. Half the bearded men of the photograph no longer existed. Their names might not be mentioned, their memory only invoked with curses —except for the old man with the slanting Tartar eyes, the leader of yore, who had died in time. He was revered as God-the-Father, and No. 1 as the Son; but it was whispered everywhere that he had forged the old man's will in order to come into the heritage. Those of the bearded men in the old photograph who were left had become unrecognizable. They were clean-shaven, worn out and disillusioned, full of cynical melancholy. From time to time No. 1 reached out for a new victim amongst them. Then they all beat their breasts and repented in chorus of their sins. After a fortnight, when he was still walking on crutches, Rubashov had asked for a new mission abroad. "You seem to be in rather a hurry," said No. 1, looking at him from behind clouds of smoke. After twenty years in the leadership of the Party they were still on formal terms with each other. Above No. 1's head hung the portrait of the Old Man; next to it the photograph with the numbered heads had hung, but it was now gone. The colloquy was short, it had lasted only a few minutes, but on leaving No. 1 had shaken his hand with peculiar emphasis. Rubashov had afterwards cogitated a long time over the meaning of this handshake; and over the look of strangely knowing irony which No. 1 had given him from behind his smoke-clouds. Then Rubashov had hobbled out of the room on his crutches; No. 1 did not accompany him to the door. The next day he had left for Belgium.

On the boat he recovered slightly and thought over his task. Little Loewy with the sailor's pipe came to meet him on his arrival. He was the local leader of the dock-workers' section of the Party; Rubashov liked him at once. He showed Rubashov through the docks and the twisting harbour streets as proudly as if he had made it all himself. In every pub he had acquaintances, dock workers, sailors and prostitutes; he was everywhere offered drinks and returned salutations by raising his pipe to his ear. Even the traffic policeman on the marketplace winked at him as they passed, and the sailor comrades from foreign ships, who could not make themselves understood, slapped him tenderly on the deformed shoulder. Rubashov saw all this with a mild surprise. No, Little Loewy was not odious and detestable.

The dock workers' section in this town was one of the best organized sections of the Party in the world.

In the evening Rubashov, Little Loewy and a couple of others sat in one of the harbour pubs. A certain Paul was amongst them, the section's organization Secretary. He was an ex-wrestler, bald-headed, pock-marked, with big sticking-out ears. He wore a sailor's black sweater under his coat, and a black bowler on his head. He had the gift of waggling his ears, thereby lifting his bowler and letting it drop again. With him was a certain Bill, an ex-sailor who had written a novel about the sailor's life, had been famous for a year and then quickly forgotten again; now he wrote articles for Party newspapers. The others were dock workers, heavy men and steadfast drinkers. New people kept coming in, sat down or stood at the table, paid a round of drinks and lounged out again. The fat pub-keeper sat down to their table whenever he had a free moment. He could play the mouth-organ. Quite a lot was drunk.

Rubashov had been introduced by Little Loewy as a "comrade from Over There" without further commentary. Little Loewy was the only one who knew his identity. As the people at the table saw that Rubashov either was not in a communicative mood, or had reasons not to be, they did not ask him many questions; and those which they did ask referred to the material conditions of life "over there", the wages, the land problem, the development of industry. Everything they said revealed a surprising knowledge of technical detail, coupled with an equally surprising ignorance of the general situation and political atmosphere "over there". They inquired about the development of production in the light metal industry, like children asking the exact size of the grapes of Canaan. An old dock worker, who had stood at the bar for a time without ordering anything until Little Loewy called him over for a drink, said to Rubashov, after having shaken hands with him: "You look very like old Rubashov." "That I have often been told," said Rubashov. "Old Rubashov—there's a man for you," said the old man, emptying his glass. It was not a month ago that Rubashov had been set free, and not six weeks since he knew that he would remain alive. The fat pub-keeper played his mouth-organ. Rubashov lit a cigarette and ordered drinks all round. They drank to his health and to the health of the people "over there", and the Secretary Paul moved his bowler hat up and down with his ears.

Later on Rubashov and Little Loewy remained for some time together in a café. The owner of the café had let down the blinds and piled the chairs on the tables, and was asleep against the counter, while Little Loewy told Rubashov the story of his life. Rubashov had not asked him for it, and at once foresaw com-plications for next day: he could not help it that all comrades felt an urge to tell him their life history. He had really meant to go, but he felt suddenly very tired—he had, after all, overrated his strength; so he stayed on and listened.

It turned out that Little Loewy was not a native of the country, although he spoke the language like one and knew everybody in the place. Actually he was born in a South German town, had learnt the carpenter's trade, and had played the guitar and given lectures on Darwinism on the revolutionary youth club's Sunday excursions. During the disturbed months before the Dictatorship came to power, when the Party was in urgent need of weapons, a daring trick was played in that particular town: one Sunday afternoon, fifty rifles, twenty revolvers and two light machine guns with munitions were carried away in a furniture-van from the police station in the busiest quarter of the city. The people in the van had shown some sort of written order, covered with official stamps, and were accompanied by two apparent policemen in real uniforms. The weapons were found later in another town during a search in the garage of a Party member. The affair was never fully cleared up, and the day after it happened Little Loewy vanished from the town. The Party had promised him a passport and identity papers, but the arrangement broke down. That is to say, the messenger from the upper

Party spheres who was to bring him passport and money
for the journey, did not appear at the pre-arranged
meeting-place.

"It's always like that with us," added Little Loewy
philosophically. Rubashov kept quiet.

In spite of that, Little Loewy managed to get away
and eventually to cross the frontier. As there was a
warrant of arrest out for him, and as his photograph
with the deformed shoulder was posted up in every
police station, it took him several months of wandering
across country. When he had started off to meet the
comrade from the "upper spheres" he had just enough
money in his pocket for three days. "I had always
thought before that it was only in books that people
chewed the bark of trees," he remarked. "Young plane
trees taste best." The memory impelled him to get up
and fetch a couple of sausages from the counter. Rubashov remembered prison soup and hunger strikes, and
ate with him.

At last Little Loewy crossed over the French frontier.
As he had no passport, he was arrested after a few days,
told to betake himself to another country and released.
"One might just as well have told me to climb to the
moon," he observed. He turned to the Party for help;
but in this country the Party did not know him and told
him they would first have to make inquiries in his native
country. He wandered on; after a few days he was
arrested again and sentenced to three months' imprisonment. He served his sentence, and gave his cell companion,
a tramp, a course of lectures about the resolutions of the
last Party Congress. In return the latter let him into the
secret of making a living by catching cats and selling
their skins. When the three months were over, he was
taken by night to a wood on the Belgian frontier. The
gendarmes gave him bread, cheese and a packet of
French cigarettes. "Go straight on," they said. "In half
an hour you will be in Belgium. If we ever catch you
over here again, we'll knock your head off."

For several weeks Little Loewy drifted about in Belgium. He again turned to the Party for help, but re-

ceived the same answer as in France. As he had had enough of plane trees, he tried the cat trade. It was fairly easy to catch cats, and one obtained for a skin, if it were young and not mangy, the equivalent of half a loaf of bread and a packet of pipe tobacco. Between the capture and the selling, however, lay a rather unpleasant operation. It was quickest if one grasped the cat's ears in one hand, and its tail in the other, and broke its back over one's knee. The first few times one was seized by nausea: later on one got used to it. Unfortunately, Little Loewy was arrested again after a few weeks, for in Belgium, too, one was supposed to have identity papers. Followed in due course expulsion, release, second arrest, imprisonment. Then one night two Belgian gendarmes took him to a wood on the French frontier. They gave him bread, cheese and a packet of Belgian cigarettes. "Go straight on," they said. "In half an hour you will be in France. If we catch you over here again, we'll knock your head off."

In the course of the next year, Little Loewy was smuggled backwards and forwards over the frontier three times, by complicity of the French authorities or, as the case might be, the Belgian. He gathered that this game had been played for years with several hundred of his kind. He applied again and again to the Party, for his chief anxiety was that he should lose contact with the movement. "We received no notification of your arrival from your organisation," the Party told him. "We must wait for the answer to our inquiries. If you are a Party member, keep Party discipline." Meanwhile Little Loewy continued his cat trade and let himself be shoved to and fro across the frontier. Also the dictatorship broke out in his own country. A further year passed and Little Loewy, slightly the worse for his travels, began to spit blood and dream of cats. He suffered from the delusion that everything smelled of cats, his food, his pipe and even the kindly old prostitutes who sometimes gave him shelter. "We have still received no answer to our inquiries," said the Party. After another year it turned out that all those comrades who could have given the re-

quired information about Little Loewy's part were either
murdered, locked-up or had disappeared. "We are afraid
we cannot do anything for you," said the Party. "You
should not have come without an official notification.
Perhaps you left even without the Party's permission.
How can we know? A lot of spies and *provocateurs*
try to creep into our ranks. The Party must be on its
guard."

"What are you telling me this for?" asked Rubashov.
He wished he had left before.

Little Loewy fetched himself beer from the tap, and
saluted with his pipe. "Because it is instructive," he said.
"Because it is a typical example. I could tell you of
hundreds of others. For years the best of us have been
crushed in that way. The Party is becoming more and
more fossilized. The Party has gout and varicose veins
in every limb. One cannot make a revolution like that."

I could tell you more about it, thought Rubashov,
but said nothing.

However, Little Loewy's story came to an unexpectedly happy end. While serving one of his countless
sentences of imprisonment, he was given ex-wrestler
Paul as cell companion. Paul was at that time a dock
worker; he was in jail for having, during a strike riot,
remembered his professional past and applied the grip
known as a double Nelson to a policeman. This grip consisted in passing one's arms through the opponent's armpits from behind, locking one's hands behind his neck,
and pressing his head down until the neck vertebra began
to crack. In the ring this had always brought him considerable applause, but he had learned to his regret that
in the class struggle the double Nelson was not done.
Little Loewy and ex-wrestler Paul became friends. It
turned out that Paul was the Administrative Secretary
of the Dockers' Section of the Party; when they came
out, he procured papers and work for Loewy and obtained his reintegration in the Party. So Little Loewy
could again lecture to the dockers on Darwinism and
on the latest Party Congress as though nothing had happened. He was happy and forgot the cats and his anger

against the Party bureaucrats. After half a year, he became Political Secretary of the local section. All's well that ends well.

And Rubashov wished with his whole heart, old and tired as he felt, that it should end well. But he knew for what task he had been sent here, and there was only one revolutionary virtue which he had not learned, the virtue of self-deception. He looked quietly at Little Loewy through his glasses. And while Little Loewy, who did not understand the meaning of this look, became slightly embarrassed and saluted smilingly with his pipe, Rubashov was thinking of the cats. He noticed with horror that his nerves were going wrong and that he had perhaps drunk too much, for he could not get rid of the obsession that he must take Little Loewy by his ears and legs and break him over his knee, deformed shoulder and all. He was feeling ill and stood up to go. Little Loewy saw him home; he gathered that Rubashov was in a sudden fit of depression, and was respectfully silent. A week later Little Loewy hanged himself.

Between that evening and Little Loewy's death lay several undramatic meetings of the Party cell. The facts were simple.

Two years ago the Party had called up the workers of the world to fight the newly established dictatorship in the heart of Europe by means of a political and economic boycott. No goods coming from the enemy's country should be bought, no consignments for its enormous armament industry should be allowed to pass. The sections of the Party executed these orders with enthusiasm. The dock workers in the small port refused to load or unload cargoes coming from that country or destined for it. Other trade unions joined them. The strike was hard to carry through; conflicts with the police resulted in wounded and dead. The final result of the struggle was still uncertain when a little fleet of five curious, old-fashioned black cargo boats sailed into the port. Each of them had the name of a great leader of the Revolution painted on its stern, in the strange

alphabet used "over there", and from their bows waved
the flag of the Revolution. The striking workers greeted
them with enthusiasm. They at once began to unload
the cargo. After several hours it came to light that the
cargo consisted of certain rare minerals and was destined for the war industry of the boycotted country.

The dockers' section of the Party immediately called
a committee meeting, where people came to blows. The
dispute spread through the movement all over the country.
The reactionary Press exploited the event with derision.
The police ceased their attempts to break the strike, pro-
claimed their neutrality and let the harbour workers decide for themselves whether they would unload the cargo
of the curious black fleet or not. The Party leadership
called the strike off and gave orders to unload the cargo.
They gave reasonable explanations and cunning arguments for the behaviour of the Country of the Revolution, but few were convinced. The section split; the
majority of the old members left. For months the Party
led the shadow of an existence; but gradually, as the
industrial distress of the country grew, it regained its
popularity and strength.

Two years had passed. Another hungry dictatorship in the south of Europe began a war of plunder
and conquest in Africa. Again the Party called for a
boycott. They received an even more enthusiastic response than on the previous occasion. For this time the
governments themselves in nearly every country in the
world had decided to cut off the aggressor's supply of
raw materials.

Without raw materials and particularly without petrol,
the aggressor would be lost. This was the state of
affairs, when again the curious little black fleet set out
on her way. The biggest of the ships bore the name of a
man who had raised his voice against war and had been
slain; at their mastheads waved the flag of the Revolution and in their holds they carried the petrol for the
aggressor. They were only a day's journey away from
this port, and Little Loewy and his friends knew as yet

nothing of their approach. It was Rubashov's task to prepare them for it.

On the first day he had said nothing—only felt his ground. On the morning of the second day the discussion began in the Party meeting-room.

The room was big, bare, untidy and furnished with that lack of care which made the Party's offices in every town in the world look exactly alike. It was partly a result of poverty, but chiefly of an ascetic and gloomy tradition. The walls were covered with old election posters, political slogans and typed notices. In one corner stood a dusty old duplicator. In another lay a heap of old clothes destined for the families of strikers; next to them piles of yellowing leaflets and brochures. The long table consisted of two parallel planks laid over a couple of trestles. The windows were smeared with paint as in an unfinished building. Over the table a naked electric bulb hung on a cord from the ceiling, and next to it a sticky paper fly-catcher. Round the table sat hunchbacked Little Loewy, ex-wrestler Paul, the writer Bill and three others.

Rubashov spoke for some time. The surroundings were familiar to him; their traditional ugliness made him feel at home. In these surroundings he was again fully convinced of the necessity and utility of his mission and could not understand why, in the noisy pub the night before, he had had that feeling of uneasiness. He explained objectively and not without warmth the real state of things, without as yet mentioning the practical object for his coming. The world boycott against the aggressor had failed because of the hypocrisy and greed of the European governments. Some of them still kept up an appearance of sticking to the boycott, the others not even that. The aggressor needed petrol. In the past the Country of the Revolution had covered a considerable part of this need. If now it stopped the supplies, other countries would greedily spring into the breach: indeed they asked nothing better than to push the Country of the Revolution from the world markets.

Romantic gestures of that sort would only hamper the
development of industry Over There, and with it the
revolutionary movement all over the world. So the in-
ference was clear.

Paul and the three dock-hands nodded. They were
slow thinkers; everything the comrade from Over There
was telling them sounded quite convincing; it was only
a theoretical discourse, of no immediate consequence to
them. They did not see the actual point he was aiming
at; none of them thought of the black flotilla which was
approaching their harbour. Only Little Loewy and the
writer with the twisted face exchanged a quick glance.
Rubashov noticed it. He finished a shade more drily,
without warmth in his voice:

"That is really all I had to tell you as far as principle
is concerned. You are expected to carry out the decisions of the C.C. and to explain the ins and outs of the
matter to the politically less developed comrades, if any
of them should have any doubts. For the moment I
have no more to say."

There was silence for a minute. Rubashov took his
pince-nez off and lit a cigarette. Little Loewy said in a
casual tone of voice:

"We thank the speaker. Does anybody wish to ask
any questions?"

Nobody did. After a while one of the three dock
workers said awkwardly:

"There is not much to be said to it. The comrades
Over There must know what they are about. We, of
course, must continue to work for the boycott. You can
trust us. In our port nothing will get through for the
swine."

His two colleagues nodded. Wrestler Paul confirmed:
"Not here," made a bellicose grimace and waggled his
ears for fun.

For a moment Rubashov believed he was faced by an
oppositional faction; he only realized gradually that the
others had really not grasped the point. He looked at
Little Loewy, in the hope that he would clear up the
misunderstanding. But Little Loewy held his eyes lowered

and was silent. Suddenly the writer said with a nervous twitch:

"Couldn't you choose another harbour this time for your little transactions? Must it always be us?"

The dockers looked at him in surprise; they did not understand what he meant by "transaction"; the idea of the small black fleet which was approaching their coast through mist and smoke was further than ever from their minds. But Rubashov had expected this question:

"It is both politically and geographically advisable," he said. "The goods will be conveyed from there by land. We have, of course, no reason to keep anything secret: still, it is more prudent to avoid a sensation which the reactionary Press might exploit."

The writer again exchanged a glance with Little Loewy. The dock-hands looked at Rubashov uncomprehendingly; one could see them working it out slowly in their heads. Suddenly Paul said in a changed, hoarse voice:

"What, actually, are you talking about?"

They all looked at him. His neck was red, and he was looking at Rubashov with bulging eyes. Little Loewy said with restraint:

"Have you only just noticed?"

Rubashov looked from one to the other, and then said quietly:

"I omitted to tell you the details. The five cargo boats of the Commissariat for Foreign Trade are expected to arrive tomorrow morning, weather permitting."

Even now it took several minutes before they had all understood. Nobody said a word. They all looked at Rubashov. Then Paul stood up slowly, flung his cap to the ground, and left the room. Two of his colleagues turned their heads after him. Nobody spoke. Then Little Loewy cleared his throat and said:

"The Comrade speaker has just explained to us the reasons for this business: if they do not deliver the supplies, others will. Who else wishes to speak?"

The docker who had already spoken shifted on his chair and said:

"We know that tune. In a strike there are always people who say: if I don't do the work, someone else will take it. We've heard enough of that. That's how blacklegs talk."

Again there was a pause. One heard outside the front door being slammed by Paul. Then Rubashov said:

"Comrades, the interests of our industrial development Over There come before everything else. Sentimentality does not get us any further. Think that over."

The docker shoved his chin forward and said:

"We have already thought it over. We've heard enough of it. You Over There must give the example. The whole world looks to you for it. You talk of solidarity and sacrifice and discipline, and at the same time you use your fleet for plain blacklegging."

At that Little Loewy lifted his head suddenly; he was pale; he saluted Rubashov with his pipe and said low and very quickly:

"What the comrade said is also my opinion. Has anyone anything further to say? The meeting is closed."

Rubashov limped out of the room on his crutches. Events followed their prescribed and inevitable course. While the little old-fashioned fleet was entering the harbour, Rubashov exchanged a few telegrams with the competent authorities Over There. Three days later the leaders of the dockers' section were expelled from the Party and Little Loewy was denounced in the official Party organ as an *agent provocateur*. Another three days later Little Loewy had hanged himself.

13

The night was even worse. Rubashov could not sleep until dawn. Shivers ran over him at regular intervals; his tooth was throbbing. He had the sensation that all the association centres of his brain were sore and inflamed; yet he lay under the painful compulsion to conjure up pictures and voices. He thought of young Richard in the black Sunday suit, with his inflamed eyes "But you can't throw me to the wolves, comrade. . . ." He thought of little deformed Loewy: "Who else wishes to speak?" There were so many who did wish to speak. For the movement was without scruples; she rolled towards her goal unconcernedly and deposed the corpses of the drowned in the windings of her course. Her course had many twists and windings; such was the law of her being. And whosoever could not follow her crooked course was washed on to the bank, for such was her law. The motives of the individual did not matter to her. His conscience did not matter to her, neither did she care what went on in his head and his heart. The Party knew only one crime: to swerve from the course laid out; and only one punishment: death. Death was no mystery in the movement; there was nothing exalted about it: it was the logical solution to political divergences.

Not before the early hours of the morning did Rubashov, exhausted, fall asleep on his bunk. He was woken again by the bugle blast which heralded a new day; shortly afterwards he was fetched by the old warder and two officials in uniform, to be conducted to the doctor.

Rubashov had hoped to be able to read the name-cards on the cell-doors of Hare-lip and of No. 402, but he was taken in the opposite direction. The cell to his right was empty. It was one of the last cells of that end of the corridor; the wing of isolation cells was shut off by a heavy concrete door, which the old man opened with much fumbling. They now passed through a long gallery, Rubashov with the old warder in front, the two men in uniform behind. Here all the cards on the cell-doors bore several names; they heard talking, laughter and even singing coming from the cells; Rubashov knew at once that they were in the section for petty criminals. They passed the barber's shop, of which the door stood open; a prisoner with the sharp bird's face of the old convict was just being shaved; two peasants were having their heads shorn: all three turned their heads curiously as Rubashov and his escort marched past. They came to a door with a red cross painted on it. The warder knocked respectfully, and he

and Rubashov went in; the two uniformed men waited
outside.

The infirmary was small and the air stuffy; it smelled
of carbolic and tobacco. A bucket and two pans were
filled to the brim with cotton-wool swabs and dirty
bandages. The doctor sat at a table with his back to
them, reading the newspaper and chewing bread and
dripping. The newspaper lay on a heap of instruments,
pincers and syringes. When the warder had shut the
door, the doctor turned slowly round. He was bald and
had an unusually small skull, covered with white fluff,
which reminded Rubashov of an ostrich.

"He says he's got toothache," said the old man.

"Toothache?" said the doctor, looking past Rubashov.
"Open your mouth, and be quick about it."

Rubashov looked at him through his glasses.

"I beg to point out," he said quietly, "that I am a
political prisoner and entitled to correct treatment."

The doctor turned his head to the warder:

"Who is this bird?"

The warder gave Rubashov's name. For a second
Rubashov felt the round ostrich eyes rest on him. Then
the doctor said:

"Your cheek is swollen. Open your mouth."

Rubashov's tooth was not aching at the moment. He
opened his mouth.

"You have no teeth left at all in the left side of your
upper jaw," said the doctor, probing with his finger in
Rubashov's mouth. Suddenly Rubashov became pale and
had to lean against the wall.

"There it is!" said the doctor. "The root of the right
eye-tooth is broken off and has remained in the jaw."

Rubashov breathed deeply several times. The pain
was throbbing from his jaw to his eye and right to the
back of his head. He felt each pulsation of the blood
singly, at regular intervals. The doctor had sat down
again and spread out his newspaper. "If you like I can
extract the root for you," he said and took a mouthful of
bread and dripping. "We have, of course, no anæs-

thetics here. The operation takes anything from half an
hour to an hour."

Rubashov heard the doctor's voice through a mist. He
leant against the wall and breathed deeply. "Thank you,"
he said. "Not now." He thought of Hare-lip and the
"steambath" and of the ridiculous gesture yesterday,
when he had stubbed out the cigarette on the back of
his hand. Things will go badly, he thought.

When he was back in his cell, he let himself drop on
the bunk and fell asleep at once.

At noon, when the soup came, he was no longer
omitted; from then on he received his rations regularly.
The toothache lessened and remained within bearable
limits. Rubashov hoped the abscess in the root had
opened by itself.

Three days later he was brought up for examination
for the first time.

14

It was eleven o'clock in the morning when they
came to fetch him. By the warder's solemn expression,
Rubashov guessed at once where they were going. He
followed the warder, with the serene nonchalance which
had always come to him in moments of danger, as an
unexpected gift of mercy.

They went the same way as three days ago when
going to the doctor. The concrete door again opened
and crashed shut; strange, thought Rubashov, how
quickly one grows used to an intense environment; he
felt as if he had been breathing the air of this corridor for years, as if the stale atmosphere of all the
prisons he had known had been stored away here.

They passed the barber's shop and the doctor's door
which was shut; three prisoners stood outside, guarded
by a sleepy warder, waiting their turn.

Beyond the doctor's door was new ground for Rubashov. They passed a spiral staircase leading down into
the depths. What was down there—store-rooms, punish-

ment cells? Rubashov tried to guess, with the interest of
the expert. He did not like the look of that staircase.

They crossed a narrow, windowless courtyard; it was
a blind shaft, rather dark, but over it hung the open
sky. On the other side of the courtyard the corridors
were brighter; the doors were no longer of concrete,
but of painted wood, with brass handles; busy officials
passed them; behind a door a wireless was playing; behind another one heard a typewriter. They were in the
administrative department.

They stopped at the last door, at the end of the corridor; the warder knocked. Inside someone was tele-
phoning; a quiet voice called out: "A minute, please,"
and went on patiently saying "Yes" and "Quite" into
the receiver. The voice seemed familiar to Rubashov,
but he could not place it. It was an agreeably masculine
voice, slightly husky; he had certainly heard it somewhere before. "Come in," said the voice; the warder
opened the door and shut it immediately behind Rubashov. Rubashov saw a desk; behind it sat his old college
friend and former battalion commander, Ivanov; he was
looking at him smilingly while putting back the receiver.
"So here we are again," said Ivanov.

Rubashov still stood at the door. "What a pleasant
surprise," he said drily.

"Sit down," said Ivanov with a polite gesture. He had
risen; standing, he was half a head taller than Rubashov. He looked at him smilingly. They both sat down
—Ivanov behind the desk, Rubashov in front of it. They
stared at each other for some time and with unre-
strained curiosity—Ivanov with his almost tender smile,
Rubashov expectant and watchful. His glance slid to
Ivanov's right leg under the table.

"Oh, that's all right," said Ivanov. "Artificial leg with
automatic joints and rustless chromium-plating; I can
swim, ride, drive a car and dance. Will you have a
cigarette?"

He held out a wooden cigarette case to Rubashov.

Rubashov looked at the cigarettes and thought of his
first visit to the military hospital after Ivanov's leg had

been amputated. Ivanov had asked him to procure veronal for him, and in a discussion which lasted the whole afternoon, had tried to prove that every man had a right to suicide. Rubashov had finally asked for time to reflect, and had in the same night been transferred to another sector of the front. It was only years later that he had met Ivanov again. He looked at the cigarettes in the wooden case. They were hand-made, of loose, blonde American tobacco.

"Is this still an unofficial prelude, or have the hostilities started?" asked Rubashov. "In the latter case, I won't have one. You know the etiquette."

"Rubbish," said Ivanov.

"Well then, rubbish," said Rubashov and lit one of Ivanov's cigarettes. He inhaled deeply, trying not to let his enjoyment be seen. "And how is the rheumatism in your shoulders?" he asked.

"All right, thank you," said Ivanov, "and how is your burn?"

He smiled and pointed innocently at Rubashov's left hand. On the back of the hand, between the bluish veins, in the place where three days ago he had stubbed out his cigarette, was a blister the size of a copper coin. For a minute both looked at Rubashov's hand lying in his lap. How does he know that? thought Rubashov. He has had me spied on. He felt more shame than anger; he took one last deep pull at his cigarette and threw it away. "As far as I am concerned the unofficial part is over," he said.

Ivanov blew smoke rings and watched him with the same tenderly ironic smile. "Don't become aggressive," he said.

"Make allowances," said Rubashov. "Did I arrest you or did you people arrest me?"

"We arrested you," said Ivanov. He put out his cigarette, lit another one and held out the box to Rubashov, who did not move. "The devil take you," said Ivanov. "Do you remember the story of the veronal?" He bent forward and blew the smoke of his cigarette into Rubashov's face.

"I do not want you to be shot," he said slowly. He leaned back again in his chair. "The devil take you," he repeated, smiling again.

"Touching of you," said Rubashov. "Why actually do you people intend to have me shot?"

Ivanov let a few seconds go by. He smoked and drew figures with his pencil on the blotting-paper. He seemed to be searching for the exact words.

"Listen, Rubashov," he said finally. "There is one thing I would like to point out to you. You have now repeatedly said 'you'—meaning State and Party, as opposed to 'I'—that is, Nicolas Salmanovitch Rubashov. For the public, one needs, of course, a trial and legal justification. For us, what I have just said should be enough."

Rubashov thought this over; he was somewhat taken aback. For a moment it was as if Ivanov had hit a tuning fork, to which his mind responded of its own accord. All he had believed in, fought for and preached during the last forty years swept over his mind in an irresistible wave. The individual was nothing, the Party was all; the branch which broke from the tree must wither. . . . Rubashov rubbed his pince-nez on his sleeve. Ivanov was sitting back in his chair, smoking; he was no longer smiling. Suddenly Rubashov's eye was caught by a square patch on the wall lighter than the rest of the wall-paper. He knew at once that the picture with the bearded heads and the numbered names had hung there —Ivanov followed his glance without changing his expression.

"Your argument is somewhat anachronistic," said Rubashov. "As you quite rightly remarked, we were accustomed always to use the plural 'we' and to avoid as far as possible the first person singular. I have rather lost the habit of that form of speech; you stick to it. But who is this 'we' in whose name you speak to-day? It needs re-defining. That is the point."

"Entirely my own opinion," said Ivanov. "I am glad that we have reached the heart of the matter so soon. In other words: you are convinced that 'we'—that is to say, the Party, the State and the masses behind it—no longer represent the interests of the Revolution."

"I should leave the masses out of it," said Rubashov.

"Since when have you this supreme contempt for the plebs?" asked Ivanov. "Has that, too, a connection with the grammatical change to the first person singular?"

He leant across his desk with a look of benevolent mockery. His head now hid the light patch on the wall and suddenly the scene in the picture gallery occurred to Rubashov, when Richard's head had come between him and the folded hands of the *Pietà*. In the same instant a spasm of pain throbbed from his jaw up to his forehead and ear. For a second he shut his eyes. "Now I am paying," he thought. An instant later he did not know whether he had not spoken aloud.

"How do you mean?" Ivanov's voice asked. It sounded close to his ear, mocking and slightly surprised.

The pain faded; a peaceful stillness pervaded his mind. "Leave the masses out of it," he repeated. "You understand nothing about them. Nor, probably, do I any more. Once, when the great 'we' still existed, we understood them as no one had ever understood them before. We had penetrated into their depths, we worked in the amorphous raw material of history itself. . . ."

Without noticing it, he had taken a cigarette out of Ivanov's case, which still lay open on the table. Ivanov bent forward and lit it for him.

"At that time," Rubashov went on, "we were called the Party of the Plebs. What did the others know of history? Passing ripples, little eddies and breaking waves. They wondered at the changing forms of the surface and could not explain them. But we had descended into the depths, into the formless, anonymous masses, which at all times constituted the substance of history; and we were the first to discover her laws of motion. We had discovered the laws of her inertia, of the slow changing of her molecular structure, and of her sudden eruptions. That was the greatness of our doctrine. The Jacobins were moralists; we were empirics. We dug in the primeval mud of history and there we found her laws. We knew more than ever men have known about mankind; that is why our revolution succeeded. And now you have buried it all again. . . ."

Ivanov was sitting back with his legs stretched out, listening and drawing figures on his blotting-paper.

"Go on," he said. "I am curious to know what you are driving at."

Rubashov was smoking with relish. He felt the nicotine making him slightly dizzy after his long abstinence.

"As you notice, I am talking my head off my neck," he said and looked up smilingly at the faded patch on the wall where the photograph of the old guard had once hung. This time Ivanov did not follow his glance. "Well," said Rubashov, "one more makes no difference. Everything is buried; the men, their wisdom and their hopes. You killed the 'We'; you destroyed it. Do you really maintain that the masses are still behind you? Other usurpers in Europe pretend the same thing with as much right as you. . . ."

He took another cigarette and lit it himself this time, as Ivanov did not move.

"Forgive my pompousness," he went on, "but do you really believe the people are still behind you? It bears you, dumb and resigned, as it bears others in other countries, but there is no response in its depths. The masses have become deaf and dumb again, the great silent x of history, indifferent as the sea carrying the ships. Every passing light is reflected on its surface, but underneath is darkness and silence. A long time ago we stirred up the depths, but that is over. In other words" —he paused and put on his pince-nez—"in those days we made history; now you make politics. That's the whole difference."

Ivanov leant back in his chair and blew smoke rings. "I'm sorry, but the difference is not quite clear to me," he said. "Perhaps you'll be kind enough to explain."

"Certainly," said Rubashov. "A mathematician once said that algebra was the science for lazy people—one does not work out x, but operates with it as if one knew it. In our case, x stands for the anonymous masses, the people. Politics mean operating with this x without worrying about its actual nature. Making history is to recognize x for what it stands for in the equation."

"Pretty," said Ivanov. "But unfortunately rather abstract. To return to more tangible things: you mean, therefore, that 'we'—namely, Party and State—no longer represent the interests of the Revolution, of the masses or, if you like, the progress of humanity."

"This time you have grasped it," said Rubashov smiling. Ivanov did not answer his smile.

"When did you develop this opinion?"

"Fairly gradually: during the last few years," said Rubashov.

"Can't you tell me more exactly? One year? Two? Three years?"

"That's a stupid question," said Rubashov. "At what age did you become adult? At seventeen? At eighteen and a half? At nineteen?"

"It's you who are pretending to be stupid," said Ivanov. "Each step in one's spiritual development is the result of definite experiences. If you really want to know: I became a man at seventeen, when I was sent into exile for the first time."

"At that time you were quite a decent fellow," said Rubashov. "Forget it." He again looked at the light patch on the wall and threw away his cigarette.

"I repeat my question," said Ivanov and bent forward slightly. "For how long have you belonged to the organized opposition?"

The telephone rang. Ivanov took the receiver off, said, "I am busy," and hung it up again. He leant back in his chair, leg stretched out, and waited for Rubashov's answer.

"You know as well as I do," said Rubashov, "that I never joined an oppositional organization."

"As you like," said Ivanov. "You put me into the painful position of having to act the bureaucrat." He put a hand in a drawer and pulled out a bundle of files.

"Let's start with 1933," he said and spread the papers

out in front of him. "Outbreak of the dictatorship and crushing of the Party in the very country where victory seemed closest. You are sent there illegally, with the task of carrying through a purging and reorganization of the ranks. . . ."

Rubashov had leant back and was listening to his biography. He thought of Richard, and of the twilight in the avenue in front of the museum, where he had stopped the taxi.

". . . Three months later: you are arrested. Two years' imprisonment. Behaviour exemplary, nothing can be proved against you. Release and triumphal return. . . ."

Ivanov paused, threw him a quick glance and went on:

"You were much fêted on your return. We did not meet then; you were probably too busy. . . . I did not take it amiss, by the way. After all, one could not expect you to look up all your old friends. But I saw you twice at meetings, up on the platform. You were still on crutches and looked very worn-out. The logical thing would have been for you to go to a sanatorium for a few months, and then to take some Government post—after having been four years away on foreign mission. But after a fortnight you were already applying for another mission abroad. . . ."

He bent forward suddenly, moving his face closer to Rubashov:

"Why——?" he asked, and for the first time his voice was sharp. "You did not feel at ease here, presumably? During your absence certain changes had taken place in the country, which you evidently did not appreciate."

He waited for Rubashov to say something; but Rubashov was sitting quietly in his chair, rubbing his pince-nez on his sleeve, and did not answer.

"It was shortly after the first crop of the opposition had been convicted and liquidated. You had intimate friends amongst them. When it became known what degree of decay the opposition had attained, there was an outbreak of indignation throughout the country. You said nothing. After a fortnight, you went abroad, although you could not yet walk without crutches. . . ."

To Rubashov it seemed that he smelt again the smell of the docks in the little port, a mixture of seaweed and petrol; wrestler Paul wagging his ears; Little Loewy saluting with his pipe. . . . He had hanged himself on a beam in his attic. The dilapidated old house trembled every time a lorry passed; Rubashov had been told that on the morning when Little Loewy was found, his body had turned slowly on its own axis, so that at first they thought he still moved. . . .

"The mission successfully concluded, you were nominated leader of our Trade Delegation in B. This time, too, you carried out your duties irreproachably. The new commercial treaty with B. is a definite success. In appearance your behaviour remains exemplary and spotless. But six months after you took over this post, your two closest collaborators, one of whom is your secretary, Arlova, have to be recalled under the suspicion of oppositional conspiracy. This suspicion is confirmed by the inquiry. You are expected to disavow them publicly. You remain silent. . . .

"Another six months later you are yourself recalled. The preparations for the second trial of the opposition are proceeding. Your name occurs repeatedly at the trial; Arlova refers to you for her exculpation. Under these circumstances, to maintain your silence would look like a confession of guilt. You know that and yet you refuse to make a public declaration until the Party sends you an ultimatum. Only then, when your head is at stake, do you condescend to give a declaration of loyalty, which automatically finishes Arlova. Her fate you know. . . ."

Rubashov was silent, and noticed that his tooth was aching again. He knew her fate. Also Richard's. Also Little Loewy's. Also his own. He looked at the light patch on the wall, the only trace left by the men with the numbered heads. Their fate, too, was known to him. For once History had taken a run, which at last

promised a more dignified form of life for mankind;
now it was over. So why all this talk and all this
ceremony? If anything in human beings could survive
destruction, the girl Arlova lay somewhere in the great
emptiness, still staring with her good cow's eyes at Comrade Rubashov, who had been her idol and had sent her
to her death. . . . His tooth became worse and worse.

"Shall I read you the public statement you made at
that time?" asked Ivanov.

"No, thank you," said Rubashov, and noticed that
his voice sounded hoarse.

"As you remember, your statement—which one
could also describe as a confession—ended with a sharp
condemnation of the opposition and with a declaration of unconditional adhesion both to the policy of
the Party and to the person of No. 1."

"Stop this," said Rubashov in a flat voice. "You know
how this sort of statement is produced. If not, so much
the better for you. For God's sake, stop this comedy."

"We have nearly finished," said Ivanov. "We are now
only two years from the present time. During these two
years you were head of the State Aluminum Trust. A
year ago, on the occasion of the third trial of the opposition, the principal accused mentioned your name
repeatedly in somewhat obscure contexts. Nothing
tangible is revealed, but the suspicion grows in the ranks
of the Party. You make a new public statement, in which
you proclaim anew your devotion to the policy of the
Leadership and condemn the criminality of the opposition in still sharper terms. . . . That was six months
ago. And to-day you admit that for years already you
have considered the policy of the Leadership to be
wrong and harmful. . . ."

He paused and leant back again comfortably in his
chair.

"Your first declarations of loyalty," he continued,
"were therefore merely means to a definite end. I beg
you to take note that I am not moralizing. We both
grew up in the same tradition and have on these matters the same conception. You were convinced that

our policy was wrong and that your own was right. To say that openly at that time would have meant your expulsion from the Party, with the resulting impossibility to continue your work for your own ideas. So you had to throw out ballast in order to be able to serve the policy which, in your opinion, was the only right one. In your place, I would, of course, have acted in the same way. So far everything is in order."

"And what follows?" asked Rubashov.

Ivanov had again his former amiable smile.

"What I don't understand," he said, "is this. You now openly admit that for years you have had the conviction that we were ruining the Revolution; and in the same breath you deny that you belonged to the opposition and that you plotted against us. Do you really expect me to believe that you sat watching us with your hands in your lap—while, according to your conviction, we led country and Party to destruction?"

Rubashov shrugged his shoulders. "Perhaps I was too old and used up. . . . But believe what you like," he said.

Ivanov lit another cigarette. His voice became quiet and penetrating:

"Do you really want me to believe that you sacrificed Arlova and denied those"—he jerked his chin towards the light patch on the wall—"only in order to save your own head?"

Rubashov was silent. Quite a long time passed. Ivanov's head bent even closer over the writing desk.

"I don't understand you," he said. "Half an hour ago you made me a speech full of the most impassioned attacks against our policy, any fraction of which would have been enough to finish you off. And now you deny such a simple logical deduction as that you belonged to an oppositional group, for which, in any case, we hold all the proofs."

"Really?" said Rubashov. "If you have all the proofs, why do you need my confession? Proofs of what, by the way?"

"Amongst others," said Ivanov slowly, "proofs of a projected attempt on No. 1's life."

Again there was a silence. Rubashov put on his pince-nez.

"Allow me to ask you a question in my turn," he said. "Do you really believe this idiocy or do you only pretend to?"

In the corners of Ivanov's eyes appeared the same nearly tender smile as before:

"I told you. We have proofs. To be more exact: confessions. To be still more exact: the confession of the man who was actually to commit the attempt on your instigation."

"Congratulations," said Rubashov. "What is his name?"

Ivanov went on smiling.

"An indiscreet question."

"May I read that confession? Or be confronted with the man?"

Ivanov smiled. He blew the smoke of his cigarette with friendly mockery into Rubashov's face. It was unpleasant to Rubashov, but he did not move his head.

"Do you remember the veronal?" said Ivanov slowly. "I think I have already asked you that. Now the rôles are interchanged: to-day it is you who are about to throw yourself head first down the precipice. But not with my help. You then convinced me that suicide was petty bourgeois romanticism. I shall see that you do not succeed in committing it. Then we shall be quits."

Rubashov was silent. He was thinking over whether Ivanov was lying or sincere—and at the same time he had the strange wish, almost a physical impulse, to touch the light patch on the wall with his fingers. "Nerves," he thought. "Obsessions. Stepping only on the black tiles, murmuring senseless phrases, rubbing my pince-nez on my sleeve—there, I am doing it again. . . ."

"I am curious to know," he said aloud, "what scheme you have for my salvation. The way in which you have examined me up till now seems to have exactly the opposite aim."

Ivanov's smile became broad and beaming. "You old

fool," he said, and, reaching over the table, he grasped Rubashov's coat button. "I was obliged to let you explode once, else you would have exploded at the wrong time. Haven't you even noticed that I have no stenographer present?"

He took a cigarette out of the case and forced it into Rubashov's mouth without letting go his coat button. "You're behaving like an infant. Like a romantic infant," he added. "Now we are going to concoct a nice little confession and that will be all for to-day."

Rubashov at last managed to free himself from Ivanov's grip. He looked at him sharply through his pince-nez. "And what would be in this confession?" he asked.

Ivanov beamed at him unabatedly. "In the confession will be written," he said, "that you admit, since such and such a year, to have belonged to such and such a group of the opposition; but that you emphatically deny having organized or planned an assassination; that, on the contrary, you withdrew from the group when you learned of the opposition's criminal and terrorist plans."

For the first time during their discussion, Rubashov smiled, too.

"If that is the object of all this talk," he said, "we can break it off immediately."

"Let me finish what I was going to say," said Ivanov without any impatience. "I knew, of course, that you would stall. Let's first consider the moral or sentimental side of the matter. You do not give away anybody by what you admit. The whole bunch was arrested long before you, and half of them have been already liquidated; you know that yourself. From the rest, we can obtain other confessions than this harmless stuff—in fact, any confession we like. . . . I take it that you understand me and that my frankness convinces you."

"In other words: you yourself don't believe the story of the plot against No. 1," said Rubashov. "Then, why don't you confront me with this mysterious X, who made this alleged confession?"

"Think it over a bit," said Ivanov. "Put yourself in

my place—after all, our positions might equally well be
reversed—and find out the answer for yourself."

Rubashov thought it over. "You were given definite
instructions from above for the handling of my case," he
said.

Ivanov smiled. "That's a bit too sharply put. In
actual fact, it is not yet decided whether your case
should belong to category A or category P. You know
the terms?"

Rubashov nodded; he knew them.

"You begin to understand," said Ivanov. "A means:
administrative case, P means: public trial. The great
majority of political cases are tried administratively—
that is to say, those who would be no good in a public
trial. . . . If you fall into category A, you will be removed from my authority. The trial by the Administrative Board is secret and, as you know, somewhat
summary. There is no opportunity for confrontations
and that sort of thing. Think of . . ." Ivanov cited
three or four names, and gave a fugitive glance at the
light patch on the wall. When he turned towards
Rubashov again, the latter noticed for the first time a
tormented look in his face, a fixedness in his eye, as
though he were not focusing him, Rubashov, but a point
at some distance behind him.

Ivanov repeated again, in a lower tone, the names of
their former friends. "I knew them as well as you did,"
he went on. "But you must allow that we are as convinced that you and they would mean the end of the
Revolution as you are of the reverse. That is the
essential point. The methods follow by logical deduction.
We can't afford to lose ourselves in judicial subtleties.
Did you, in your time?"

Rubashov said nothing.

"It all depends," Ivanov went on, "on your being
classed in category P, and on the case remaining in
my hands. You know from what point of view those
cases are selected, which are given a public trial. I have
to prove a certain willingness on your part. For that I
need your deposition with a partial confession. If you

play the hero, and insist on giving the impression that there is nothing to be done with you, you will be finished off on the grounds of X's confession. On the other hand, if you make a partial confession, a basis is given for a more thorough examination. On this basis, I shall be able to obtain a confrontation; we will refute the worst points of the accusation and plead guilty within certain carefully defined limits. Even so, we shan't be able to make it cheaper than twenty years; that means, in fact, two or three years, and then an amnesty; and in five years you will be back in the ring again. Now have the goodness to think it over calmly before answering."

"I have already thought it over," said Rubashov. "I reject your proposition. Logically, you may be right. But I have had enough of this kind of logic. I am tired and I don't want to play this game any more. Be kind enough to have me taken back to my cell."

"As you like," said Ivanov. "I did not expect that you would agree at once. This kind of conversation usually has a retarded effect. You have a fortnight's time. Ask to be taken to me again when you have thought the matter over, or send me a written declaration. For I have no doubt that you will send one."

Rubashov stood up; Ivanov also rose; again he ranged half a head above Rubashov. He pressed an electric bell next to his desk. While they waited for the warder to come and fetch Rubashov, Ivanov said:

"You wrote in your last article, a few months ago, that this next decade will decide the fate of the world in our era. Don't you want to be here for that?"

He smiled down at Rubashov. In the corridor steps were approaching; the door was opened. Two warders came in and saluted. Without a word, Rubashov stepped between them; they started the march back to his cell. The noises in the corridors had now died out; from some cells came a subdued snoring, which sounded like moaning. All over the building the yellow, stale electric light was burning.

The Second Hearing

> When the existence of the Church is threat-
> ened, she is released from the command-
> ments of morality. With unity as the end,
> the use of every means is sanctified, even
> cunning, treachery, violence, simony, prison,
> death. For all order is for the sake of the
> community, and the individual must be sacri-
> ficed to the common good.
>
> DIETRICH VON NIEHEIM,
> BISHOP OF VERDEN:
> *De schismate libri III*, A.D. 1411

1

*Extract from the diary of N. S. Rubashov, on the fifth day
of imprisonment*

". . . The ultimate truth is penultimately always a
falsehood. He who will be proved right in the end appears to be wrong and harmful before it.

"But who will be proved right? It will only be known
later. Meanwhile he is bound to act on credit and to sell
his soul to the devil, in the hope of history's absolution.

"It is said that No. 1 has Machiavelli's *Prince*
lying permanently by his bedside. So he should: since
then, nothing really important has been said about the
rules of political ethics. We were the first to replace
the nineteenth century's liberal ethics of 'fair play' by
the revolutionary ethics of the twentieth century. In that
also we were right: a revolution conducted according
to the rules of cricket is an absurdity. Politics can be
relatively fair in the breathing spaces of history; at its
critical turning points there is no other rule possible
than the old one, that the end justifies the means. We
introduced neo-Machiavellism into this country; the
others, the counter-revolutionary dictatorships, have
clumsily imitated it. We were neo-Machiavellians in the

name of universal reason—that was our greatness; the others in the name of a national romanticism, that is their anachronism. That is why we will in the end be absolved by history; but not they. . . .

"Yet for the moment we are thinking and acting on credit. As we have thrown overboard all conventions and rules of cricket-morality, our sole guiding principle is that of consequent logic. We are under the terrible compulsion to follow our thought down to its final consequence and to act in accordance to it. We are sailing without ballast; therefore each touch on the helm is a matter of life or death.

"A short time ago, our leading agriculturist, B., was shot with thirty of his collaborators because he maintained the opinion that nitrate artificial manure was superior to potash. No. 1 is all for potash; therefore B. and the thirty had to be liquidated as saboteurs. In a nationally centralized agriculture, the alternative of nitrate of potash is of enormous importance: it can decide the issue of the next war. If No. 1 was in the right, history will absolve him, and the execution of the thirty-one men will be a mere bagatelle. If he was wrong . . .

"It is that alone that matters who is objectively in the right. The cricket-moralists are agitated by quite another problem: whether B. was subjectively in good faith when he recommended nitrogen. If he was not, according to their ethics he should be shot, even if it should subsequently be shown that nitrogen would have been better after all. If he was in good faith, then he should be acquitted and allowed to continue making propaganda for nitrate, even if the country should be ruined by it. . . .

"That is, of course, complete nonsense. For us the question of subjective good faith is of no interest. He who is in the wrong must pay; he who is in the right will be absolved. That is the law of historical credit; it was our law.

"History has taught us that often lies serve her better than the truth; for man is sluggish and has to be led *through the desert for forty years before each step in his development. And he has to be driven through the desert with threats and promises, by imaginary terrors and imaginary consolations, so that he should not sit down prematurely to rest and divert himself by worshipping golden calves.*

"We have learnt history more thoroughly than the others. We differ from all others in our logical consistency. We know that virtue does not matter to history, and that crimes remain unpunished; but that every error had its consequences and venges itself unto the seventh generation. Therefore we concentrated all our efforts on preventing error and destroying the very seeds of it. Never in history has so much power over the future of humanity been concentrated in so few hands as in our case. Each wrong idea we follow is a crime committed against future generations. Therefore we have to punish wrong ideas as others punish crimes: with death. We were held for madmen because we followed every thought down to its final consequence and acted accordingly. We were compared to the inquisition because, like them, we constantly felt in ourselves the whole weight of responsibility for the superindividual life to come. We resembled the great Inquisitors in that we persecuted the seeds of evil not only in men's deeds, but in their thoughts. We admitted no private sphere, not even inside a man's skull. We lived under the compulsion of working things out to their final conclusions. Our minds were so tensely charged that the slightest collision caused a mortal short-circuit. Thus we were fated to mutual destruction.

"I was one of those. I have thought and acted as I had to; I destroyed people whom I was fond of, and gave power to others I did not like. History put me where I stood; I have exhausted the credit which she accorded me; if I was right I have nothing to repent of; if wrong, I will pay.

"But how can the present decide what will be judged truth in the future? We are doing the work of prophets without their gift. We replaced vision by logical de-

duction; but although we all started from the same point of departure, we came to divergent results. Proof disproved proof, and finally we had to recur to faith— to axiomatic faith in the rightness of one's own reasoning. That is the crucial point. We have thrown all ballast overboard; only one anchor holds us: faith in one's self. Geometry is the purest realization of human reason; but Euclid's axioms cannot be proved. He who does not believe in them sees the whole building crash.

"No. 1 has faith in himself, tough, slow, sullen and unshakable. He has the most solid anchor-chain of all. Mine has worn thin in the last few years. . . .

"The fact is: I no longer believe in my infallibility. That is why I am lost."

2

The day after the first hearing of Rubashov, the Examining Magistrate Ivanov and his colleague Gletkin were sitting in the canteen after dinner. Ivanov was tired; he had propped his artificial leg up on a second chair and undone the collar of his uniform. He poured out some of the cheap wine which the canteen provided, and silently wondered at Gletkin, who sat straight up on his chair in his starched uniform, which creaked at every movement. He had not even taken off his revolver belt, although he must have been pretty tired, too. Gletkin emptied his glass; the conspicuous scar on his clean-shaven head had reddened slightly. Besides them, only three other officers were in the canteen at a distant table; two were playing chess, the third looking on.

"What is to happen about Rubashov?" asked Gletkin.

"He is in rather a bad way," answered Ivanov. "But he is still as logical as ever. So he will capitulate."

"That I don't believe," said Gletkin.

"He will," said Ivanov. "When he has thought out everything to its logical conclusion, he will capitulate. Therefore the essential thing is to leave him in peace and not to disturb him. I have allowed him paper, pencil and cigarettes—to accelerate the process of thought."

"I consider that wrong," said Gletkin.

"You don't like him," said Ivanov. "You had a scene with him a few days ago, I believe?"

Gletkin thought of the scene when Rubashov had sat on his bunk and pulled his shoe over his ragged sock. "That does not matter," he said. "His personality does not matter. It is the method which I consider wrong. It will never make him give in."

"When Rubashov capitulates," said Ivanov, "it won't be out of cowardice, but by logic. It is no use trying the hard method with him. He is made out of a certain material which becomes the tougher the more you hammer on it."

"That is just talk," said Gletkin. "Human beings able to resist any amount of physical pressure do not exist. I have never seen one. Experience shows me that the resistance of the human nerve system is limited by Nature."

"I wouldn't like to fall into your hands," said Ivanov smilingly, but with a trace of uneasiness. "Anyhow, you are a living refutation of your own theory."

His smiling glance rested for a second on the scar on Gletkin's skull. The story of that scar was well-known. When, during the Civil War, Gletkin had fallen into the enemy's hands, they had tied a lighted candlewick on to his shaven skull, to extract from him certain information. A few hours later his own people recaptured the position and found him unconscious. The wick had burnt right to the end; Gletkin had kept silence.

He looked at Ivanov with his expressionless eyes. "That's only talk, too," he said. "I did not give in because I fainted. If I had stayed conscious another minute, I should have spoken. It is a question of constitution."

He emptied his glass with a deliberate gesture; his cuffs crackled as he put it down on the table again. "When I came to, I was convinced at first that I *had* spoken. But the two N.C.O.s who were freed together with me asserted the contrary. So I was decorated. It is all a question of constitution; the rest is just fairy tales."

Ivanov was drinking too. He had already drunk quite a lot of the cheap wine. He shrugged his shoulders.

"Since when have you had this notable constitution theory? After all, during the first years these methods did not exist. At that time we were still full of illusions. Abolition of punishment and of retaliation for crime; sanatoriums with flower gardens for the a-social elements. It's all humbug."

"I don't believe it is," said Gletkin. "You are a cynic. In a hundred years we will have all that. But first we have to get through. The quicker, the better. The only illusion was, to believe the time had already come. When I first was put here, I was also under that illusion. Most of us were—in fact, the entire apparatus up to the top. We wanted to start at once with the flower gardens. That was a mistake. In a hundred years we will be able to appeal to the criminal's reason and social instincts. To-day we have still to work on his physical constitution, and crush him, physically and mentally, if necessary."

Ivanov wondered whether Gletkin was drunk. But he saw by his quiet, expressionless eyes that he was not. Ivanov smiled at him rather vaguely. "In a word, I am the cynic and you are the moralist."

Gletkin said nothing. He sat stiffly on his chair in his starched uniform; his revolver-belt smelled of fresh leather.

"Several years ago," said Gletkin after a while, "a little peasant was brought to me to be cross-examined. It was in the provinces, at the time when we still believed in the flower-garden theory, as you call it. Cross-examinations were conducted in a very gentlemanly way. The peasant had buried his crops; it was at the beginning of the collectivization of the land. I kept strictly to the prescribed etiquette. I explained to him in a friendly way that we needed the corn to feed the growing city population and for export, in order to build up our industries; so would he please tell me where he had hidden his crops. The peasant had his head drawn into his shoulders when he was brought into my room, expecting a beating. I knew his kind; I am myself country-born. When, instead of beating him, I began to reason with him, to talk to him as an equal and call him 'citizen,' he took me for a half-wit. I saw it in his eyes. I talked at him for half an hour. He never opened his mouth and alternately picked his nose and his ears. I went on talking, although I saw that he held the whole thing for a superb joke and was not listening at all. Arguments simply did not penetrate his ears. They were blocked up by the wax of centuries of patriarchal mental paralysis. I held strictly to the regulations; it never even occurred to me that there were other methods. . . .

"At that time I had twenty to thirty such cases daily. My colleagues the same. The Revolution was in danger of foundering on these little fat peasants. The workers were undernourished; whole districts were ravaged by starvation typhus; we had no credit with which to build up our armament industry, and we were expecting to be attacked from month to month. Two hundred millions in gold lay hidden in the woollen stockings of these fellows and half the crops were buried underground. And, when cross-examining them, we addressed them as 'citizen,' while they blinked at us with their sly-stupid eyes, took it all for a superb joke and picked their noses.

"The third hearing of my man took place at two o'clock at night; I had previously worked for eighteen hours on end. He had been woken up; he was drunk with sleep and frightened; he betrayed himself. From that time I cross-examined my people chiefly at night. . . . Once a woman complained that she had been kept standing outside my room the whole night, awaiting her turn. Her legs were shaking and she was completely tired out; in the middle of the hearing she fell asleep. I woke her up; she went on talking, in a sleepy mumbling voice, without fully realizing what she was saying, and fell asleep again. I woke her once more, and she admitted everything and signed the statement without reading it, in order that I should let her sleep. Her husband had hidden two machine guns in his barn and persuaded the farmers of his village to burn the corn because the Anti-Christ had appeared to him in a dream. That the wife had been kept waiting on her feet the whole night was due to the carelessness of my sergeant; from then onwards I encouraged carelessness of that kind; stubborn cases had to stand upright on one spot for as long as forty-eight hours. After that the wax had melted out of their ears, and one could talk to them. . . ."

The two chess-players in the other corner of the room threw over the chess-men and started a new game. The third man had already left. Ivanov watched Gletkin while he talked. His voice was as sober and expressionless as ever.

"My colleagues had similar experiences. It was the only possible way to obtain results. The regulations were observed; not a prisoner was actually touched. But it happened that they had to witness—so to speak accidentally—the execution of their fellow prisoners. The effect of such scenes is partly mental, partly physical. Another example: there are showers and baths for reasons of hygiene. That in winter the heating and hot-water pipes did not always function, was due to technical difficulties; and the duration of the baths depended on the attendants. Sometimes, again, the heating and hot-water apparatus functioned all too well; that equally depended on the attendants. They were all old comrades; it was not necessary to give them detailed instructions; they understood what was at stake."

"That'll about do," said Ivanov.

"You asked me how I came to discover my theory and I am explaining it to you," said Gletkin. "What matters is, that one should keep in mind the logical necessity of it all; otherwise one is a cynic, like you. It is getting late and I must go."

Ivanov emptied his glass and settled his artificial leg on the chair; he again had rheumatic pains in the stump. He was annoyed with himself for having started this conversation.

Gletkin paid. When the canteen waiter had gone, he asked:

"What is going to be done about Rubashov?"

"I have told you my opinion," said Ivanov. "He should be left in peace."

Gletkin stood up. His boots creaked. He stood by the chair on which Ivanov's leg rested.

"I recognize his past merits," he said. "But to-day he has become as harmful as my fat peasant was; only more dangerous."

Ivanov looked up into Gletkin's expressionless eyes.

"I have given him a fortnight's time for reflection," he said. "Until that is over I want him to be left in peace."

Ivanov had spoken in his official tone. Gletkin was his subordinate. He saluted and left the canteen with creaking boots.

Ivanov remained seated. He drank another glass, lit a cigarette and blew the smoke out in front of him. After a while he stood up and limped over to the two officers to watch their game of chess.

3

Since his first hearing, Rubashov's standard of life had improved miraculously. Already on the following morning the old turnkey had brought him paper, pencil, soap and a towel. At the same time he gave Rubashov prison vouchers to the value of the cash he had had in his possession when he was arrested, and explained to him that he now had the right to order tobacco and extra food from the prisoners' canteen.

Rubashov ordered his cigarettes and some food. The old man was just as surly and monosyllabic as ever, but he shuffled up promptly with the things Rubashov had asked for. Rubashov thought for a moment of demanding a doctor from outside the prison, but he forgot about it. His tooth did not hurt for the moment, and when he had washed and had had something to eat, he felt much better.

The courtyard had been cleared of snow, and groups

of prisoners walked round it for their daily exercise. It had been interrupted because of the snow; only Hare-lip and his companion had been allowed daily ten minutes' walk, perhaps because of special doctor's orders; every time that they entered or left the yard, Hare-lip had looked up to Rubashov's window. The gesture was so clear as to exclude any possibility of doubt.

When Rubashov was not working at his notes or walking up and down his cell, he stood at the window with his forehead against the pane, and watched the prisoners during their round of exercise. This occurred in groups of twelve at a time, who circled round the yard in pairs at a distance of ten paces from each other. In the middle of the yard stood four uniformed officials who saw that the prisoners did not talk; they formed the axis of the roundabout, which turned slowly and steadily for exactly twenty minutes. Then the prisoners were conducted back into the building through the door on the right, while simultaneously a new group entered the yard through the left door, and went through the same monotonous roundabout until the next relief.

During the first few days Rubashov had looked for familiar faces, but found none. That relieved him: for the moment he wanted to avoid any possible reminder of the outside world, anything which might distract him from his task. His task was to work his thoughts to a conclusion, to come to terms with the past and future, with the living and the dead. He had still ten days left of the term set by Ivanov.

He could only hold his thoughts by writing them down; but writing exhausted him so much that he could at the most force himself to it for an hour or two a day. The rest of the time his brain worked on its own account.

Rubashov had always believed that he knew himself rather well. Being without moral prejudices, he had no illusions about the phenomenon called the "first person singular," and had taken for granted, without particular emotion, that this phenomenon was endowed with certain impulses which people are generally reluctant to admit. Now, when he stood with his forehead against the window or suddenly stopped on the third black tile, he made unexpected discoveries. He found out that those processes wrongly known as "monologues" are really dialogues of a special kind; dialogues in which one partner remains silent while the other, against all grammatical rules, addresses him as "I" instead of "you", in order to creep into his confidence and to fathom his intentions; but the silent partner just remains silent, shuns observation and even refuses to be localized in time and space.

Now, however, it seemed to Rubashov that the habitually silent partner spoke sometimes, without being addressed and without any visible pretext; his voice sounded totally unfamiliar to Rubashov, who listened in honest wonder and found that his own lips were moving. These experiences held nothing mystic or mysterious; they were of a quite concrete character; and by his observations Rubashov gradually became convinced that there was a thoroughly tangible component in this first person singular, which had remained silent through all these years and now had started to speak.

This discovery preoccupied Rubashov far more intensely than did the details of his interview with Ivanov. He considered it as settled that he would not accept Ivanov's proposals, and that he would refuse to go on with the game; in consequence, he had only a limited time still to live; and this conviction formed the basis of his reflections.

He did not think at all of the absurd story of a plot against No. 1's life; he was far more interested in the personality of Ivanov himself. Ivanov had said that their rôles could equally well have been reversed; in that he was doubtless right. He himself and Ivanov were twins in their development; they did not come from the same ovum, yet were nourished by the same umbilical cord of a common conviction; the intense environment of the Party had etched and moulded the character of both during the decisive years of development. They had the same moral standard, the same philosophy, they thought in the same terms. Their positions might just as well have been the other way round. Then Rubashov would have sat behind the desk and Ivanov in front of it; and from that position Rubashov would probably have used the same arguments as had Ivanov. The rules of the game were fixed. They only admitted variations in detail.

The old compulsion to think through the minds of others had again taken hold of him; he sat in Ivanov's place and saw himself through Ivanov's eyes, in the position of the accused, as once he had seen Richard and Little Loewy. He saw this degraded Rubashov, the shadow of the former companion, and he understood the mixture of tenderness and contempt with which Ivanov had treated him. During their discussion, he had repeatedly asked himself whether Ivanov was sincere or hypocritical; whether he was laying traps for him, or really wanted to show him a way of escape. Now, putting himself in Ivanov's position, he realized that Ivanov was sincere—as much so or as little, as he himself had been towards Richard or Little Loewy.

These reflections also had the form of a monologue, but along familiar lines; that newly discovered entity, the silent partner, did not participate in them. Although it was supposed to be the person addressed in all monologues, it remained dumb, and its existence was limited to a grammatical abstraction called the "first person singular". Direct questions and logical meditations did not induce it to speak; its utterances occurred without visible cause and, strangely enough, always accompanied by a sharp attack of toothache. Its mental sphere seemed to be composed of such various and disconnected parts as the folded hands of the *Pietà*, Little Loewy's cats, the tune of the song with the refrain of "come to dust", or a particular sentence which Arlova had once spoken on a particular occasion. Its means of expression were equally fragmentary: for instance, the compulsion to rub one's pince-nez on one's sleeve, the impulse to touch the light patch on the wall

of Ivanov's room, the uncontrollable movements of
the lips which murmured such senseless sentences as
"I shall pay", and the dazed state induced by day-
dreams of past episodes in one's life.

Rubashov tried to study this newly discovered entity
very thoroughly during his wanderings through the cell;
with the shyness of emphasizing the first person singular
customary in the Party, he had christened it the "grammatical fiction". He probably had only a few weeks left
to live, and he felt a compelling urge to clear up this
matter, to "think it to a logical conclusion". But the
realm of the "grammatical fiction" seemed to begin just
where the "thinking to a conclusion" ended. It was obviously an essential part of its being, to remain out of
the reach of logical thought, and then to take one unawares, as from an ambush, and attack one with day-
dreams and toothache. Thus, Rubashov passed the entire seventh day of his imprisonment, the third after the
first hearing, re-living a past period of his existence—
namely, his relation with the girl Arlova, who had been
shot.

The exact moment in which, in spite of his resolutions,
he had slid into the day-dream was as impossible to
establish afterwards as the moment in which one falls
asleep. On the morning of this seventh day, he had
worked on his notes, then, presumably, he had stood
up to stretch his legs a bit—and only when he heard
the rattling of the key in the lock did he wake up to
the fact that it was already midday, and that he had
walked back and forth in the cell for hours on end. He
even had hung the blanket round his shoulders because,
presumably also for several hours, he had been
rhythmically shaken by a kind of ague and had felt
the nerve of his tooth pulsing in his temples. He ab-
sently spooned out his bowl which the orderlies had
filled with their ladles, and continued his walk. The
warder, who observed him from time to time through
the spy-hole, saw that he had shiveringly hunched up his
shoulders and that his lips were moving.

Once more Rubashov breathed the air of his erstwhile

office in the Trade Delegation, which was filled with the peculiarly familiar odor of Arlova's big, well-formed and sluggish body; once more he saw the curve of her bowed neck over the white blouse, bent over her note-book while he dictated, and her round eyes following his wanderings through the room in the intervals between the sentences. She always wore white blouses, of the same kind as Rubashov's sisters had worn at home, embroidered with little flowers at the high neck, and always the same cheap ear-rings, which stood out a little from her cheeks as she bent over her note-book. In her slow, passive way, she was as if made for this job, and had an unusually quietening effect on Rubashov's nerves when he was overworked. He had taken over his new post as leader of the Trade Delegation in B. immediately after the incident with Little Loewy, and had thrown himself into work head first; he was grateful to the C.C. for providing him with this bureaucratic activity. It was exceedingly rare that leading men out of the International were transferred to the diplomatic services. No. 1 presumably had special intentions with him, for usually the two hierarchies were kept strictly apart, were not allowed to have contact with each other, and sometimes even followed opposite policies. Only when seen from the higher viewpoint of the spheres around No. 1 did the apparent contradictions resolve themselves and the motives became clear.

Rubashov needed some time to get used to his new way of life; it amused him that he now had a diplomatic passport, which was even authentic and in his own name; that, in formal clothes, he had to take part in receptions; that policemen stood to attention for him, and that the inconspicuously dressed men in black bowlers who sometimes followed him about were doing it solely out of tender care for his safety.

At first he felt slightly estranged by the atmosphere in the rooms of the Trade Delegation, which was attached to the legation. He understood that in the bourgeois world one had to be representative and play their game, but he considered that the game was played rather too well here, so that it was hardly possible to distinguish appearance from reality. When the First Secretary of the legation drew Rubashov's attention to certain necessary changes in his dress and in his style of living—the First Secretary had before the Revolution forged money in the service of the Party—he did not do this in a comradely, humorous way, but with such underlined consideration and tact that the scene became embarrassing and got on Rubashov's nerves.

Rubashov had twelve subordinates, each with a clearly defined rank; there were First and Second Assistants, First and Second Book-keepers, Secretaries and Assistant Secretaries. Rubashov had the feeling that the whole bunch of them regarded him as something between a national hero and a robber chief. They treated him with exaggerated respect and indulgently superior tolerance. When the Secretary to the legation had to report to him about a document, he made an effort to express himself in the simple terms one would use to a savage or a child. Rubashov's private secretary, Arlova, got on his nerves the least; only he could not understand why she wore such ridiculously high-heeled, patent-leather shoes with her pleasant, simple blouses and skirts.

It was nearly a month before he first spoke to her in a conversational tone. He was tired by dictating and walking up and down, and suddenly became aware of the silence in the room. "Why do you never say anything, Comrade Arlova?" he asked, and sat down in the comfortable chair behind his writing-desk.

"If you like," she answered in her sleepy voice, "I will always repeat the last word of the sentence."

Every day she sat on her chair in front of the desk, in her embroidered blouse, her heavy, shapely bust bent over the note-book, with bowed head and ear-rings hanging parallel to her cheeks. The only jarring element was the patent leather shoes with pointed heels, but she never crossed her legs, as most of the women did whom Rubashov knew. As he always walked up and down while dictating, he usually saw her from behind or half in profile, and the thing he remembered most clearly was the curve of her bent neck. The back of her neck was neither fluffy nor shaved; the skin was white and taut over the vertebræ; below were the embroidered flowers on the edge of her white blouse.

In his youth Rubashov had not had much to do with women; nearly always they were comrades, and nearly always the start of the affair had been a discussion prolonged so late into the night that whichever was the other's guest missed the last tram home.

After that unsuccessful attempt at a conversation, another fortnight passed. At first Arlova had really repeated the last word of the dictated sentence in her drowsy voice; then she had given it up, and when Rubashov paused, the room was again still and saturated with her sisterly perfume. One afternoon, to his own surprise, Rubashov stopped behind her chair, put both his hands lightly on her shoulders, and asked her whether she would go out with him in the evening. She did not jerk back and her shoulders kept still under his touch; she nodded in silence and did not even turn her head. It was not a habit of Rubashov's to make frivolous jokes, but later in the same night he could not forbear saying with a smile: "One would think you were still taking down dictation." The outline of her large, well-shaped breast seemed as familiar against the darkness of the room as though she had always been there. Only the ear-rings now lay flat on the pillow. Her eyes had the same expression as ever, when she pronounced that sentence which could no more leave Rubashov's memory than the folded hands of the *Pietà*, and the smell of sea-weed in the harbour town:

"You will always be able to do what you like with me."

"But why?" asked Rubashov, astonished and slightly startled.

She did not answer. Probably she was already asleep. Asleep, her breathing was as inaudible as waking. Rubashov had never noticed that she breathed at all. He had never seen her with shut eyes. It made her face strange to him; it was much more expressive with shut eyes than with open. Strange to him also were the dark shadows of her armpits; her chin, otherwise lowered to her breast, stuck out steeply like a dead woman's. But the light, sisterly scent of her body was familiar to him, even asleep.

The next day and all the following days, she sat again in her white blouse, bent over the desk; the next night and all the following nights the paler silhouette of her breast was raised against the dark bedroom curtain. Rubashov lived by day and by night in the atmosphere of her large, lazy body. Her behaviour during work remained unaltered, her voice and the expression of her eyes was the same; never did they contain the least suggestion of an allusion. From time to time, when Rubashov was tired by dictating, he stopped behind her chair and leaned his hands on her shoulders; he said nothing, and under the blouse her warm shoulders did not move; then he found the phrase he had been searching for, and, resuming his wandering through the room, he went on dictating.

Sometimes he added sarcastic commentaries to what he was dictating; then she stopped writing and waited, pencil in hand, until he had finished; but she never smiled at his sarcasms and Rubashov never discovered what she thought of them. Only once, after a particularly dangerous joke of Rubashov's, referring to certain personal habits of No. 1's she said suddenly, in her sleepy voice: "You ought not to say such things in front of other people; you ought to be more careful altogether. . . ." But from time to time, particularly when instructions and circulars from above arrived, he felt a need to give vent to his heretical witticisms.

It was the time of preparation for the second great trial of the opposition. The air in the legation had become peculiarly thin. Photographs and portraits disappeared from walls overnight; they had hung there for years, nobody had looked at them, but now the light patches leaped to the eye. The staff restricted their conversation to service matters; they spoke to each other with a careful and reserved politeness. At meals in the

Legation canteen, when conversation was unavoidable, they stuck to the stock phrases of official terminology, which, in the familiar atmosphere, appeared grotesque and rather uneasy; it was as though, between requests for salt-cellar and mustard-pot, they called out to each other the catch-words of the latest Congress manifesto. Often it happened that somebody protested against a supposed false interpretation of what he had just said, and called his neighbours to witness, with precipitate exclamations of "I did not say that", or "That is not what I meant". The whole thing gave Rubashov the impression of a queer and ceremonious marionette-play with figures, moving on wires, each saying their set piece. Arlova alone, with her silent, sleepy manner, seemed to remain unchanged.

Not only the portraits on the walls, but also the shelves in the library were thinned out. The disappearance of certain books and brochures happened discreetly, usually the day after the arrival of a new message from above. Rubashov made his sarcastic commentaries on it while dictating to Arlova, who received them in silence. Most of the works on foreign trade and currency disappeared from the shelves—their author, the People's Commissar for Finance, had just been arrested; also nearly all old Party Congress reports treating the same subject; most books and reference-books on the history of antecedents of the Revolution; most works by living authors of jurisprudence and philosophy; all pamphlets dealing with the problems of birth control; the manuals on the structure of the People's Army; treatises on trade unionism and the right to strike in the People's state; practically every study of the problems of political constitution more than two years old, and, finally, even the volumes of the *Encyclopædia* published by the Academy—a new revised edition being promised shortly.

New books arrived, too; the classics of social science appeared with new footnotes and commentaries, the old histories were replaced by new histories, the old memoirs of dead revolutionary leaders were replaced by

new memoirs of the same defunct. Rubashov remarked
jokingly to Arlova that the only thing left to be done
was to publish a new and revised edition of the back
numbers of all newspapers.

In the meantime, a few weeks ago, an order had
come from "above", to appoint a librarian who would
take the political responsibility for the contents of the
Legation library. They had appointed Arlova to this
post. At first Rubashov had mumbled something about
a "kindergarten" and had held the whole thing for an
imbecility, up to the evening when, at the weekly meeting
of the legation Party cell, Arlova had been sharply attacked from several sides. Three or four speakers,
amongst whom was the First Secretary, rose and complained that some of the most important speeches of
No. 1 were not to be found in the library, that on the
other hand it was still full of oppositional works, and
that books by politicians who had since been unmasked
as spies, traitors and agents of foreign Powers had until
quite recently occupied prominent positions in the shelves;
so that one could hardly avoid a suspicion of an intentional demonstration. The speakers were dispassionate
and cuttingly business-like; they used carefully selected
phrases. It seemed as though they were giving each
other the cues for a prearranged text. All speeches
ended with the conclusion that the Party's chief duty
was to be watchful, to denounce abuses mercilessly,
and that whoever did not fulfil this duty made himself
an accomplice of the vile *saboteurs*. Arlova, summoned
to make a statement, said with her usual equanimity,
that she was far from having any evil intent, and that
she had followed every instruction given to her; but
while she was speaking in her deep, slightly blurred
voice, she let her glance rest a long time on Rubashov,
which she otherwise never did in the presence of others.
The meeting ended with the resolution to give Arlova a
"serious warning".

Rubashov, who knew only too well the methods
lately brought into use in the Party, became uneasy. He
guessed that there was something in store for Arlova

and felt helpless, because there was nothing tangible to fight against.

The air in the Legation became even thinner. Rubashov stopped making personal comments while dictating, and that gave him a singular feeling of guilt. There was apparently no change in his relations with Arlova, but this curious feeling of guilt, which was solely due to the fact that he no longer felt capable of making witty remarks while dictating, prevented him stopping behind her chair and putting his hands on her shoulders, as he used to do. After a week, Arlova stayed away from his room one evening, and did not come the following evenings either. It was three days before Rubashov could bring himself to ask her the reason. She answered something about a migraine in her sleepy voice and Rubashov did not press her any further. From then on she did not come again, with one exception.

This was three weeks after the cell meeting which had pronounced the "serious warning", and a fortnight after she had first stopped visiting him. Her behaviour was almost as usual, but the whole evening Rubashov had the feeling that she was waiting for him to say something decisive. He only said, however, that he was glad she was back again, and that he was overworked and tired—which actually was the case. In the night he noticed repeatedly that she was awake and staring into the dark. He could not get rid of this tormenting sense of guilt; also his toothache had started again. That was her last visit to him.

Next day, before Arlova had appeared in his office, the Secretary told Rubashov, in a manner which was supposed to be confidential, but with each sentence carefully formulated, that Arlova's brother and sister-in-law had been arrested a week ago "over there". Arlova's brother had married a foreigner; they were both accused of having treasonable connections with her native country in the service of the opposition.

A few minutes later Arlova arrived for work. She sat, as always, on her chair in front of the desk, in her embroidered blouse, slightly bent forward. Rubashov walked up and down behind her, and all the time he had before his eyes her bent neck, with the skin slightly stretched over the neck-bones. He could not take his eyes off this piece of skin, and felt an uneasiness which amounted to physical discomfort. The thought would not leave him that "over there" the condemned were shot through the back of the neck.

At the next meeting of the Party cell Arlova was dismissed from her post as librarian because of political untrustworthiness, on the motion of the First Secretary. No comment was made and there was no discussion. Rubashov, who was suffering from almost intolerable toothache, had excused himself from attending the meeting. A few days afterwards Arlova and another member of the staff were recalled. Their names were never mentioned by their former colleagues; but, during the months he remained in the Legation before he was himself recalled, the sisterly scent of her large, lazy body clung to the walls of his room and never left them.

4

ARIE, YE WRETCHED OF THE EARTH.

Since the morning of the tenth day after Rubashov's arrest, his new neighbour to the left, the occupant of No. 406, tapped out the same line at regular intervals, always with the same spelling mistake: "ARIE" instead of "ARISE". Rubashov had tried to start a conversation with him several times. As long as Rubashov was tapping, his new neighbour listened in silence; but the only answer he ever received was a row of disconnected letters and to conclude always the same crippled verse:

ARIE, YE WRETCHED OF THE EARTH.

The new neighbour had been put in there the night before. Rubashov had woken, but had only heard muffled sounds and the locking of cell No. 406. In the morning after the first bugle-blast, No. 406 had at once started to tap: ARIE, YE WRETCHED OF THE EARTH. He tapped quickly and deftly, with the technique of a virtuoso, so that his spelling mistake and the senselessness of his other messages must have had not technical but mental causes. Probably the new neighbour's mind was deranged.

After breakfast, the young officer in No. 402 gave the sign that he wanted conversation. Between Rubashov and No. 402 a sort of friendship had developed. The officer with the eye-glass and the turned-up moustache must have been living in a state of chronic boredom, for he was always grateful to Rubashov for the smallest crumbs of conversation. Five or six times during the day he would humbly beg Rubashov:

DO TALK TO ME. . . .

Rubashov was rarely in the mood for it; neither did he know quite what to talk about to No. 402. Usually No. 402 tapped out classical anecdotes of the officer's mess. When the point had been reached, there would be a painful silence. They were dusty old anecdotes, of a patriarchal obscenity; one imagined how, having tapped them to a conclusion, No. 402 would wait for roars of laughter and stare despairingly at the dumb, whitewashed wall. Out of sympathy and politeness, Rubashov occasionally tapped out a loud HA-HA! with his pince-nez as a laughter-substitute. Then there would be no holding No. 402; he imitated an outburst of merriment, by drumming against the wall with fists and boots: HA-HA! HA-HA! and making occasional pauses, to make sure Rubashov was joining in. If Rubashov remained silent, he was reproachful: YOU DIDN'T LAUGH. . . . If, in order to be left in peace, Rubashov gave one or two HA-HA's, No. 402 informed him afterwards: WE HAD JOLLY GOOD FUN.

Sometimes he reviled Rubashov. Occasionally, if he got no answer, he would tap out the whole of a military song with an endless number of verses. It sometimes happened, when Rubashov was walking to and fro, sunk in a day-dream or in meditation, that he started humming the refrain of an old march, the sign for which his ear had unconsciously registered.

And yet No. 402 was useful. He had been there for more than two years already; he knew the ropes, he was in communication with several neighbours and heard all the gossip; he seemed informed of everything which happened in the building.

On the morning after the arrival of No. 406, when the officer opened the usual conversation, Rubashov asked him whether he knew who was his new neighbour. To which 402 replied:

RIP VAN WINKLE.

No. 402 was fond of speaking in riddles, in order to bring an element of excitement into the conversation. Rubashov searched his memory. He remembered the story of the man who had slept for twenty-five years and found an unrecognizable world on his awakening.

HAS HE LOST HIS MEMORY? asked Rubashov.

No. 402, satisfied by his effect, told Rubashov what he knew. No. 406 had once been a teacher of sociology in a small state in the south-east of Europe. At the end of the last War he took part in the revolution which had broken out in his country, as in most countries of Europe at that time. A "Commune" was created, which led a romantic existence for a few weeks, and met the usual bloody end. The leaders of the revolution had been amateurs, but the repression which followed was carried out with professional thoroughness; No. 406, to whom the Commune had given the sonorous title of "State Secretary for the Enlightenment of the People", was condemned to death by hanging. He waited a year for his execution, then the sentence was commuted to lifelong imprisonment. He served twenty years of it.

He served twenty years, most of the time in solitary confinement, without communication with the outside world, and without newspapers. He was to all intents and purposes forgotten; the administration of justice in that south-eastern country still was of a rather patriarchal character. A month ago he was suddenly released by an amnesty—Rip Van Winkle, who, after more than twenty years of sleep and darkness, finds himself on earth again.

He took the first train hither, to the land of his dreams. Fourteen days after his arrival he was arrested. Perhaps, after twenty years of solitary confinement, he had become too talkative. Perhaps he had told people what he had imagined the life would be like over here—during the days and nights in his cell. Perhaps he had asked for the addresses of old friends, the heroes of the Revolution, without knowing that they were nothing but traitors and spies. Perhaps he had laid a wreath on the wrong grave, or had wished to pay a call on his illustrious neighbour, Comrade Rubashov.

Now he could ask himself which was better: two decades of dreams on a palliasse in a dark cell or two weeks' reality in the light of day. Perhaps he was no longer quite sane. That was the story of Rip Van Winkle. . . .

Some time after No. 402 had tapped out his long report, Rip Van Winkle again started; five or six times he repeated his mutilated verse, ARIE, YE WRETCHED OF THE EARTH, and then fell silent.

Rubashov lay on his bunk, with eyes shut. The "grammatical fiction" was again making itself felt; it did not express itself in words, only in a vague uneasiness which meant:

"For that too you must pay, for that too you are responsible; for you acted while he dreamed."

In the same afternoon Rubashov was taken to be shaved.

This time the procession consisted only of the old warder and one uniformed guard; the old man shuffled along two steps ahead, the soldier marched along two steps behind Rubashov. They passed No. 406; but there was still no name-card on the door. In the barber's shop there was only one of the two prisoners who ran it; it was obviously being seen to that Rubashov did not make too many contacts.

He sat down in the armchair. The establishment was comparatively clean; there was even a mirror. He took off his pince-nez and glanced at his face in the glass; he saw no change, except for the stubble on his cheeks.

The barber worked in silence, rapidly and carefully. The door of the room remained open; the warder had shuffled off; the uniformed guard stood leaning against the door-post and watched the procedure. The tepid lather on

his face made Rubashov feel happy; he felt a slight temptation to yearn after the little pleasures of life. He would
have liked to chat to the barber; but he knew it was forbidden, and he did not want to make trouble for the
barber, whose broad, open face he liked. By his physi-
ognomy, Rubashov would have taken him more for a
locksmith or a mechanic. When the soaping was over,
after the first stroke of the razor, the barber asked whether the blade did not scratch, addressing him as "Citizen
Rubashov".

It was the first sentence spoken since Rubashov had
entered the room, and in spite of the barber's matter-of-
fact tone, it acquired a special significance. Then there
was silence again; the guard in the doorway lit a cigarette;
the barber trimmed Rubashov's goatee and head with
quick, precise movements. While he stood bent over Rubashov, the latter caught his eye for a moment; in the
same instant the barber pushed two fingers under Rubashov's collar, as if to reach the hair on his neck more
easily; as he drew out his fingers, Rubashov felt the
scratching of a little ball of paper under his collar. A few
minutes later the operation was over and Rubashov was
conducted back to his cell. He sat down on the bed,
with his eye on the spy-hole to make sure he was not
observed, extracted the bit of paper, flattened it and read
it. It consisted of only three words, apparently scribbled
in a great hurry:

"Die in silence."

Rubashov threw the scrap of paper into the bucket and
started again on his wanderings. It was the first message
which had reached him from outside. In the enemy country he had often had messages smuggled to him in prison;
they had summoned him to raise his voice in protest, to
hurl the accusation back at his accusers. Were there also
moments in history, in which the revolutionary had to
keep silent? Were there turning points in history, where
only one thing was required of him, only one thing was
right: to die in silence?

Rubashov's thoughts were interrupted by No. 402, who

had started tapping immediately on his return; he was bursting with curiosity and wanted to find out where Rubashov had been taken.

TO BE SHAVED, explained Rubashov.

I FEARED THE WORST ALREADY, tapped No. 402 feelingly.

AFTER YOU, tapped back Rubashov.

As usual, No. 402 was a grateful audience.

HA-HA! he expressed. YOU ARE A DEVIL OF A FELLOW. . . .

Strangely enough, this archaic compliment filled Rubashov with a kind of satisfaction. He envied No. 402, whose caste possessed a rigid code of honour prescribing how to live and how to die. To that one could cling. For his own kind there was no text-book; everything had to be worked out.

Even for dying there was no etiquette. What was more honourable: to die in silence—or to abase oneself publicly, in order to be able to pursue one's aims? He had sacrificed Arlova because his own existence was more valuable to the Revolution. That was the decisive argument his friends had used to convince him; the duty to keep oneself in reserve for later on, was more important than the commandments of petty bourgeois morality. For those who had changed the face of history, there was no other duty than to stay here and be ready. "You can do what you like with me," Arlova had said, and so he had done. Why should he treat himself with more consideration? "The coming decade will decide the fate of our era," Ivanov had quoted. Could he abscond out of mere personal disgust and tiredness and vanity? And what if, after all, No. 1 were in the right? If here, in dirt and blood and lies, after all and in spite of everything, the grandiose foundations of the future were being laid? Had not history always been an inhumane, unscrupulous builder, mixing its mortar of lies, blood and mud?

Die in silence—fade into darkness—that was easily said. . . .

Rubashov stopped suddenly on the third black tile from the window; he had caught himself repeating the

words "die in silence" aloud several times, in an ironically disapproving tone, as if to emphasize their full absurdity. . . .

And only now did he become aware that his decision
to refuse Ivanov's offer was not half as unshakable as he
had believed. Now it seemed to him even questionable,
whether he had ever seriously intended to reject the offer
and to walk off the stage without a word.

5

The improvement in Rubashov's standard of life went
on. On the morning of the eleventh day he was taken for
the first time into the yard for exercise.

The old jailor fetched him shortly after breakfast, accompanied by the same guard as had escorted the expedi-
tion to the barber. The warder informed Rubashov that
from to-day onwards he was allowed daily twenty minutes' exercise in the courtyard. Rubashov was attached to
the "first round", which started after breakfast. Then the
warder reeled off the regulations: conversation during the
walk with one's neighbour, or any other prisoner, was
prohibited; so was making signs to each other, exchang-
ing written messages or stepping out of the line; any disre-
gard of the regulations would be punished by immediate
withdrawal of the privilege of exercise; serious infractions
of discipline with up to four weeks' imprisonment in a
darkened cell. Then the warder slammed Rubashov's cell
from outside, and the three of them started on their way.
After a few steps the warder stopped and opened the door
of No. 406.

Rubashov, who had remained next to the uniformed
guard at some distance from the door, saw inside the cell
the legs of Rip Van Winkle, who was lying on his bunk.
He wore black, buttoned boots and check trousers, frayed
at the bottom, but still giving a painfully well-brushed effect. The warder once more reeled off his regulations;
the checked trouser legs slid rather falteringly off the bunk
and a little old man appeared in the doorway, blinking.
His face was covered with grey stubble; with his impres-
sive trousers he wore a black waistcoat with a metal

watch-chain and a black cloth coat. He stood in the doorway, examining Rubashov with earnest curiosity; then he gave him a short, friendly nod, and the four of them moved on. Rubashov had expected to find a person who was mentally deranged; now he changed his opinion. In spite of a nervous twitching of his eyebrow, caused probably by years of confinement in a darkened cell, Rip Van Winkle's eyes were clear and of a childlike friendliness. He walked rather laboriously, but with short, decided steps, and threw Rubashov a friendly look from time to time. Going down the stairs, the little old man stumbled suddenly and would have fallen, had not the guard caught his arm in time. Rip Van Winkle murmured a few words, in too low a voice for Rubashov to hear, but which evidently expressed his polite thanks; the guard grinned stupidly. Then, through an open gate, they entered the yard, where the other prisoners were already arranged in pairs. From the middle of the yard, where the guards stood, two short whistles sounded and the round started.

The sky was clear, of a curiously pale blue, the air was filled with the crystalline tang of the snow. Rubashov had forgotten to bring his blanket and shivered. Rip Van Winkle had hung round his shoulders a grey, worn-out cover, which the warder had handed him on entering the yard. He walked in silence beside Rubashov, with small firm steps, blinking up occasionally at the pale blue over their heads; the grey blanket fell to his knees, enclosing him like a bell. Rubashov worked out which of the windows belonged to his cell; it was dark and dirty, like all the others; one could see nothing behind it. He kept his eyes for a time on No. 402's window, but there too one could only see the blind, barred window-pane. No. 402 was not allowed out for exercise; neither was he taken to the barber's or to be examined; Rubashov had never heard him being let out of his cell.

They walked in silence in slow circles round the yard. Between the grey stubble, Rip Van Winkle's lips moved hardly perceptibly; he was murmuring something to himself which Rubashov did not understand at first; then he noticed that the old man was humming the tune of "Arise, ye wretched of the earth". Mad he was not, but in the seven thousand days and nights of imprisonment he had apparently become somewhat peculiar. Rubashov observed him sideways and tried to imagine what it meant to be cut off from the world for two decades. Twenty years ago motor-cars had been rare and oddly shaped; there was no wireless, and the names of the political leaders of to-day were unknown. Nobody foresaw the new mass movements, the great political landslides, nor the twisted roads, the bewildering stages which the Revolutionary State was to go through; at that time one believed that the gates of Utopia stood open, and that mankind stood on its threshold. . . .

Rubashov found that by no stretch of his imagination could he picture his neighbour's state of mind, in spite of all his practice in the art of "thinking through others' minds". He could do it without much effort as far as Ivanov was concerned, or No. 1, or even the officer with the monocle; but with Rip Van Winkle he failed. He looked at him sideways; the old man had just turned his head towards him; he was smiling; holding the blanket round his shoulders with both hands, he was walking beside him with his short steps, humming almost inaudibly the tune of "Arise, ye wretched of the earth".

When they had been conducted back into the building, at his cell-door, the old man turned round once again and nodded to Rubashov; his eyes blinked with a suddenly changed expression, terrified and hopeless; Rubashov thought he was going to call out to him, but the warder had already slammed the door of 406. When Rubashov was shut into his cell, he went at once to the wall; but Rip Van Winkle was silent and gave no answer to his tapping.

No. 402, on the other hand, who had looked at them from his window, wanted to be told everything about the walk, down to the smallest detail. Rubashov had to inform him how the air had smelled, whether it had been cold or just cool, whether he had met any other prisoners in the corridor, and whether he had, after all, been able to exchange a few words with Rip Van Winkle. Rubashov patiently answered every question; compared with No.

402, who was never allowed out, he felt a privileged person; he was sorry for him and had almost a feeling of guilt.

The next day and the day after, Rubashov was fetched for his walk at the same hour after breakfast. Rip Van Winkle was always his companion in the round about. They circled slowly side by side, each with a blanket over his shoulders, both in silence; Rubashov sunk in thought, from time to time glancing attentively through his pince-nez at the other prisoners or at the windows of the building; the old man, with the growing stubble of beard and his gentle, childlike smile, humming his eternal song.

Up to their third walk together they had not exchanged a word, although Rubashov saw that the officials did not seriously try to enforce the rule of silence, and that the other pairs in the circle talked almost incessantly; they did so looking stiffly ahead and speaking with the prison technique familiar to Rubashov, hardly moving their lips.

The third day, Rubashov had brought his note-book and pencil with him; the note-book stuck out of his left outside pocket. After ten minutes the old man noticed it; his eyes lit up. He glanced covertly at the warders in the centre of the circle, who were holding an animated conversation and did not seem interested in the prisoners; then he rapidly pulled pencil and note-book out of Rubashov's pocket and began to scribble something, under cover of his bell-like blanket. He finished it quickly, tore off the page, and pressed it into Rubashov's hand; he retained, however, block and pencil and went on scribbling. Rubashov made certain their guards were paying no attention to them, and looked at the page. Nothing was written on it, it was a drawing: a geographical sketch of the country they were in, drawn with astonishing accuracy. It showed the principal towns, mountains and rivers, and had a flag planted in the middle, bearing the symbol of the Revolution.

When they had gone half the way round again, No. 406 tore off a second page and pressed it into Rubashov's hand. It contained the same drawing over again, an exact-

ly identical map of the Country of the Revolution. No.
406 looked at him and waited smilingly for the effect. Rubashov became slightly embarrassed under his gaze and
murmured something indicative of his appreciation. The
old man winked at him:

"I can also do it with my eyes shut," he said.

Rubashov nodded.

"You don't believe me," said the old man smiling, "but
I have been practising it for twenty years."

He looked quickly at the guards, shut his eyes, and
without altering his pace, began to draw on a new page
under the bell of his blanket. His eyes were tightly shut
and he held his chin up stiffly, like a blind man. Rubashov looked anxiously at the guard; he was afraid the old
man would stumble or fall out of the row. But in another
half-round the drawing was finished, a trifle more wobbly
than the others, but equally accurate; only the symbol
on the flag in the middle of the country had become dis-
proportionately large.

"Now do you believe me?" whispered No. 406, and
smiled at him happily. Rubashov nodded. Then the old
man's face darkened; Rubashov recognized the expression of fear, which fell on him every time he was shut into
his cell.

"It can't be helped," he whispered to Rubashov. "I was
put in the wrong train."

"How do you mean?" asked Rubashov.

Rip Van Winkle smiled at him, gently and sadly. "They
took me to the wrong railway station on my departure,"
he said, "and they thought I didn't notice. Don't tell anybody that I know," he whispered, indicating the guards
with a wink.

Rubashov nodded. Soon afterwards the whistle sounded which announced the end of the walk.

Passing through the gate, they had one more moment
unobserved. No. 406's eyes were again clear and friendly:

"Perhaps the same thing happened to you?" he asked
Rubashov sympathetically.

Rubashov nodded.

"One must not give up hope. One day we will get

there all the same——," said Rip Van Winkle, pointing to the crumpled-up map in Rubashov's hand.

Then he shoved note-book and pencil back into Rubashov's pocket. On the stairs he was again humming his eternal tune.

6

The day before the term set by Ivanov expired, at the serving out of supper, Rubashov had the feeling that there was something unusual in the air. He could not explain why; the food was doled out according to routine, the melancholy tune of the bugle sounded punctually at the prescribed time; yet it seemed to Rubashov that there was something tense about the atmosphere. Perhaps one of the orderlies had looked at him a shade more expressively than usual; perhaps the voice of the old warder had had a curious undertone. Rubashov did not know, but he was unable to work; he felt the tension in his nerves, as rheumatic people feel a storm.

After the "Last Post" had died away, he spied out into the corridor; the electric bulbs, lacking current, burnt at half strength and shed their dim light on to the tiles; the silence of the corridor seemed more final and hopeless than ever. Rubashov lay down on his bunk, stood up again, forced himself to write a few lines, stubbed out his cigarette and lit a new one. He looked down into the yard: it was thawing, the snow had become dirty and soft, the sky was clouded over; on the parapet opposite, the sentinel with his rifle was marching up and down. Once more Rubashov looked through the judas into the corridor: silence, desolation and electric light.

Against his custom, and in spite of the late hour, he started a conversation with No. 402. ARE YOU ASLEEP? he tapped.

For a while there was no answer and Rubashov waited with a feeling of disappointment. Then it came—quieter and slower than usual:

NO. DO YOU FEEL IT TOO?

FEEL—WHAT? asked Rubashov. He breathed heavily; he was lying on the bunk, tapping with his pince-nez.

Again No. 402 hesitated a while. Then he tapped so subduedly that it sounded as if he were speaking in a very low voice:

IT'S BETTER FOR YOU TO SLEEP. . . .

Rubashov lay still on his bunk and was ashamed that No. 402 should speak to him in such a paternal tone. He lay on his back in the dark and looked at his pince-nez, which he held against the wall in his half-raised hand. The silence outside was so thick that he heard it humming in his ears. Suddenly the wall ticked again:

FUNNY—THAT YOU FELT IT AT ONCE. . . .

FELT WHAT? EXPLAIN! tapped Rubashov, sitting up on the bunk.

No. 402 seemed to think it over. After a short hesitation he tapped:

TO-NIGHT POLITICAL DIFFERENCES ARE BEING SETTLED. . . .

Rubashov understood. He sat leaning against the wall, in the dark, waiting to hear more. But No. 402 said no more. After a while, Rubashov tapped:

EXECUTIONS?

YES, answered 402 laconically.

HOW DO YOU KNOW? asked Rubashov.

FROM HARE-LIP.

AT WHAT TIME?

DON'T KNOW. And, after a pause: SOON.

KNOW THE NAMES? asked Rubashov.

NO, answered No. 402. After another pause he added: OF YOUR SORT. POLITICAL DIVERGENCIES.

Rubashov lay down again and waited. After a while he put on his pince-nez, then he lay still, one arm under his neck. From outside nothing was to be heard. Every movement in the building was stifled, frozen into the dark.

Rubashov had never witnessed an execution—except, nearly, his own; but that had been during the Civil War. He could not well picture to himself how the same thing looked in normal circumstances, as part of an orderly routine. He knew vaguely that the executions were carried out at night in the cellars, and that the delinquent was killed by a bullet in the neck; but the details of it he did not know. In the Party death was no mystery, it had no romantic aspect. It was a logical consequence, a factor with which one reckoned and which bore rather an abstract character. Also death was rarely spoken of, and the word "execution" was hardly ever used; the customary expression was "physical liquidation". The words "physical liquidation" again evoked only one concrete idea: The cessation of political activity. The act of dying in itself was a technical detail, with no claim to interest; death as a factor in a logical equation had lost any intimate bodily feature.

Rubashov stared into the darkness through his pince-nez. Had the proceedings already started? Or was it still to come? He had taken off shoes and socks; his bare feet at the other end of the blanket stuck up palely in the darkness. The silence became even more unnatural. It was not the usual comforting absence of noise; it was a silence which had swallowed all sound and smothered it, a silence vibrating like a taut drum-skin. Rubashov stared at his bare feet and slowly moved the toes. It looked grotesque and uncanny, as though the white feet led a life of their own. He was conscious of his own body with unusual intensity, felt the lukewarm touch of the blanket on his legs and the pressure of his hand under his neck. Where did the "physical liquidation" take place? He had the vague idea that it must take place below, under the stairs which led down, beyond the barber's room. He smelled the leather of Gletkin's revolver belt and heard the crackling of his uniform. What did he say to his victim? "Stand with your face to the wall"? Did he add "please"? Or did he say: "Don't be afraid. It won't hurt . . ."? Perhaps he shot without any warning, from behind, while they were walking along—but the victim would be constantly turning his head round. Perhaps he hid the revolver in his sleeve, as the dentist hides his forceps. Perhaps others were also present. How did they look? Did the man fall forwards or backwards? Did he call out? Perhaps it was necessary to put a second bullet in him to finish him off.

Rubashov smoked and looked at his toes. It was so quiet

that one heard the crackling of the burning cigarette paper. He took a deep pull on his cigarette. Nonsense, he said to himself. Penny novelette. In actual fact, he had never believed in the technical reality of "physical liquidation". Death was an abstraction, especially one's own. Probably it was now all over, and what is past has no reality. It was dark and quiet, and No. 402 had stopped tapping.

He wished that outside somebody might scream to tear this unnatural silence. He sniffed and noticed that for some time already he had the scent of Arlova in his nostrils. Even the cigarettes smelled of her; she had carried a leather case in her bag and every cigarette out of it had smelled of her powder. . . . The silence persisted. Only the bunk creaked slightly when he moved.

Rubashov was just thinking of getting up and lighting another cigarette when the ticking in the wall started again. THEY ARE COMING, said the ticking.

Rubashov listened. He heard his pulses hammering in his temples and nothing else. He waited. The silence thickened. He took off his pince-nez and tapped:

I HEAR NOTHING. . . .

For a whole while No. 402 did not answer. Suddenly he tapped, loudly and sharply:

NO. 380. PASS IT ON.

Rubashov sat up quickly. He understood: the news had been tapped on through eleven cells, by the neighbours of No. 380. The occupants of the cells between 380 and 402 formed an acoustic relay through darkness and silence. They were defenceless, locked within their four walls; this was their form of solidarity. Rubashov jumped from his bunk, pattered over bare-footed to the other wall, posted himself next to the bucket, and tapped to No. 406:

ATTENTION. NO. 380 IS TO BE SHOT NOW. PASS IT ON.

He listened. The bucket stank; its vapours had replaced the scent of Arlova. There was no answer. Rubashov pattered hastily back to the bunk. This time he tapped not with the pince-nez, but with his knuckles:

WHO IS NO. 380?

There was again no answer. Rubashov guessed that, like himself, No. 402 was moving pendulum-like between the two walls of his cell. In the eleven cells beyond him, the inhabitants were hurrying noiselessly, with bare feet, backwards and forwards between the walls. Now No. 402 was back again at his wall; he announced:

THEY ARE READING THE SENTENCE TO HIM. PASS IT ON.

Rubashov repeated his previous question:

WHO IS HE?

But No. 402 had gone again. It was no use passing the message on to Rip Van Winkle, yet Rubashov pattered over to the bucket side of the cell and tapped it through; he was driven by an obscure sense of duty, the feeling that the chain must not be broken. The proximity of the bucket made him feel sick. He pattered back to the bed and waited. Still not the slightest sound was heard from outside. Only the wall went on ticking:

HE IS SHOUTING FOR HELP.

HE IS SHOUTING FOR HELP, Rubashov tapped to 406. He listened. One heard nothing. Rubashov was afraid that the next time he went near the bucket he would be sick.

THEY ARE BRINGING HIM. SCREAMING AND HITTING OUT. PASS IT ON, tapped No. 402.

WHAT IS HIS NAME? Rubashov tapped quickly, before 402 had quite finished his sentence. This time he got an answer:

BOGROV. OPPOSITIONAL. PASS IT ON.

Rubashov's legs suddenly became heavy. He leant against the wall and tapped through to No. 406:

MICHAEL BOGROV, FORMER SAILOR ON BAT-TLESHIP POTEMKIN, COMMANDER OF THE EASTERN FLEET, BEARER OF THE FIRST REV-OLUTIONARY ORDER, LED TO EXECUTION.

He wiped the sweat from his forehead, was sick into the bucket and ended his sentence:

PASS IT ON.

He could not call back to his memory the visual image

of Bogrov, but he saw the outlines of his gigantic figure,
his awkward, trailing arms, the freckles on his broad, flat
face with the slightly turned-up nose. They had been room-
mates in exile after 1905; Rubashov had taught him reading, writing and the fundamentals of historical thought;
since then, wherever Rubashov might happen to be, he received twice a year a hand-written letter, ending invariably
with the words: "Your comrade, faithful unto the grave,
Bogrov."

THEY ARE COMING, tapped No. 402 hastily, and
so loudly that Rubashov, who was still standing next to
the bucket with his head leaning against the wall, heard
it across the cell! STAND AT THE SPY-HOLE. DRUM.
PASS IT ON.

Rubashov stiffened. He tapped the message through to
No. 406: STAND AT THE SPY-HOLE. DRUM. PASS
IT ON. He pattered through the dark to the cell door
and waited. All was silent as before.

In a few seconds there came again the ticking in the
wall: NOW.

Along the corridor came the low, hollow sound of subdued drumming. It was not tapping nor hammering: the
men in the cells 380 to 402, who formed the acoustic
chain and stood behind their doors like a guard of honour in the dark, brought out with deceptive resemblance
the muffled, solemn sound of a roll of drums, carried by
the wind from the distance. Rubashov stood with his eyes
pressed to the spy-hole, and joined the chorus by beating
with both hands rhythmically against the concrete door.
To his astonishment, the stifled wave was carried on to
the right, through No. 406 and beyond; Rip Van Winkle
must have understood after all; he too was drumming. At
the same time Rubashov heard to his left, at some distance
still from the limits of his range of vision, the grinding
of iron doors being rolled back on their slidings. The drumming to his left became slightly louder; Rubashov knew
that the iron door which separated the isolation cells
from the ordinary ones, had been opened. A bunch of keys
jangled, now the iron door was shut again; now he heard
the approach of steps, accompanied by sliding and slip-

ping noises on the tiles. The drumming to the left rose in a wave, a steady, muffled crescendo. Rubashov's field of vision, limited by cells No. 401 and 407, was still empty. The sliding and squealing sounds approached quickly, now he distinguished also a moaning and whimpering, like the whimpering of a child. The steps quickened, the drumming to the left faded slightly, to the right it swelled.

Rubashov drummed. He gradually lost the sense of time and of space, he heard only the hollow beating as of jungle tom-toms; it might have been apes that stood behind the bars of their cages, beating their chests and drumming; he pressed his eye to the judas, rising and falling rhythmically on his toes as he drummed. As before, he saw only the stale, yellowish light of the electric bulb in the corridor; there was nothing to be seen save the iron doors of Nos. 401 to 407, but the roll of drums rose, and the creaking and whimpering approached. Suddenly shadowy figures entered his field of vision: they were there. Rubashov ceased to drum and stared. A second later they had passed.

What he had seen in these few seconds, remained branded on Rubashov's memory. Two dimly lit figures had walked past, both in uniform, big and indistinct, dragging between them a third, whom they held under the arms. The middle figure hung slack and yet with doll-like stiffness from their grasp, stretched out at length, face turned to the ground, belly arched downwards. The legs trailed after, the shoes skated along on the toes, producing the squealing sound which Rubashov had heard from the distance. Whitish strands of hair hung over the face turned towards the tiles, with the mouth wide open. Drops of sweat clung to it; out of the mouth spittle ran thinly down the chin. When they had dragged him out of Rubashov's field of vision, further to the right and down the corridor, the moaning and whimpering gradually faded away; it came to him only as a distant echo, consisting of three plaintive vowels: "u-a-o". But before they had turned the corner at the end of the corridor, by the barber's shop, Bogrov bellowed out loudly twice, and this time Rubashov heard not only the vowels, but the whole word;

it was his own name, he heard it clearly: Ru-ba-shov.

Then, as if at a signal, silence fell. The electric lamps were burning as usual, the corridor was empty as usual. Only in the wall No. 406 was ticking:

ARIE, YE WRETCHED OF THE EARTH.

Rubashov was lying on his bunk again, without knowing how he had got there. He still had the drumming in his ears, but the silence was now a true silence, empty and relaxed. No. 402 was presumably asleep. Bogrov, or what had remained of him, was presumably dead by now.

"Rubashov, Rubashov. . . ." That last cry was branded ineffaceably in his acoustic memory. The optic image was less sharp. It was still difficult for him to identify with Bogrov that doll-like figure with wet face and stiff, trailing legs, which had been dragged through his field of vision in those few seconds. Only now did the white hair occur to him. What had they done to Bogrov? What had they done to this sturdy sailor, to draw this childish whimpering from his throat? Had Arlova whimpered in the same way when she was dragged along the corridor?

Rubashov sat up and leant his forehead against the wall behind which No. 402 slept; he was afraid he was going to be sick again. Up till now, he had never imagined Arlova's death in such detail. It had always been for him an abstract occurrence; it had left him with a feeling of strong uneasiness, but he had never doubted the logical rightness of his behaviour. Now, in the nausea which turned his stomach and drove the wet perspiration from his forehead, his past mode of thought seemed lunacy. The whimpering of Bogrov unbalanced the logical equation. Up till now Arlova had been a factor in this equation, a small factor compared to what was at stake. But the equation no longer stood. The vision of Arlova's legs in their high-heeled shoes trailing along the corridor upset the mathematical equilibrium. The unimportant factor had grown to the immeasurable, the absolute; Bogrov's whining, the inhuman sound of the voice which had called out his name, the hollow beat of the drumming, filled his ears; they smothered the thin voice of reason, covered it as the surf covers the gurgling of the drowning.

Exhausted, Rubashov fell asleep, sitting—his head leaning against the wall, the pince-nez before his shut eyes.

7

He groaned in his sleep; the dream of his first arrest had come back; his hand, hanging slackly from the bed, strained for the sleeve of his dressing-gown; he waited for the blow to hit him at last, but it did not come.

Instead, he woke up, because the electric light in his cell was turned on suddenly. A figure stood next to his bed, looking at him. Rubashov could hardly have slept a quarter of an hour, but after that dream he always needed several minutes to find himself again. He blinked in the bright light, his mind worked laboriously through the habitual hypotheses, as though he were carrying out an unconscious ritual. He was in a cell; but not in the enemy country—that was only dreamed. So he was free—but the colour-print of No. 1 hanging over his bed was lacking, and over there stood the bucket. Besides Ivanov was standing at his bedside and blowing cigarette smoke into his face. Was that also dreamed? No, Ivanov was real, the bucket was real. He was in his own country, but it had become an enemy country; and Ivanov, who had been his friend, had now also become an enemy; and the whimpering of Arlova was not a dream either. But no, it had not been Arlova, but Bogrov, who had been dragged past like a wax-doll; Comrade Bogrov, faithful unto the grave; and he had called out his name; that was not dreamed. Arlova, on the other hand, had said: "You can do whatever you like with me. . . ."

"Do you feel ill?" asked Ivanov.

Rubashov blinked at him, blinded by the light. "Give me my dressing-gown," he said.

Ivanov watched him. The right side of Rubashov's face was swollen. "Would you like some brandy?" Ivanov asked. Without waiting for a reply, he hobbled to the spy-hole and called out something into the corridor. Rubashov's eyes followed him, blinking. His dazedness would not go. He was awake, but he saw, heard and thought in a mist.

"Have you been arrested too?" he asked.

"No," said Ivanov quietly. "I only came to visit you. I think you have a temperature."

"Give me a cigarette," said Rubashov. He inhaled deeply once or twice, and his gaze became clearer. He lay down again, smoking, and looked at the ceiling. The cell door opened; the warder brought a bottle of brandy and a glass. This time it was not the old man, but a lean youth in uniform, with steel-rimmed spectacles. He saluted Ivanov, handed the brandy and glass over to him and shut the door from outside. One heard his steps receding down the corridor.

Ivanov sat down on the edge of Rubashov's bunk and filled the glass. "Drink," he said. Rubashov emptied the glass. The mistiness in his head cleared, events and persons—his first and second imprisonment, Arlova, Bo-grov, Ivanov—arranged themselves in time and space.

"Are you in pain?" asked Ivanov.

"No," said Rubashov. The only thing he did not yet understand was what Ivanov was doing in his cell.

"Your cheek is badly swollen. Probably you also have a temperature."

Rubashov stood up from the bunk, looked through the spy-hole into the corridor, which was empty, and walked up and down the cell once or twice until his head became quite clear. Then he stopped in front of Ivanov, who was sitting on the end of the bunk, patiently blowing smoke-rings.

"What are you doing here?" he asked.

"I want to talk to you," Ivanov said. "Lie down again and drink some more brandy."

Rubashov blinked at him ironically through his pince-nez. "Until now," he said, "I was tempted to believe you were acting in good faith. Now I see that you are a swine. Get out of here."

Ivanov did not move. "Be good enough to give the reasons for this assertion," he said.

Rubashov leaned his back against the wall of No. 406 and looked down at Ivanov. Ivanov was smoking with equanimity.

"Point one," said Rubashov. "You knew of my friendship with Bogrov. Therefore you take care that Bogrov—or what was left of him—is taken past my cell on his last journey, as a reminder. To make sure that I do not miss this scene, Bogrov's execution is discreetly announced beforehand, on the assumption that this news will be tapped through to me by my neighbours, which, in fact, happens. A further finesse of the producer's is to inform Bogrov of my presence here, just before he is dragged off —on the further assumption that this final shock will draw from him some audible manifestation; which also happens. The whole thing is calculated to put me into a state of depression. In this darkest hour, Comrade Ivanov appears as a saviour, with a bottle of brandy under his arm. Follows a touching scene of reconciliation, we fall into each other's arms, exchange moving war memories and incidentally sign the statement with my confession. Whereupon the prisoner sinks into a gentle slumber; Comrade Ivanov leaves on the tip of his toes with the statement in his pocket, and is promoted a few days later. . . . Now have the goodness to get out of here."

Ivanov did not move. He blew smoke into the air, smiled and showed his gold teeth. "Do you really think I have such a primitive mind?" he asked. "Or, to be more exact: do you really believe I am such a bad psychologist?"

Rubashov shrugged. "Your tricks disgust me," he said. "I cannot throw you out. If you have a trace of decency left in you, you will now leave me alone. You can't imagine how you all disgust me."

Ivanov lifted the glass from the floor, filled it and drank it. "I propose the following agreement," he said. "You let me speak for five minutes without interrupting me, and listen with a clear head to what I am saying. If after that you still insist on my going—I will go."

"I'm listening," said Rubashov. He stood leaning against the wall opposite Ivanov and glanced at his watch.

"In the first place," said Ivanov, "in order to remove any possible doubts or illusions you may have: Bogrov has in fact been shot. Secondly, he has been in prison for several months, and at the end was tortured for several days. If you mention this during the public trial, or even so much as tap it through to your neighbours, I am done for. About the reasons for treating Bogrov like that, we will speak later. Thirdly, it was intentional that he was taken past your cell, and intentional that he was told of your presence here. Fourthly, this filthy trick, as you call it, was not arranged by me, but by my colleague Gletkin, against my express instructions."

He paused. Rubashov stood leaning against the wall and said nothing.

"I should never have made such a mistake," Ivanov went on; "not out of any regard for your feelings, but because it is contrary to my tactics and to my knowledge of your psychology. You have recently shown a tendency to humanitarian scruples and other sentimentalities of that sort. Besides, the story of Arlova still lies on your stomach. The scene with Bogrov must only intensify your depression and moralistic leanings—that could be foreseen; only a bungler in psychology like Gletkin could have made such a mistake. Gletkin has been dinning into my ears for the last ten days that we should use 'hard methods' on you. For one thing, he doesn't like you because you showed him the holes in your socks; for another, he is used to dealing with peasants. . . . So much for the elucidation of the affair with Bogrov. The brandy, of course, I ordered because you were not in full possession of your wits when I came in. It is not in my interest to make you drunk. It is not in my interest to lay you open to mental shocks. All that only drives you further into your moral exaltation. I need you sober and logical. My only interest is that you should calmly think your case to a conclusion. For, when you have thought the whole thing to a conclusion—then, and only then, will you capitulate. . . ."

Rubashov shrugged his shoulders; but before he could say anything, Ivanov cut in:

"I know that you are convinced that you won't capitulate. Answer me only one thing: *if* you became convinced of the logical necessity and the objective rightness of capitulating—would you then do it?"

Rubashov did not answer at once. He felt dully that the conversation had taken a turn which he should not have allowed. The five minutes had passed, and he had not thrown out Ivanov. That alone, it seemed to him, was a betrayal of Bogrov—and of Arlova; and of Richard and Little Loewy.

"Go away," he said to Ivanov. "It's no use." He noticed only now that he had for some time been walking up and down his cell in front of Ivanov.

Ivanov was sitting on the bunk. "By your tone of voice, I notice," he said, "that you recognize your mistake concerning my part in the Bogrov affair. Why, then, do you want me to go? Why don't you answer the question I asked? . . ." He bent forward a little and looked Rubashov mockingly in the face; then he said slowly, emphasizing each word: *"Because you are afraid of me.* Because my way of thinking and of arguing is your own, and you are afraid of the echo in your own head. In a moment you will be calling out: Get thee behind me, Satan. . . ."

Rubashov did not answer. He was walking to and fro by the window, in front of Ivanov. He felt helpless and incapable of clear argument. His consciousness of guilt, which Ivanov called "moral exaltation", could not be expressed in logical formula—it lay in the realm of the "grammatical fiction". At the same time, every sentence spoken by Ivanov did in fact evoke an echo in him. He felt he ought never to have let himself be drawn into this discussion. He felt as if he were on a smooth, slanting plane, down which one slid irresistibly.

"Apage Satanas!" repeated Ivanov and poured himself out another glass. "In old days, temptation was of carnal nature. Now it takes the form of pure reason. The values change. I would like to write a Passion play in which God and the Devil dispute for the soul of Saint Rubashov. After a life of sin, he has turned to God—to a God with the double chin of industrial liberalism and the charity of the

Salvation Army soups. Satan, on the contrary, is thin, ascetic and a fanatical devotee of logic. He reads Machiavelli, Ignatius of Loyola, Marx and Hegel; he is cold and un-
merciful to mankind, out of a kind of mathematical mer-
cifulness. He is damned always to do that which is most
repugnant to him: to become a slaughterer, in order to
abolish slaughtering, to sacrifice lambs so that no more
lambs may be slaughtered, to whip people with knouts so
that they may learn not to let themselves be whipped,
to strip himself of every scruple in the name of a higher
scrupulousness, and to challenge the hatred of mankind
because of his love for it—an abstract and geometric love.
Apage Satanas! Comrade Rubashov prefers to become a
martyr. The columnists of the liberal Press, who hated
him during his lifetime, will sanctify him after his death.
He has discovered a conscience, and a conscience renders
one as unfit for the revolution as a double chin. Conscience eats through the brain like a cancer, until the whole
of the grey matter is devoured. Satan is beaten and with-
draws—but don't imagine that he grinds his teeth and spits
fire in his fury. He shrugs his shoulders; he is thin and
ascetic; he has seen many weaken and creep out of his
ranks with pompous pretexts. . . ."

Ivanov paused and poured himself another glass of
brandy. Rubashov walked up and down in front of the window. After a while he said:

"Why did you execute Bogrov?"

"Why? Because of the submarine question," said Ivanov. "It concerned the problem of tonnage—an old quar-
rel, the beginnings of which must be familiar to you.

"Bogrov advocated the construction of submarines of
large tonnage and a long range of action. The Party is in
favour of small submarines with a short range. You can
build three times as many small submarines for your
money as big ones. Both parties had valid technical arguments. The experts made a big display of technical sketch-
es and algebraic formulæ; but the actual problem lay in
quite a different sphere. Big submarines mean: a policy
of aggression, to further world revolution. Small submarines mean: coastal defense—that is, self-defense and

postponement of world revolution. The latter is the point of view of No. 1, and the Party.

"Bogrov had a strong following in the Admiralty and amongst the officers of the old guard. It would not have been enough to put him out of the way; he also had to be discredited. A trial was projected to unmask the partisans of big tonnage as *saboteurs* and traitors. We had already brought several little engineers to the point of being willing to confess publicly to whatever we liked. But Bogrov wouldn't play the game. He declaimed up to the very end of big tonnage and world revolution. He was two decades behind the times. He would not understand that the times are against us, that Europe is passing through a period of reaction, that we are in the hollow of a wave and must wait until we are lifted by the next. In a public trial he would only have created confusion amongst the people. There was no other way possible than to liquidate him administratively. Would not you have done the same thing in our position?"

Rubashov did not answer. He stopped walking, and again remained leaning against the wall of No. 406, next to the bucket. A cloud of sickening stench rose from it. He took off his pince-nez and looked at Ivanov out of red-rimmed, hunted eyes.

"You did not hear him whimpering," he said.

Ivanov lit a new cigarette on the stump of the old one; he too found the stench of the bucket rather overpowering.

"No," he said. "I did not hear it. But I have heard and seen similar things. What of it?"

Rubashov was silent. It was no use to try and explain it. The whimpering and the muffled drumming again penetrated his ears, like an echo. One could not express that. Nor the curve of Arlova's breast with its warm, steep point. One could express nothing. "Die in silence," had been written on the message given him by the barber.

"What of it?" repeated Ivanov. He stretched out his leg and waited. As no answer came, he went on speaking:

"If I had a spark of pity for you," he said, "I would now leave you alone. But I have not a spark of pity. I drink; for a time, as you know, I drugged myself; but the vice of pity I have up till now managed to avoid. The smallest dose of it, and you are lost. Weeping over humanity and bewailing oneself—you know our race's pathological leaning to it. Our greatest poets destroyed themselves by this poison. Up to forty, fifty, they were revolutionaries—then they became consumed by pity and the world pronounced them holy. You appear to have the same ambition, and to believe it to be an individual process, personal to you, something unprecedented. . . ." He spoke rather louder and puffed out a cloud of smoke. "Beware of these ecstasies," he said: "Every bottle of spirits contains a measurable amount of ecstasy. Unfortunately, only few people, particularly amongst our fellow countrymen, ever realize that the ecstasies of humility and suffering are as cheap as those induced chemically. The time when I woke from the anæsthetic, and found that my body stopped at the left knee, I also experienced a kind of absolute ecstasy of unhappiness. Do you remember the lectures you gave me at the time?" He poured out another glass and emptied it.

"My point is this," he said; "one may not regard the world as a sort of metaphysical brothel for emotions. That is the first commandment for us. Sympathy, conscience, disgust, despair, repentance, and atonement are for us repellent debauchery. To sit down and let oneself be hypnotized by one's own navel, to turn up one's eyes and humbly offer the back of one's neck to Gletkin's revolver—that is an easy solution. The greatest temptation for the like of us is: to renounce violence, to repent, to make peace with oneself. Most great revolutionaries fell before this temptation, from Spartacus to Danton and Dostoevsky; they are the classical form of betrayal of the cause. The temptations of God were always more dangerous for mankind than those of Satan. As long as chaos dominates the world, God is an anachronism; and every compromise with one's own conscience is perfidy. When the accursed inner voice speaks to you, hold your hands over your ears. . . ."

He felt for the bottle behind him and poured out another glass. Rubashov noticed that the bottle was already half empty. You also could do with a little solace, he thought.

"The greatest criminals in history," Ivanov went on, "are not of the type Nero and Fouché, but of the type Gandhi and Tolstoy. Gandhi's inner voice has done more to prevent the liberation of India than the British guns. To sell oneself for thirty pieces of silver is an honest transaction; but to sell oneself to one's own conscience is to abandon mankind. History is *a priori* amoral; it has no conscience. To want to conduct history according to the maxims of the Sunday school means to leave everything as it is. You know that as well as I do. You know the stakes in this game, and here you come talking about Bogrov's whimpering. . . ."

He emptied his glass and added:

"Or with conscience pricks because of your fat Arlova."

Rubashov knew from before that Ivanov could hold a lot; one did not notice any change in his behaviour, beyond a slightly more emphatic way of speaking than usual. You do need consolation, thought Rubashov again, perhaps more than I do. He sat down on the narrow stool opposite Ivanov and listened. All this was not new to him; he had defended the same point of view for years, with the same or similar words. The difference was that at that time he had known those inner processes of which Ivanov spoke so contemptuously, merely as an abstraction; but since then he had experienced the "grammatical fiction" as a physical reality in his own body. But had these irrational processes become more admissible merely because he had a personal acquaintance with them now? Was it any the less necessary to fight the "mystical intoxication" merely because one had oneself become intoxicated by it? When a year ago he had sent Arlova to her death, he had not had enough imagination to picture the details of an execution. Would he now behave differently merely because he now knew some of its aspects? Either it was right—or it was wrong to sacrifice Richard, Arlova and Little Loewy. But what had

Richard's stutter, the shape of Arlova's breast or Bogrov's whimpering to do with the objective rightness or wrongness of the measure itself?

Rubashov began again to walk up and down his cell. He felt that everything he had experienced since his imprisonment had been only a prelude; that his cogitations had led him to a dead end—on to the threshold of what Ivanov called the "metaphysical brothel"—and that he must begin again from the beginning. But how much time was there left? He stopped, took the glass out of Ivanov's hand and drained it. Ivanov watched him.

"That's better," he said with a fleeting smile. "Monologues in the form of a dialogue are a useful institution. I hope I reproduced the voice of the tempter effectively. A pity that the opposite party is not represented. But that is part of its tricks, that it never lets itself be drawn into a rational discussion. It always attacks a man in defenceless moments, when he is alone and in some effective *mise en scène:* from burning thorn-bushes or cloud-covered mountain tops—and with a special preference for a sleeping victim. The methods of the great moralist are pretty unfair and theatrical. . . ."

Rubashov was no longer listening. Walking up and down, he was wondering whether to-day, if Arlova were still alive he would sacrifice her again. This problem fascinated him; it seemed to contain the answer to all other questions. . . . He stopped in front of Ivanov and asked him:

"Do you remember 'Raskolnikov'?"

Ivanov smiled at him with irony. "It was to be expected that you would sooner or later come to that. *Crime and Punishment* . . . You are really becoming childish or senile. . . ."

"Wait a bit. Wait a bit," said Rubashov, walking up and down agitatedly. "All this is just talk, but now we are getting nearer the point. As far as I remember, the problem is, whether the student Raskolnikov has the right to kill the old woman? He is young and talented; he has as it were an unredeemed pledge on life in his pocket; she is old and utterly useless to the world. But the equation does not stand. In the first place, circumstances oblige him to murder a second person; that is the unforeseeable and illogical consequence of an apparently simple and logical action. Secondly, the equation collapses in any case, because Raskolnikov discovers that twice two are not four when the mathematical units are human beings. . . ."

"Really," said Ivanov. "If you want to hear my opinion, every copy of the book should be burnt. Consider a moment what this humanitarian fog-philosophy would lead to, if we were to take it literally; if we were to stick to the precept that the individual is sacrosanct, and that we must not treat human lives according to the rules of arithmetic. That would mean that a battalion commander may not sacrifice a patrolling party to save the regiment. That we may not sacrifice fools like Bogrov, and must risk our coastal towns being shot to pieces in a couple of years. . . ."

Rubashov shook his head:

"Your examples are all drawn from war—that is, from abnormal circumstances."

"Since the invention of the steam engine," replied Ivanov, "the world has been permanently in an abnormal state; the wars and revolutions are just the visible expressions of this state. Your Raskolnikov is, however, a fool and a criminal; not because he behaves logically in killing the old woman, but because he is doing it in his personal interest. The principle that the end justifies the means is and remains the only rule of political ethics; anything else is just vague chatter and melts away between one's fingers. . . . If Raskolnikov had bumped off the old woman at the command of the Party—for example, to increase strike funds or to instal an illegal Press—then the equation would stand, and the novel with its misleading problem would never have been written, and so much the better for humanity."

Rubashov did not answer. He was still fascinated by the problem as to whether to-day, after the experiences of the last few months and days, he would again send Arlova to her death. He did not know. Logically, Ivanov was right in everything he said; the invisible opponent was silent,

and only indicated its existence by a dull feeling of uneasiness. And in that, too, Ivanov was right, that this behaviour of the "invisible opponent", in never exposing
itself to argument and only attacking people at defenceless
moments, showed it in a very dubious light. . . .

"I don't approve of mixing ideologies," Ivanov continued. "There are only two conceptions of human ethics,
and they are at opposite poles. One of them is Christian
and humane, declares the individual to be sacrosanct,
and asserts that the rules of arithmetic are not to be
applied to human units. The other starts from the basic
principle that a collective aim justifies all means, and
not only allows, but demands, that the individual should
in every way be subordinated and sacrificed to the
community—which may dispose of it as an experimen-
tation rabbit or a sacrificial lamb. The first conception could be called anti-vivisection morality, the second, vivisection morality. Humbugs and dilettantes have
always tried to mix the two conceptions; in practice, it
is impossible. Whoever is burdened with power and
responsibility finds out on the first occasion that he has
to choose; and he is fatally driven to the second alternative. Do you know, since the establishment of Chris-
tianity as a state religion, a single example of a state
which really followed a Christian policy? You can't point
out one. In times of need—and politics are chronically in
a time of need—the rulers were always able to evoke
'exceptional circumstances', which demanded exceptional
measures of defence. Since the existence of nations
and classes, they live in a permanent state of mutual
self-defence, which forces them to defer to another time
the putting into practice of humanism. . . ."

Rubashov looked through the window. The melted
snow had again frozen and sparkled, an irregular surface of yellow-white crystals. The sentinel on the wall
marched up and down with shouldered rifle. The sky
was clear but moonless; above the machine-gun turret
shimmered the Milky Way.

Rubashov shrugged his shoulders. "Admit," he said,
"that humanism and politics, respect for the individual

and social progress, are incompatible. Admit that Gandhi
is a catastrophe for India; that chasteness in the choice
of means leads to political impotence. In negatives we
agree. But look where the other alternative has led
us. . . ."

"Well," asked Ivanov. "Where?"

Rubashov rubbed his pince-nez on his sleeve, and
looked at him shortsightedly. "What a mess," he said,
"what a mess we have made of our golden age."

Ivanov smiled. "Maybe," he said happily. "Look at the
Gracchi and Saint-Just and the Commune of Paris. Up to
now, all revolutions have been made by moralizing dilettantes. They were always in good faith and perished because of their dilettantism. We for the first time are consequent. . . ."

"Yes," said Rubashov. "So consequent, that in the interests of a just distribution of land we deliberately let
die of starvation about five million farmers and their
families in one year. So consequent were we in the liberation of human beings from the shackles of industrial ex-
ploitation that we sent about ten million people to do
forced labour in the Arctic regions and the jungles of
the East, under conditions similar to those of antique
galley slaves. So consequent that, to settle a difference
of opinion, we know only one argument: death, whether
it is a matter of submarines, manure, or the Party line to
be followed in Indo-China. Our engineers work with the
constant knowledge that an error in calculation may take
them to prison or the scaffold; the higher officials in our
administration ruin and destroy their subordinates, because they know that they will be held responsible for
the slightest slip and be destroyed themselves; our poets
settle discussions on questions of style by denunciations
to the Secret Police, because the expressionists consider
the naturalistic style counter-revolutionary, and *vice
versa*. Acting consequentially in the interests of the
coming generations, we have laid such terrible priva-
tions on the present one that its average length of life is
shortened by a quarter. In order to defend the existence
of the country, we have to take exceptional measures and

make transition-stage laws, which are in every point contrary to the aims of the Revolution. The people's standard of life is lower than it was before the Revolution; the labour conditions are harder, the discipline is more inhuman, the piece-work drudgery worse than in colonial countries with native coolies; we have lowered the age limit for capital punishment down to twelve years; our sexual laws are more narrow-minded than those of England, our leader-worship more Byzantine than that of the reactionary dictatorships. Our Press and our schools cultivate Chauvinism, militarism, dogmatism, conformism and ignorance. The arbitrary power of the Government is unlimited, and unexampled in history; freedom of the Press, of opinion and of movement are as thoroughly exterminated as though the proclamation of the Rights of Man had never been. We have built up the most gigantic police apparatus, with informers made a national institution, and with the most refined scientific system of physical and mental torture. We whip the groaning masses of the country towards a theoretical future happiness, which only we can see. For the energies of this generation are exhausted; they were spent in the Revolution; for this generation is bled white and there is nothing left of it but a moaning, numbed, apathetic lump of sacrificial flesh. . . . Those are the consequences of our consequentialness. You called it vivisection morality. To me it sometimes seems as though the experimenters had torn the skin off the victim and left it standing with bared tissues, muscles and nerves. . . ."

"Well, and what of it?" said Ivanov happily. "Don't you find it wonderful? Has anything more wonderful ever happened in history? We are tearing the old skin off mankind and giving it a new one. That is not an occupation for people with weak nerves; but there was once a time when it filled you with enthusiasm. What has so changed you that you are now as pernickety as an old maid?"

Rubashov wanted to answer: "Since then I have heard Bogrov call out my name." But he knew that this answer did not make sense. So he answered instead:

"To continue with the same metaphor: I see the flayed body of this generation: but I see no trace of the new skin. We all thought one could treat history like one experiments in physics. The difference is that in physics one can repeat the experiment a thousand times, but in history only once. Danton and Saint-Just can be sent to the scaffold only once; and if it should turn out that big submarines would after all have been the right thing, Comrade Bogrov will not come to life again."

"And what follows?" asked Ivanov. "Should we sit with idle hands because the consequences of an act are never quite to be foreseen, and hence all action is evil? We vouch for every act with our heads—more cannot be expected of us. In the opposite camp they are not so scrupulous. Any old idiot of a general can experiment with thousands of living bodies; and if he makes a mistake, he will at most be retired. The forces of reaction and counter-revolution have no scruples or ethical problems. Imagine a Sulla, a Galliffet, a Koltschak reading Raskolnikov. Such peculiar birds as you are found only in the trees of revolution. For the others it is easier. . . ."

He looked at his watch. The cell window had turned a dirty grey; the newspaper which was stuck over the broken pane swelled and rustled in the morning breeze. On the rampart opposite, the sentry was still doing his hundred steps up and down.

"For a man with your past," Ivanov went on, "this sudden revulsion against experimenting is rather naïve. Every year several million people are killed quite pointlessly by epidemics and other natural catastrophes. And we should shrink from sacrificing a few hundred thousand for the most promising experiment in history? Not to mention the legions of those who die of undernourishment and tuberculosis in coal and quicksilver mines, rice-fields and cotton plantations. No one takes any notice of them; nobody asks why or what for; but if here we shoot a few thousand objectively harmful people, the humanitarians all over the world foam at the mouth. Yes, we liquidated the parasitic part of the peasantry and let it die of starvation. It was a surgical operation which had to be done once and for all; but in the good old days before the Revolution just as many died in any dry year—only senselessly and pointlessly. The victims of the Yellow River floods in China amount sometimes to hundreds of thousands. Nature is generous in her senseless experiments on mankind. Why should mankind not have the right to experiment on itself?"

He paused; Rubashov did not answer. He went on:

"Have you ever read brochures of an anti-vivisectionist society? They are shattering and heartbreaking; when one reads how some poor cur which has had its liver cut out, whines and licks his tormentor's hands, one is just as nauseated as you were to-night. But if these people had their say, we would have no serums against cholera, typhoid, or diphtheria. . . ."

He emptied the rest of the bottle, yawned, stretched and stood up. He limped over to Rubashov at the window, and looked out.

"It's getting light," he said. "Don't be a fool, Rubashov. Everything I brought up to-night is elementary knowledge, which you know as well as I. You were in a state of nervous depression, but now it is over." He stood next to Rubashov at the window, with his arm round Rubashov's shoulders; his voice was nearly tender. "Now go and sleep it off, old warhorse; to-morrow the time is up, and we will both need a clear head to concoct your deposition. Don't shrug your shoulders—you are yourself at least half convinced that you will sign. If you deny it, it's just moral cowardice. Moral cowardice has driven many to martyrdom."

Rubashov looked out into the grey light. The sentry was just doing a right-about turn. Above the machine-gun turret the sky was pale grey, with a shade of red. "I'll think it over again," said Rubashov after a while.

When the door had closed behind his visitor, Rubashov knew that he had already half-surrendered. He threw himself on the bunk, exhausted and yet strangely relieved. He felt hollowed-out and sucked dry, and at the same time as if a weight had been lifted from him.

Bogrov's pathetic appeal had in his memory lost some of its acoustic sharpness. Who could call it betrayal if, instead of the dead, one held faith with the living?

While Rubashov slept quietly and dreamlessly—the toothache had also quietened down—Ivanov, on the way to his room, paid a visit to Gletkin. Gletkin sat at his desk in full uniform, and was working through files. For years he had had the habit of working right through the night three or four times a week. When Ivanov entered the room, Gletkin stood up to attention.

"It is all right," said Ivanov. "To-morrow he will sign. But I had to sweat to repair your idiocy."

Gletkin did not answer; he stood stiffly in front of his desk. Ivanov, who remembered the sharp scene he had had with Gletkin before his visit to Rubashov's cell and knew that Gletkin did not forget a rebuff so easily, shrugged his shoulders and blew cigarette smoke into Gletkin's face. "Don't be a fool," he said. "You all still suffer from personal feelings. In his place, you would be even more stubborn."

"I have a backbone, which he hasn't," said Gletkin.

"But you're an idiot," said Ivanov. "For that answer you ought to be shot before him."

He hobbled to the door and banged it from outside.

Gletkin sat down to his desk again. He did not believe Ivanov would succeed, and at the same time he was afraid of it. Ivanov's last sentence had sounded like a threat, and with him one never knew what was a joke and what serious. Perhaps he did not know himself—like all these intellectual cynics. . . .

Gletkin shrugged his shoulders, shoved his collar and crackling cuffs into place, and went on with his work on the pile of documents.

The Third Hearing

Darkness at Noon

IS BETTER FOR YOU TO SLEEP

> *Occasionally words must serve to veil the facts. But this must happen in such a way that no one become aware of it; or, if it should be noticed, excuses must be at hand, to be produced immediately.*
>
> MACHIAVELLI:
> *Instructions to Raffaello Girolami*
> But let your communication be, Yea, yea;
> Nay, nay; for whatsoever is more than these
> cometh of evil.
>
> Matt. v. 37

1

Extract from N. S. Rubashov's diary. 20th Day of Prison. ". . . VLADIMIR BOGROV *has fallen out of the swing. A hundred and fifty years ago, the day of the storming of the Bastille, the European swing, after long inaction, again started to move. It had pushed off from tyranny with gusto; with an apparently uncheckable impetus, it had swung up towards the blue sky of freedom. For a hundred years it had risen higher and higher into the spheres of liberalism and democracy. But, see, gradually the pace slowed down, the swing neared the summit and turning-point of its course; then, after a second of immobility, it started the movement backwards, with ever-increasing speed. With the same impetus as on the way up, the swing carried its passengers back from freedom to tyranny again. He who had gazed upwards instead of clinging on, became dizzy and fell out.*

"Whoever wishes to avoid becoming dizzy must try to find out the swing's law of motion. We seem to be faced with a pendulum movement in history, swinging from absolutism to democracy, from democracy back to absolute dictatorship.

"The amount of individual freedom which a people may conquer and keep, depends on the degree of its

political maturity. The aforementioned pendulum motion seems to indicate that the political maturing of the masses does not follow a continuous rising curve, as does the growing up of an individual, but that it is governed by more complicated laws.

"The maturity of the masses lies in the capacity to recognize their own interests. This, however, pre-supposes a certain understanding of the process of production and distribution of goods. A people's capacity to govern itself democratically is thus proportionate to the degree of its understanding of the structure and functioning of the whole social body.

"Now, every technical improvement creates a new complication to the economic apparatus, causes the appearance of new factors and combinations, which the masses cannot penetrate for a time. Every jump of technical progress leaves the relative intellectual development of the masses a step behind, and thus causes a fall in the political-maturity thermometer. It takes sometimes tens of years, sometimes generations, for a people's level of understanding gradually to adapt itself to the changed state of affairs, until it has recovered the same capacity for self-government as it had already possessed at a lower stage of civilization. Hence the political maturity of the masses cannot be measured by an absolute figure, but only relatively, i.e. in proportion to the stage of civilization at that moment.

"When the level of mass-consciousness catches up with the objective state of affairs, there follows inevitably the conquest of democracy, either peaceably or by force. Until the next jump of technical civilization—the discovery of the mechanical loom, for example—again sets back the masses in a state of relative immaturity, and renders possible or even necessary the establishment of some form of absolute leadership.

"This process might be compared to the lifting of a ship through a lock with several chambers. When it first enters a lock chamber, the ship is on a low level relative to the capacity of the chamber; it is slowly lifted up until the water-level reaches its highest point. But this

grandeur is illusory, the next lock chamber is higher still, the levelling process has to start again. The walls of the lock chambers represent the objective state of control of natural forces, of the technical civilization; the water-level in the lock chamber represents the political maturity of the masses. It would be meaningless to measure the latter as an absolute height above sea-level; what counts is the relative height of the level in the lock chamber.

"*The discovery of the steam engine started a period of rapid objective progress, and, consequently, of equally rapid subjective political retrogression. The industrial era is still young in history, the discrepancy is still great between its extremely complicated economic structure and the masses' understanding of it. Thus it is comprehensible that the relative political maturity of the nations in the first half of the twentieth century is less than it was 200 B.C. or at the end of the feudal epoch.*

"*The mistake in socialist theory was to believe that the level of mass-consciousness rose constantly and steadily. Hence its helplessness before the latest swing of the pendulum, the ideological self-mutilation of the peoples. We believed that the adaptation of the masses' conception of the world to changed circumstances was a simple process, which one could measure in years; whereas, according to all historical experience, it would have been more suitable to measure it by centuries. The peoples of Europe are still far from having mentally digested the consequences of the steam engine. The capitalist system will collapse before the masses have understood it.*

"*As to the Fatherland of the Revolution, the masses there are governed by the same laws of thought as anywhere else. They have reached the next higher lock chamber, but they are still on the lowest level of the new basin. The new economic system which has taken the place of the old is even more incomprehensible to them. The laborious and painful rise must start anew. It will probably be several generations before the people manage to understand the new state of affairs, which they themselves created by the Revolution.*

"Until then, however, a democratic form of government is impossible, and the amount of individual freedom which may be accorded is even less than in other countries. Until then, our leaders are obligated to govern as though in empty space. Measured by classical liberal standards, this is not a pleasant spectacle. Yet all the horror, hypocrisy and degradation which leap to the eye are merely the visible and inevitable expression of the law described above. Woe to the fool and the æsthete who only ask how and not why. But woe also unto the opposition in a period of relative immaturity of the masses, such as this.

"In perods of maturity it is the duty and the function of the opposition to appeal to the masses. In periods of mental immaturity, only demagogues invoke the 'higher judgment of the people'. In such situations the opposition has two alternatives: to seize the power by a coup d'état, *without being able to count on the support of the masses or in mute despair to throw themselves out of the swing—'to die in silence'.*

"There is a third choice which is no less consistent, and which in our country has been developed into a system: the denial and suppression of one's own conviction when there is no prospect of materializing it. As the only moral criterion which we recognize is that of social utility, the public disavowal of one's conviction in order to remain in the Party's ranks is obviously more honourable than the quixotism of carrying on a hopeless struggle.

"Questions of personal pride; prejudices such as exist elsewhere against certain forms of self-abasement; personal feelings of tiredness, disgust and shame—are to be cut off root and branch. . . ."

2

Rubashov had begun to write his meditations on the "swing" immediately after the first bugle blast on the morning which followed Bogrov's execution and Ivanov's visit. When his breakfast was brought in, he drank a mouthful of coffee and let the rest get cold. His handwriting, which during the last few days had borne a somewhat flabby and unsteady character, again became firm and disciplined; the letters became smaller, the swinging open loops gave way to sharp angles. When he read it through, he noticed the change.

At eleven o'clock in the morning he was fetched for exercise as usual, and had to stop. Arrived in the courtyard, he was given as neighbour in the roundabout, not old Rip Van Winkle, but a thin peasant with bast shoes. Rip Van Winkle was not to be seen in the yard, and Rubashov only now remembered that at breakfast he had missed the habitual "Arie, ye wretched of the earth." Apparently, the old man had been taken away, God only knew where; a poor, ragged, last year's moth which had miraculously and uselessly survived its appointed life-term, to reappear at the wrong season, flutter round blindly a couple of times, and in a corner fall to dust.

The peasant at first trotted along in silence beside Rubashov, watching him from the side. After the first round he cleared his throat several times, and after a further round he said:

"I come from the province D. Have you ever been there, your honour?"

Rubashov answered in the negative. D. was an out-of-the-way province in the east, of which he only had a rather vague idea.

"It certainly is a long way to go," said the peasant. "You must ride on camels to get there. Are you a political gentleman, your honour?"

Rubashov admitted it. The peasant's bast shoes had the soles half torn off; he was walking with bare toes on the trampled snow. He had a thin neck, and he constantly nodded his head while speaking, as though repeating the amen of a litany.

"I too am a political person," he said; "namely, I am a reactionary. They say all reactionaries must be sent away for ten years. Do you think they will send me away for ten years, your honour?"

He nodded, and squinted anxiously at the warders in the centre of the roundabout, who formed a small group, stamping their feet, and paying no attention to the prisoners.

"What have you done?" asked Rubashov.

"I was unmasked as a reactionary at the pricking of the children," said the peasant. "Every year the Government sends a commission out to us. Two years ago, it sent us papers to read and a whole lot of images of itself. Last year it sent a threshing machine and brushes for the teeth. This year it sent little glass pipes with needles, to prick the children. There was a woman in man's trousers; she wanted to prick all the children one after the other. When she came to my house, I and my wife barred the door and unmasked ourselves as reactionaries. Then we all together burnt the papers and the images and broke up the threshing machine; and then a month afterwards they came to take us away."

Rubashov murmured something and thought over the continuation of his essay on self-government. It occurred to him that he had once read about the natives of New Guinea, who were intellectually on a level with this peasant, yet lived in complete social harmony and possessed surprisingly developed democratic institutions. They had reached the highest level of a lower lock basin. . . .

The peasant next to Rubashov took his silence as a sign of disapproval and shrunk even more into himself. His toes were frozen blue; he sighed from time to time; resigned in his fate, he trotted along beside Rubashov.

As soon as Rubashov was back in his cell, he went on writing. He believed he had made a discovery in the "law of relative maturity" and wrote in a state of extreme tension. When the midday meal was brought in, he had just finished. He ate up his portion and lay back contentedly on his bunk.

He slept for an hour, quietly and dreamlessly, and woke up feeling refreshed. No. 402 had been tapping on his wall for some time; he was obviously feeling neglected. He enquired after Rubashov's new neighbour in the roundabout, whom he had observed from the window, but Rubashov interrupted him. Smiling to himself, he tapped with his pince-nez:

I AM CAPITULATING.

He waited curiously for the effect.

For a long while nothing came; No. 402 was silenced. His answer came a whole minute later:

I'D RATHER HANG. . . .

Rubashov smiled. He tapped:

EACH ACCORDING TO HIS KIND.

He had expected an outbreak of anger from No. 402. Instead, the tapping sign sounded subdued, as it were, resigned:

I WAS INCLINED TO CONSIDER YOU AN EXCEPTION. HAVE YOU NO SPARK OF HONOUR LEFT?

Rubashov lay on his back, his pince-nez in his hand. He felt contented and peaceful. He tapped:

OUR IDEAS OF HONOUR DIFFER.

No. 402 tapped quickly and precisely:

HONOUR IS TO LIVE AND DIE FOR ONE'S BELIEF.

Rubashov answered just as quickly:

HONOUR IS TO BE USEFUL WITHOUT VANITY.

No. 402 answered this time louder and more sharply:

HONOUR IS DECENCY—NOT USEFULNESS.

WHAT IS DECENCY? asked Rubashov, comfortably spacing the letters. The more calmly he tapped, the more furious became the knocking in the wall.

SOMETHING YOUR KIND WILL NEVER UNDERSTAND, answered No. 402 to Rubashov's question. Rubashov shrugged his shoulders:

WE HAVE REPLACED DECENCY BY REASON, he tapped back.

No. 402 did not answer any more.

Before supper Rubashov read through again what he had written. He made one or two corrections, and made a

copy of the whole text in the form of a letter, addressed
to the Public Prosecutor of the Republic. He underlined
the last paragraphs which treated of the alternative cours-
es of action open to the opposition, and ended the document with this concluding sentence:

"The undersigned, N. S. Rubashov, former member of
the Central Committee of the Party, former Commissar
of the People, former Commander of the 2nd Division of
the Revolutionary Army, bearer of the Revolutionary
Order for Fearlessness before the Enemy of the People,
has decided, in consideration of the reasons exposed
above, utterly to renounce his oppositional attitude and
to denounce publicly his errors."

3

Rubashov had been waiting for two days to be taken
before Ivanov. He had thought this would follow immediately after he had handed the document announcing his
capitulation to the old warder; it happened to be the
same day as the term set by Ivanov expired. But apparently one was no longer in such a hurry about him.
Possibly Ivanov was studying his "Theory of Relative
Maturity"; more probably, the document had already
been forwarded to the competent higher authorities.

Rubashov smiled at the thought of the consternation
it must have caused amidst the "theorists" of the Central
Committee. Before the Revolution and also for a short
while after it, during the lifetime of the old leader, no distinction between "theorists" and "politicians" had existed.
The tactics to be followed at any given moment were de-
duced straight from the revolutionary doctrine in open
discussion; strategic moves during the Civil War, the req-
uisitioning of crops, the division and distribution of the
land, the introduction of the new currency, the reorganization of the factories—in fact, every administrative measure—represented an act of applied philosophy.
Each one of the men with the numbered heads on the old
photograph which had once decorated Ivanov's walls,
knew more about the philosophy of law, political econo-
my and statesmanship than all the highlights in the pro-

fessional chairs of the universities of Europe. The discussions at the congresses during the Civil War had been
on a level never before in history attained by a political
body; they resembled reports in scientific periodicals—
with the difference that on the outcome of the discussion
depended the life and well-being of millions, and the future of the Revolution.

Now the old guard was used up; the logic of history
ordained that the more stable the régime became, the
more rigid it had to become, in order to prevent the enormous dynamic forces which the Revolution had released
from turning inwards and blowing the Revolution itself
into the air. The time of philosophizing congresses was
over; instead of the old portraits, a light patch shone from
Ivanov's wallpaper; philosophical incendiarism had given
place to a period of wholesome sterility. Revolutionary
theory had frozen to a dogmatic cult, with a simplified,
easily graspable catechism, and with No. 1 as the high
priest celebrating the Mass. His speeches and articles had,
even in their style, the character of an infallible catechism; they were divided into question and answer, with a
marvellous consistency in the gross simplification of the
actual problems and facts. No. 1 doubtless had an in-
stinct for applying the "law of the relative maturity of
the masses". . . . The dilettantes in tyranny had forced
their subjects to act at command; No. 1 had taught them
to think at command.

Rubashov was amused by the thought of what the pres-
ent-day "theorists" of the Party would say to his letter.
Under actual conditions, it represented the wildest heresy;
the fathers of the doctrine, whose word was taboo, were
criticized; spades were called spades, and even No. 1's
sacrosanct person was treated objectively in its historical context. They must writhe in agony, those unfortunate
theorists of to-day, whose only task was to dress up
No. 1's jumps and sudden changes of course as the latest
revelations of philosophy.

No. 1 sometimes indulged in strange tricks on his theorists. Once he had demanded an analysis of the American
industrial crisis from the committee of experts who edited

the Party's economic periodical. This required several months to complete; at last appeared the special number in which—based on the thesis exposed by No. 1 in his last Congress speech—it was proved, over approximately three hundred pages, that the American boom was only a sham-boom, and that in actual fact America was at the bottom of a depression, which would only be overcome by the victorious revolution. On the very day on which the special number appeared, No. 1 received an American journalist and staggered him and the world, between two pulls at his pipe, by the pithy sentence:

"The crisis in America is over and business is normal again."

The members of the Committee of Experts, expecting their dismissal and possible arrest, composed in the same night letters in which they confessed their "misdemeanours committed by the setting-up of counter-revolutionary theories and misleading analyses"; they emphasized their repentance and promised public atonement. Only Isakovitch, a contemporary of Rubashov, and the only one in the Board of Editors who belonged to the old guard—preferred to shoot himself. The initiated afterwards asserted that No. 1 had set the whole affair going with the sole intention of destroying Isakovitch, whom he suspected of oppositional tendencies.

The whole thing was a pretty grotesque comedy, Rubashov thought; at bottom all this jugglery with "revolutionary philosophy" was merely a means to consolidate the dictatorship, which, though so depressing a phenomenon, yet seemed to represent a historical necessity. So much the worse for him who took the comedy seriously, who only saw what happened on the stage, and not the machinery behind it. Formerly the revolutionary policy had been decided at open congresses; now it was decided behind the scenes—that also was a logical consequence of the law of relative maturity of the masses. . . .

Rubashov yearned to work again in a quiet library with green lamps, and to build up his new theory on a historical basis. The most productive times for revolutionary philosophy had always been the time of exile, the forced rests between periods of political activity. He walked up and down in his cell and let his imagination play with the idea of passing the next two years, when he would be politically excommunicated, in a kind of inner exile; his public recantation would buy him the necessary breathing-space. The outward form of capitulation did not matter much; they should have as many *mea culpas* and declarations of faith in No. 1's infallibility as the paper would hold. That was purely a matter of etiquette—a Byzantine ceremonial which had developed out of the necessity to drill every sentence into the masses by vulgarization and endless repetition; what was presented as right must shine like gold, what was presented as wrong must be as black as pitch; political statements had to be coloured like ginger-bread figures at a fair.

These were matters of which No. 402 understood nothing, Rubashov reflected. His narrow conception of honour belonged to another epoch. What was decency? A certain form of convention, still bound by the traditions and rules of the knightly jousts. The new conception of honour should be formulated differently: to serve without vanity and unto the last consequence. . . .

"Better die than dishonour oneself," No. 402 had announced, and, one imagines, twirled his moustache. That was the classic expression of personal vanity. No. 402 tapped his sentences with his monocle; he, Rubashov, with his pince-nez; that was the whole difference. The only thing which mattered to him now was to work peacefully in a library and build up his new ideas. It would need many years, and produce a massive volume; but it would be the first useful clue to the understanding of the history of democratic institutions and throw a light on the pendulum-like movements of mass psychology, which at the present time were particularly in evidence, and which the classical class struggle theory failed to explain.

Rubashov walked rapidly up and down his cell, smiling to himself. Nothing mattered as long as he was allowed time to develop his new theory. His toothache was gone; he felt wide awake, enterprising, and full of nervous impatience. Two days had passed since the nocturnal conversation with Ivanov and the sending off of his declaration, and still nothing happened. Time, which had flown so quickly during the first two weeks of his arrest, now crawled. The hours disintegrated into minutes and seconds. He worked in fits and starts, but was brought to a standstill every time by lack of historical documentation. He stood for whole quarters of an hour at the judas, in the hope of catching sight of the warder who would take him to Ivanov. But the corridor was deserted, the electric light was burning, as always.

Occasionally he hoped Ivanov himself would come, and the whole formality of his deposition would be settled in his cell; that would be far pleasanter. This time he would not even object to the bottle of brandy. He pictured the conversation in detail; how they would together work out the pompous phraseology of the "confession", and Ivanov's cynical witticisms while they did it. Smiling, Rubashov wandered up and down through his cell, and looked at his watch every ten minutes. Had Ivanov not promised in that night to have him fetched the very next day?

Rubashov's impatience became more and more feverish; in the third night after his conversation with Ivanov he could not sleep. He lay in the dark on the bunk, listening to the faint, stifled sounds in the building, threw himself from one side to another, and for the first time since his arrest wished for the presence of a warm female body. He tried breathing regularly to help himself fall asleep, but became more and more on edge. He fought for a long time against the desire to start a conversation with No. 402, who since the question "What is decency?" had not been heard of again.

About midnight, when he had been lying awake for three hours, staring at the newspaper stuck to the broken windowpane, he could no longer hold out, and tapped against the wall with his knuckles. He waited eagerly; the wall remained silent. He tapped again and waited, feeling a hot wave of humiliation mounting in his head. No. 402 still did not answer. And yet certainly he was lying awake on

the other side of the wall, killing time by chewing the cud
of old adventures; he had confessed to Rubashov that he
could never get to sleep before one or two o'clock in the
morning, and that he had returned to the habits of his
boyhood.

Rubashov lay on his back and stared into the dark. The
mattress under him was pressed flat; the blanket was too
warm and drew an unpleasant dampness from the skin, yet
he shivered when he threw it off. He was smoking the
seventh or eighth cigarette of a chain; the stumps lay
scattered round the bed on the stone floor. The slightest
sound had died out; time stood still; it had resolved itself
into shapeless darkness. Rubashov shut his eyes and
imagined Arlova lying beside him, the familiar curve of
her breast raised against the darkness. He forgot that she
had been dragged over the corridor like Bogrov; the silence became so intense that it seemed to hum and sway.
What were the two thousand men doing who were walled
into the cells of this bee-hive? The silence was inflated by
their inaudible breath, their invisible dreams, the stifled
gasping of their fears and desires. If history were a matter of calculation, how much did the sum of two thousand
nightmares weigh, the pressure of a two-thousandfold
helpless craving? Now he really felt the sisterly scent of
Arlova; his body under the woolen blanket was covered
with sweat. . . . The cell-door was torn open janglingly;
the light from the corridor stabbed into his eyes.

He saw enter two uniformed officials with revolver-
belts, as yet unknown to him. One of the two men approached the bunk; he was tall, had a brutal face and a
hoarse voice which seemed very loud to Rubashov. He
ordered Rubashov to follow him, without explaining where
to.

Rubashov felt for his pince-nez under the blanket, put
them on, and got up from the bunk. He felt leadenly tired
as he walked along the corridor beside the uniformed
giant, who towered a head above him. The other man followed behind them.

Rubashov looked at his watch; it was two o'clock in the
morning, so he must have slept, after all. They went the

way which led towards the barber's shop—the same way as Bogrov had been taken. The second official remained three paces behind Rubashov. Rubashov felt the impulse to turn his head round as an itching in the back of his neck, but controlled it. After all, they can't bump me off so completely without ceremony, he thought, without being entirely convinced. At the moment it did not matter to him much; he only wished to get it over quickly. He tried to find out whether he was afraid or not, but was aware only of the physical discomfort caused by the strain of not turning his head round towards the man behind him.

When they turned the corner beyond the barber's shop, the narrow cellar staircase came into view. Rubashov watched the giant at his side to see whether he would slacken his pace. He still felt no fear, only curiosity and uneasiness; but when they had passed the staircase, he noticed to his surprise that his legs felt shaky, so that he had to pull himself together. At the same time he caught himself mechanically rubbing his spectacles on his sleeve; apparently, he must have taken them off before reaching the barber's shop without noticing it. It is all swindle, he thought. Above, it is possible to kid oneself, but below, from the stomach downwards, one knows. If they beat me now, I will sign anything they like; but tomorrow I will recall it. . . .

A few steps further on, the "theory of relative maturity" came to his mind again, and the fact that he had already decided to give in and to sign his submission. A great relief came over him; but at the same time he asked himself in astonishment how it was possible that he should have so completely forgotten his decisions of the last few days. The giant stopped, opened a door and stood aside. Rubashov saw a room before him similar to Ivanov's, but with unpleasantly bright lighting, which stabbed his eyes. Opposite the door, behind the desk, sat Gletkin.

The door shut behind Rubashov and Gletkin looked up from his pile of documents. "Please sit down," he said in that dry, colourless tone which Rubashov remembered from that first scene in his cell. He also recognized the broad scar on Gletkin's skull; his face was in shadow, as the only light in the room came from a tall metal standing lamp behind Gletkin's armchair. The sharp white light which streamed from the exceptionally strong bulb blinded Rubashov, so that it was only after a few seconds that he became aware of a third person—a secretary sitting behind a screen at a small table, with her back to the room.

Rubashov sat down opposite Gletkin, in front of the desk, on the only chair. It was an uncomfortable chair, without arms.

"I am commissioned to examine you during the absence of Commissar Ivanov," said Gletkin. The light of the lamp hurt Rubashov's eyes; but if he turned his profile to Gletkin, the effect of the light in the corner of his eye was nearly as unpleasant. Besides, to talk with averted head seemed absurd and embarrassing.

"I prefer to be examined by Ivanov," said Rubashov.

"The examining magistrate is appointed by the authorities," said Gletkin. "You have the right to make a statement or to refuse. In your case a refusal would amount to a disavowal of the declaration of willingness to confess, which you wrote two days ago, and would automatically bring the investigation to an end. In that eventuality I have the order to send your case back to the competent authority, which would pronounce your sentence administratively."

Rubashov thought this over quickly. Something had obviously gone wrong with Ivanov. Suddenly sent on leave, or dismissed, or arrested. Perhaps because his former friendship with Rubashov had been remembered; perhaps because he was mentally superior and too witty, and because his loyalty to No. 1 was based on logical considerations and not on blind faith. He was too clever; he was of the old school: the new school was Gletkin and his methods. . . . Go in peace, Ivanov. Rubashov had no time for pity; he had to think quickly, and the light hindered him. He took his pince-nez off and blinked; he knew that without glasses he looked naked and helpless, and that Gletkin's expressionless eyes registered every trait in his face

If he now remained silent he would be lost; there was no going back now. Gletkin was a repellent creature, but he represented the new generation; the old had to come to terms with it or be crushed; there was no other alternative. Rubashov felt suddenly old; he had never known this feeling up till now. He had never held in account the fact that he was in his fifties. He put his pince-nez on and tried to meet Gletkin's gaze, but the shrill light made his eyes water; he took it off again.

"I am ready to make a statement," he said and tried to control the irritation in his voice. "But on the condition that you cease your tricks. Put out that dazzle-light and keep these methods for crooks and counter-revolutionaries."

"You are not in a position to make conditions," said Gletkin in his calm voice. "I cannot change the lighting in my room for you. You do not seem fully to realize your position, especially the fact that you are yourself accused of counter-revolutionary activities, and that in the course of these last years you have twice admitted to them in public declarations. You are mistaken if you believe you will get off as cheaply this time."

You swine, thought Rubashov. You filthy swine in uniform. He went red. He felt himself going red and knew that Gletkin had noticed it. How old might this Gletkin be? Thirty-six or seven, at the most; he must have taken part in the Civil War as a youth and seen the outbreak of the Revolution as a mere boy. That was the generation which had started to think after the flood. It had no traditions, and no memories to bind it to the old, vanished world. It was a generation born without umbilical cord. . . . And yet it had right on its side. One must tear that umbilical cord, deny the last tie which bound one to the vain conceptions of honour and the hypocritical decency of the old world. Honour was to serve without vanity, without sparing oneself, and until the last consequence.

Rubashov's temper gradually quietened down. He kept his pince-nez in his hand and turned his face towards Gletkin. As he had to keep his eyes shut, he felt even more

naked, but this no longer disturbed him. Behind his shut
lids shimmered a reddish light. He had never had such an
intense feeling of solitude.

"I will do everything which may serve the Party," he
said. The hoarseness had gone from his voice; he kept his
eyes shut. "I beg you to state the accusation in detail. Up
till now this has not been done."

He heard rather than saw through his blinking eyes,
that a short movement went through Gletkin's stiff figure.
His cuffs on the chair-arms crackled, he breathed a shade
deeper, as if for an instant his whole body had relaxed. Rubashov guessed that Gletkin was experiencing the triumph
of his life. To have laid out a Rubashov meant the beginning of a great career; and up to a minute ago all had
still hung in the balance for Gletkin—with Ivanov's fate as
a reminder before his eyes.

Rubashov understood suddenly that he had just as much
power over this Gletkin as the latter over him. I hold
you by the throat, my lad, he thought with an ironic grimace; we each hold the other by the throat, and if I throw
myself off the swing, I drag you down with me. For a moment Rubashov played with this idea, while Gletkin, again
stiff and precise, searched in his documents; then he re-
jected the temptation and slowly shut his painful eyes.
One must burn out the last vestiges of vanity—and what
else was suicide but an inverted form of vanity? This
Gletkin, of course, believed that it was his tricks, and not
Ivanov's arguments, which had induced him to capitulate; probably Gletkin had also succeeded in persuading
the higher authorities of this, and had thus brought about
Ivanov's fall. Swine, thought Rubashov, but this time without anger. You consequential brute in the uniform we
created—barbarian of the new age which is now starting.
You don't understand the issue; but, did you understand,
you would be useless to us. . . . He noticed that the light
of the lamp had become yet another grade shriller—Rubashov knew that there were arrangements for height-
ening or decreasing the power of these reflector lamps
during a cross-examination. He was forced to turn his
head away completely and wipe his watering eyes. You

brute, he thought again. Yet it is just such a generation of brutes that we need now. . . .

Gletkin had started to read the accusation. His monotonous voice was more irritating than ever; Rubashov listened with averted head and shut eyes. He was decided to regard his "confession" as a formality, as an absurd yet necessary comedy, the tortuous sense of which could only be understood by the initiated; but the text which Gletkin was reading surpassed his worst expectations in absurdity. Did Gletkin really believe that he, Rubashov, had planned these childish plots? That for years he had thought of nothing else than to break up the building, the foundations of which he and the old guard had laid? And all of them, the men with the numbered heads, the heroes of Gletkin's boyhood—did Gletkin believe that they had suddenly fallen victims to an epidemic which rendered them all venal and corruptible and gave them but one wish—to undo the Revolution? And that with methods which these great political tacticians appeared to have borrowed from a cheap detective story?

Gletkin read monotonously, without any intonation, in the colourless, barren voice of people who have learnt the alphabet late, when already grown-up. He was just reading about the alleged negotiations with the representative of a foreign Power which, it was pretended, Rubashov had started during his stay in B., with the object of a reinstatement of the old regime by force. The name of the foreign diplomat was mentioned, also the time and place of their meeting. Rubashov listened more attentively now. In his memory flashed an unimportant little scene, which he had immediately forgotten at the time and had never thought of again. He quickly worked out the approximate date; it seemed to fit. So that was to be the rope which would hang him? Rubashov smiled and rubbed his weeping eyes with his handkerchief. . . .

Gletkin read straight on, stiffly and with deadly monotony. Did he really believe what he was reading? Was he not aware of the grotesque absurdity of the text? Now he was at the period of Rubashov's activity at the head of the aluminum trust. He read out statistics which showed the

appalling disorganization in that too hastily developed
branch of industry; the number of workers victims of accidents, the series of aeroplanes crashed as a result of defective material. This all was the consequence of his,
Rubashov's, devilish sabotage. The word "devilish" actually occurred several times in the text, in between technical terms and columns of figures. For a few seconds Rubashov entertained the hypothesis that Gletkin had gone
mad; this mixture of logic and absurdity recalled the
methodical lunacy of schizophrenia. But the accusation
had not been drawn up by Gletkin; he was only reading
it along—and either actually believed it, or at any rate
considered it credible. . . .

Rubashov turned his head to the stenographer in her
dimly lit corner. She was small, thin and wore spectacles.
She was sharpening her pencil with equanimity and did not
once turn her head towards him. Obviously, she too considered the monstrous things Gletkin was reading as
quite convincing. She was still young, perhaps twenty-five
or six; she too had grown up after the flood. What did
the name Rubashov mean to this generation of modern
Neanderthalers? There he sat in front of the blinding reflector light, could not keep open his watering eyes, and
they read to him in their colourless voices and looked
at him with their expressionless eyes, indifferently, as
though he were an object on the dissecting table.

Gletkin was at the last paragraph of the accusation. It
contained the crowning feature: the plot for an attempt on No. 1's life. The mysterious X mentioned by
Ivanov in the course of the first hearing had appeared
again. It turned out that he was an assistant manager
of the restaurant from which No. 1 had his cold lunch
brought to him on busy days. This cold snack was a
feature of No. 1's Spartan mode of life, most carefully
fostered by propaganda; and it was just by means of
this proverbial cold snack that X, on Rubashov's instigation, was to prepare a premature end for No. 1.
Rubashov smiled to himself with eyes shut; when he
opened them, Gletkin had stopped reading and was looking at him. After a few seconds of silence, Gletkin said,

in his usual even tone, more as a statement than a question:

"You have heard the accusation and plead guilty."

Rubashov tried to look into his face. He could not, and had to shut his eyes again. He had had a biting answer on his tongue; instead he said, so quietly that the thin secretary had to stretch out her head to hear:

"I plead guilty to not having understood the fatal compulsion behind the policy of the Government, and to have therefore held oppositional views. I plead guilty to having followed sentimental impulses, and in so doing to have been led into contradiction with historical necessity. I have lent my ear to the laments of the sacrificed, and thus became deaf to the arguments which proved the necessity to sacrifice them. I plead guilty to having rated the question of guilt and innocence higher than that of utility and harmfulness. Finally, I plead guilty to having placed the idea of man above the idea of mankind. . . ."

Rubashov paused and again tried to open his eyes. He blinked over to the secretary's corner, his head turned away from the light. She had just finished taking down what he had said; he believed he saw an ironic smile on her pointed profile.

"I know," Rubashov went on, "that my aberration, if carried into effect, would have been a mortal danger to the Revolution. Every opposition at the critical turning-points of history carries in itself the germ of a split in the Party, and hence the germ of civil war. Humanitarian weakness and liberal democracy, when the masses are not mature, is suicide for the Revolution. And yet my oppositional attitude was based on a craving for just these methods—in appearance so desirable, actually so deadly. On a demand for a liberal reform of the dictatorship; for a broader democracy, for the abolition of the Terror, and a loosening of the rigid organization of the Party, I admit that these demands, in the present situation, are objectively harmful and therefore counter-revolutionary in character. . . ."

He paused again, as his throat was dry and his voice

had become husky. He heard the scratching of the secretary's pencil in the silence; he raised his head a little, with eyes shut, and went on:

"In this sense, and in this sense only, can you call me a counter-revolutionary. With the absurd criminal charges made in the accusation, I have nothing to do."

"Have you finished?" asked Gletkin.

His voice sounded so brutal that Rubashov looked at him in surprise. Gletkin's brightly-lit silhouette showed behind the desk in his usual correct position. Rubashov had long sought for a simple characterization of Gletkin: "correct brutality"—that was it.

"Your statement is not new," Gletkin went on in his dry, rasping voice. "In both your preceding confessions, the first one two years ago, the second time twelve months ago, you have already publicly confessed that your attitude had been 'objectively counter-revolutionary and opposed to the interests of the people.' Both times you humbly asked the forgiveness of the Party, and vowed loyalty to the policy of the leadership. Now you expect to play the same game a third time. The statement you have just made is mere eye-wash. You admit your 'oppositional attitude', but deny the acts which are the logical consequence of it. I have already told you that this time you will not get off so easily."

Gletkin broke off as suddenly as he began. In the ensuing silence Rubashov heard the faint buzzing of the current in the lamp behind the desk. At the same time the light became another grade stronger.

"The declarations I made at that time," Rubashov said in a low voice, "were made for tactical purposes. You certainly know that a whole row of oppositional politicians were obliged to pay with such declarations for the privilege of remaining in the Party. But this time I mean it differently. . . ."

"That is to say, this time you are sincere?" asked Gletkin. He asked the question quickly, and his correct voice held no irony.

"Yes," said Rubashov quietly.

"And, before, you lied?"

"Call it that," said Rubashov.

"To save your neck?"

"To be able to go on working."

"Without a neck one cannot work. Hence, to save your neck?"

"Call it that."

In the short intervals between the questions shot out by Gletkin and his own answers, Rubashov heard only the scratching of the secretary's pencil and the buzzing of the lamp. The lamp gave off cascades of white light, and radiated a steady heat which forced Rubashov to wipe the sweat from his forehead. He strained to keep his smarting eyes open, but the intervals at which he opened them became longer and longer; he felt a growing sleepiness, and when Gletkin, after his last series of rapid questions, let several moments go by in silence, Rubashov, with a kind of distant interest, felt his chin sinking on to his chest. When Gletkin's next question jerked him up again, he had the impression of having slept for an indeterminable time.

"I repeat," Gletkin's voice said. "Your former declarations of repentance had the object of deceiving the Party as to your true opinions, and of saving your neck."

"I have already admitted that," said Rubashov.

"And your public disavowal of your secretary Arlova, had that the same object?"

Rubashov nodded dumbly. The pressure in his eye-sockets radiated over all the nerves in the right side of his face. He noticed that his tooth had started to throb again.

"You know that Citizen Arlova had constantly called on you as the chief witness for her defence?"

"I was informed of it," said Rubashov. The throbbing in his tooth became stronger.

"You doubtless also know that the declaration you made at that time, which you have just described as a lie, was decisive for the passing of the death sentence on Arlova?"

"I was informed of it."

Rubashov had the feeling that the whole right side of

his face was drawn into a cramp. His head became duller
and heavier; it was with difficulty that he prevented it
sinking on his breast. Gletkin's voice bored into his ear:

"So it is possible that Citizen Arlova was innocent?"

"It is possible," said Rubashov, with a last remainder
of irony, which lay on his tongue like a taste of blood and
gall.

". . . And was executed as a consequence of the lying
declaration you made, with the object of saving your
head?"

"That is about it," said Rubashov. "You scoundrel,"
he thought with a slack, impotent rage. "Of course
what you say is the naked truth. One would like to know
which of us two is the greater scoundrel. But he has me
by the throat and I cannot defend myself, because it is
not allowed to throw oneself out of the swing. If only
he would let me sleep. If he goes on tormenting me
for long, I'll take everything back and refuse to speak—
and then I will be done for, and he too."

". . . And after all that, you demand to be treated
with consideration?" Gletkin's voice went on, with the
same brutal correctness. "You still dare to deny criminal
activities? After all that, you demand that we should believe you?"

Rubashov gave up the efforts to keep his head straight.
Of course Gletkin was right not to believe him. Even he
himself was beginning to get lost in the labyrinth of calculated lies and dialectic pretences, in the twilight between truth and illusion. The ultimate truth always re-
ceded a step; visible remained only the penultimate lie
with which one had to serve it. And what pathetic con-
tortions and St. Vitus's dances did it compel one to!
How could he convince Gletkin that this time he was
really sincere, that he had arrived at the last station?
Always one had to convince someone, talk, argue—
while one's only wish was to sleep and to fade out. . . .

"I demand nothing," said Rubashov, and turned his
head painfully in the direction whence had come Gletkin's voice, "except to prove once more my devotion to
the Party."

"There is only one proof you can give," came Gletkin's voice, "a complete confession. We have heard enough of your 'oppositional attitude' and your lofty motives. What we need is a complete, public confession of your criminal activities, which were the necessary outcome of that attitude. The only way in which you can still serve the Party is as a warning example—by demonstrating to the masses, in your own person, the consequences to which opposition to the Party policy inevitably leads."

Rubashov thought of No. 1's cold snack. His inflamed facial nerves throbbed at full pressure, but the pain was no longer acute and burning; it now came in dull, numbing blows. He thought of No. 1's cold snack, and the muscles of his face distorted themselves into a grimace.

"I can't confess to crimes I have not committed," he said flatly.

"No," sounded Gletkin's voice. "No, that you certainly can't"—and it seemed to Rubashov that for the first time he heard something like mockery in that voice.

From that moment onwards Rubashov's recollection of the hearing was rather hazy. After the sentence "that you certainly can't," which had remained in his ear because of its peculiar intonation, there was a gap of uncertain length in his memory. Later on it seemed to him that he had fallen asleep and he even remembered a strangely pleasant dream. It must have lasted only a few seconds—a loose, timeless sequence of luminous landscapes, with the familiar poplars which had lined the drive of his father's estate, and a special kind of white cloud which as a boy he had once seen above them.

The next thing he remembered was the presence of a third person in the room, and Gletkin's voice booming over him—Gletkin must have stood up and bent forward over his desk:

"I beg you to attend the proceedings. . . . Do you recognize this person?"

Rubashov nodded. He had at once recognized Hare-lip, although he was not wearing the waterproof in which he used to wrap himself, with freezingly hunched shoulders, during his walks in the yard. A familiar row of figures flashed into Rubashov's mind: 2-3; 1-1; 4-3; 1-5; 3-2; 2-4 . . . "Hare-lip sends you his greetings." On what occasion had No. 402 given him this message?

"When and where have you known him?"

It cost Rubashov a certain effort to speak; the bitter taste had remained on his parched tongue:

"I have seen him repeatedly from my window, walking in the yard."

"And you have not known him before?"

Hare-lip stood at the door, at a distance of a few steps behind Rubashov's chair; the light of the reflector fell full on him. His face, usually yellow, was chalky white, his nose pointed, the split upper-lip with the weal of flesh trembled over the naked gum. His hands hung slackly to his knees; Rubashov, who now had his back turned to the lamp, saw him like an apparition in the footlights of a stage. A new row of figures went through Rubashov's memory: "4-5; 3-5; 4-3 . . ."—"was tortured yesterday". Almost simultaneously, the shadow of a memory which he could not seize passed through his mind—the memory of having once seen the living original of this human wreck, long before he had entered cell No. 404.

"I don't know exactly," he answered hesitantly to Gletkin's question. "Now that I see him close to, it seems to me that I have met him somewhere already."

Even before he had finished the phrase, Rubashov felt it would have been better not to have spoken it. He wished intensely that Gletkin would let him have a few minutes to pull himself together. Gletkin's way of rapping out his questions in a rapid, pauseless sequence called to his mind the image of a bird of prey hacking at its victim with its beak.

"Where have you met this man last? The exactness of your memory was once proverbial in the Party."

Rubashov was silent. He racked his memory, but could not place anywhere this apparition in the glaring light, with the trembling lips. Hare-lip did not move. He passed his tongue over the red weal on his upper-lip; his gaze wandered from Rubashov to Gletkin and back.

The secretary had stopped writing; one heard only the even buzzing of the lamp and the crackling of Gletkin's cuffs; he had leaned forward and propped his elbows on the arms of the chair to put his next question:

"So you refuse to answer?"

"I do not remember," said Rubashov.

"Good," said Gletkin. He leaned further forward, turning towards Hare-lip with the whole weight of his body, as it were:

"Will you help Citizen Rubashov's memory a little? Where did you last meet him?"

Hare-lip's face became, if possible, even whiter. His eyes lingered for a few seconds on the secretary, whose presence he had apparently only just discovered, but wandered on immediately, as though fleeing and seeking a place of rest. He again passed his tongue over his lips and said hurriedly, in one breath:

"I was instigated by Citizen Rubashov to destroy the leader of the Party by poison."

In the first moment Rubashov was only surprised by the deep, melodious voice which sounded unexpectedly from this human wreck. His voice seemed to be the only thing in him which had remained whole; it stood in uncanny contrast to his appearance. What he actually said, Rubashov seized only a few seconds later. Since Hare-lip's arrival he had expected something of the sort and scented the danger; but now he was conscious above all of the grotesqueness of the charge. A moment later he heard Gletkin again—this time behind his back, as Rubashov had turned towards Hare-lip. Gletkin's voice sounded irritated:

"I have not yet asked you that. I asked you, where you had met Citizen Rubashov last."

Wrong, thought Rubashov. He should not have emphasized that it was the wrong answer. I would not have noticed it. It seemed to him that his head was now quite clear, with a feverish wakefulness. He sought for a comparison. This witness is an automatic barrel-organ, he thought; and just now it played the wrong tune. Hare-lip's next answer came even more melodiously:

"I met Citizen Rubashov after a reception at the Trade Delegation in B. There he incited me to my terroristic plot against the life of the leader of the Party."

While he was speaking, his haunted gaze touched on Rubashov and rested there. Rubashov put on his pince-nez and answered his gaze with sharp curiosity. But in the eyes of the young man he read no prayer for forgiveness, rather fraternal trust and the dumb reproach of the helplessly tormented. It was Rubashov who first averted his gaze.

Behind his back sounded Gletkin's voice, again self-confident and brutal:

"Can you remember the date of the meeting?"

"I remember it distinctly," said Hare-lip in his unnaturally pleasant voice. "It was after the reception given on the twentieth anniversary of the Revolution."

His gaze still rested nakedly on Rubashov's eyes, as though there lay a last desperate hope of rescue. A memory rose in Rubashov's mind, hazily at first, then more clearly. Now at last he knew who Hare-lip was. But this discovery caused him almost no other sensation than an aching wonder. He turned his head to Gletkin and said quietly, blinking in the light of the lamp:

"The date is correct. I did not at first recognize Professor Kieffer's son, as I had only seen him once—before he had passed through your hands. You may be congratulated on the result of your work."

"So you admit that you know him, and that you met him on the day and occasion aforementioned?"

"I have just told you that," said Rubashov tiredly. The feverish wakefulness had vanished, and the dull hammering in his head started again. "If you had told me at once that he was the son of my unfortunate friend Kieffer, I would have identified him sooner."

"In the accusation his full name is stated," said Gletkin.

"I knew Professor Kieffer, like everybody did, only by his *nom de plume*."

"That is an unimportant detail," said Gletkin. He again

bent his whole body towards Hare-lip, as though he wanted to crush him with his weight across the space between them. "Continue your report. Tell us how this meeting came about."

Again wrong, thought Rubashov, in spite of his sleepiness. It is certainly not an unimportant detail. If I had really incited this man to this idiotic plot, I would have remembered him at the first allusion, with or without name. But he was too tired to embark on such a long explanation; besides, he would have had to turn his face to the lamp again. As it was, he could at least keep his back to Gletkin.

While they were discussing his identity, Hare-lip had stood with sunken head and trembling upper lip in the white glare. Rubashov thought of his old friend and comrade Kieffer, the great historian of the Revolution. On the famous photograph of the Congress table, where all wore beards and small numbered circles like haloes round their heads, he sat to the old leader's left. He had been his collaborator in matters of history; also his chess partner, and perhaps his sole personal friend. After the death of the "old man", Kieffer, who had known him more intimately than anyone else, was commissioned to write his biography. He worked at it for more than ten years, but it was destined never to be published. The official version of the events of the Revolution had gone through a peculiar change in these ten years, the parts played in it by the chief actors had to be re-written, the scale of values reshuffled; but old Kieffer was stubborn, and understood nothing of the inner dialectics of the new era under No. 1. . . .

"My father and I," Hare-lip went on in his unnaturally musical voice, "on our return from the International Ethnographical Congress, to which I had accompanied him, made a detour by B., as my father wanted to visit his friend, Citizen Rubashov. . . ."

Rubashov listened with a queer mixture of curiosity and melancholy. Up till now the story was correct; old Kieffer had come to see him, led by the need to

pour out his heart and also to ask counsel of him. The
evening that they spent together had probably been the
last pleasant moment in old Kieffer's life.

"We could only stay one day," Hare-lip went on, his
gaze glued to Rubashov's face, as if he sought there
strength and encouragement. "It was just the day of the
celebration of the Revolution; that is why I remember
the date so exactly. The whole day Citizen Rubashov
was busy at the reception, and could only see my
father for a few minutes. But in the evening, when the
reception in the Legation was over, he invited my father to his own apartment and my father allowed me to
accompany him. Citizen Rubashov was rather tired and
had put on his dressing-gown, but he welcomed us very
warmly. He had set out wine, cognac and cakes on a
table and greeted my father, after embracing him,
with the words: 'The farewell party for the last of the
Mohicans.' . . ."

Behind Rubashov's back Gletkin's voice interrupted:

"Did you notice at once Rubashov's intention to put
you into a state of intoxication, in order to make you
more amenable to his plans?"

It seemed to Rubashov that a slight smile flitted over
Hare-lip's ravaged face: for the first time he noticed a faint
resemblance to the young man he had seen that evening.
But the expression vanished immediately; Hare-lip blinked
and licked his split lip.

"He seemed to me rather suspect, but I did not yet
penetrate his scheme."

Poor swine, thought Rubashov, what have they made
of you? . . .

"Go on," boomed Gletkin's voice.

It took a few seconds for Hare-lip to pull himself together again after the interruption. In the meantime
one heard the thin stenographer sharpening her pencil.

"Rubashov and my father exchanged reminiscences for
a long while. They had not seen each other for years.
They talked about the time before the Revolution, about
persons of the older generation whom I only knew of by
hearsay, and about the Civil War. They talked frequently

in allusions which I could not follow, and laughed about reminiscences which I did not understand."

"Was much drunk?" asked Gletkin.

Hare-lip blinked helplessly into the light. Rubashov noticed that he swayed slightly while speaking, as though he could only with difficulty remain on his feet.

"I believe, quite a lot," Hare-lip went on. "In the last few years I had never seen my father in such a good mood."

"That was," sounded Gletkin's voice, "three months before the discovery of your father's counter-revolutionary activities, which led to his execution in a further three months?"

Hare-lip licked his lips, gazed dully into the light and remained silent. Rubashov had turned to Gletkin on a sudden impulse, but, blinded by the light, he shut his eyes and turned slowly away again, rubbing his spectacles on his sleeve. The secretary's pencil squeaked on the paper and stopped. Then again Gletkin's voice was heard:

"Were you at that time already initiated into your father's counter-revolutionary activities?"

Hare-lip licked his lips.

"Yes," he said.

"And you knew that Rubashov shared your father's opinions?"

"Yes."

"Report the principal phrases of the conversation. Leave out everything non-essential."

Hare-lip had now folded his hands behind his back and leaned his shoulders against the wall.

"After a time, my father and Rubashov changed the conversation over to the present. They spoke in depreciative phrases of the present state of affairs in the Party, and about the methods of the leadership. Rubashov and my father only referred to the leader as 'No. 1.' Rubashov said that since No. 1 sat on the Party with his broad posterior, the air underneath was no longer breathable. That was the reason why he preferred missions abroad."

Gletkin turned to Rubashov:

"That was shortly before your first declaration of loyalty to the leader of the Party?"

Rubashov turned half-way to the light. "That'll be correct," he said.

"Was Rubashov's intention to make such a declaration mentioned during the evening?" Gletkin asked Hare-lip.

"Yes. My father reproached Rubashov because of it and said he was disappointed in him. Rubashov laughed, and called my father an old fool and a Don Quixote. He said the important thing was to hold out the longest and to wait for the hour to strike."

"What did he mean by this expression: 'to wait for the hour'?"

Again the young man's gaze sought Rubashov's face with a forlorn and almost tender expression. Rubashov had the absurd notion that he was about to come over from the wall and kiss him on the forehead. He smiled at this idea, while he heard the pleasant voice answer:

"The hour in which the leader of the Party would be removed from his post."

Gletkin, who had not missed Rubashov's smile, said drily:

"These reminiscences seem to amuse you?"

"Perhaps," said Rubashov, and shut his eyes again.

Gletkin pushed a cuff into place and went on questioning Hare-lip:

"So Rubashov spoke of the hour in which the leader of the Party would be removed from his post. How was this to be brought about?"

"My father considered that one day the cup would overflow and the Party would depose him or force him to resign; and that the opposition must propagate this idea."

"And Rubashov?"

"Rubashov laughed at my father, and repeated that he was a fool and a Don Quixote. Then he declared that No. 1 was no accidental phenomenon, but the embodiment of a certain human characteristic—namely, of an absolute belief in the infallibility of one's own conviction, from which he drew the strength for his complete unscrupulousness. Hence he would never resign from power of his own free will, and could only be removed by violence. One could hope for nothing from the Party either, for No. 1 held all the threads in his hand, and had made the Party bureaucracy his accomplice, who would stand and fall with him, and knew it."

In spite of his sleepiness, it struck Rubashov that the young man had retained his words with much accuracy. He himself no longer remembered the conversation in detail, but did not doubt that Hare-lip had recounted it faithfully. He observed young Kieffer through his pince-nez with a newly-awakened interest.

Gletkin's voice boomed again:

"So Rubashov emphasized the necessity to use violence against No. 1—that is, against the leader of the Party?"

Hare-lip nodded.

"And his arguments, seconded by a liberal consumption of alcoholic drinks, made a strong impression on you?"

Young Kieffer did not answer at once. Then he said, in a slightly lower tone than before:

"I had drunk practically nothing. But everything which he said made a deep impression on me."

Rubashov bowed his head. A suspicion had risen in him which affected him almost as a physical pain and made him forget everything else. Was it possible that this unfortunate youth had in fact drawn the conclusions from his, Rubashov's, line of thought—that he stood there before him in the glare of the reflector as the consequence incarnate of his own logic?

Gletkin did not let him finish this thought. His voice rasped:

". . . And following upon this preparatory theorizing came the direct instigation to the deed?"

Hare-lip was silent. He blinked into the light.

Gletkin waited a few seconds for the answer. Rubashov, too, unintentionally raised his head. A number of seconds passed, during which one only heard the lamp humming; then came Gletkin's voice again, even more correct and colourless:

"Would you like your memory to be helped out?"

Gletkin pronounced this sentence with marked casualness, but Hare-lip quivered as though struck by a whip. He licked his lips and in his eyes appeared the flickering of naked animal terror. Then his pleasant musical voice sounded again:

"The instigation did not happen that evening, but next morning, in a *tête-à-tête* between Citizen Rubashov and myself."

Rubashov smiled. The postponement of the imaginary conversation to next day was obviously a finesse in Gletkin's *mise en scène;* that old man Kieffer should have listened cheerfully while his son was instructed to murder by poison was too improbable a story even for Neanderthal-psychology. . . . Rubashov forgot the shock which he had just received; he turned to Gletkin and asked, blinking at the light:

"I believe the defendant has the right to ask questions during a confrontation?"

"You have the right," said Gletkin.

Rubashov turned to the young man. "As far as I remember," he said, looking at him through his pince-nez, "you had just finished your studies at the University when you and your father came to see me?"

Now that for the first time he spoke directly to Hare-lip, the hopeful, trusting look returned to the latter's face. He nodded.

"So that's correct," said Rubashov. "If I again remember rightly, at that time the intention was that you should start work under your father at the Institute of Historical Research. Did you do that?"

"Yes," said Hare-lip, and added after a short hesitation: "Up to my father's arrest."

"I understand," said Rubashov. "This event made it impossible for you to stay at the Institute, and you had to find some way of earning your living. . . ." He paused, turned to Gletkin, and continued:

". . . Which proved that at the time of my meeting

with this young man neither he nor I could have foreseen his future job; hence the instigation to murder by poison becomes a logical impossibility."

The secretary's pencil came to a sudden standstill. Rubashov knew, without looking at her, that she had ceased recording, and had turned her pointed, mouse-like face to Gletkin. Hare-lip also stared at Gletkin and licked his upper lip; his eyes showed no relief, only bewilderment and fear. Rubashov's momentary feeling of triumph vanished; he had the strange sensation of having disturbed the smooth running of a solemn ceremony. Gletkin's voice did in fact sound even cooler and more correct than usual:

"Have you any more questions?"

"That is all for the present," said Rubashov.

"Nobody asserted that your instructions restricted the murderer to the use of poison," said Gletkin quietly. "You gave the order for assassination; the choice of the means you left to your instrument." He turned to Hare-lip. "Is that right?"

"Yes," said Hare-lip, and his voice betrayed a kind of relief.

Rubashov remembered that the accusation had stated in express terms "instigation to murder by poison", but the whole thing had suddenly become indifferent to him. Whether young Michael had really made the crazy attempt or only planned something of this sort, whether the entire confession had been artificially pumped into him, or only parts of it, now seemed to Rubashov of merely legal interest; it made no difference to his guilt. The essential point was that this figure of misery represented the consequence of his logic made flesh. The roles had been exchanged; it was not Gletkin, but he, Rubashov, who had tried to muddle a clear case by splitting hairs. The accusation, which until now had seemed to him so absurd, in fact merely inserted—though in a clumsy and uncouth manner—the missing links into a perfectly logical chain.

And yet, in one point, it seemed to Rubashov that an injustice was being done him. But he was too exhausted to put it into words.

"Have you any more questions?" asked Gletkin.

Rubashov shook his head.

"You may go," said Gletkin to Hare-lip. He pushed a bell; a uniformed warder entered and put metal handcuffs on young Kieffer. Before he was led away, at the door, Hare-lip turned his head once more to Rubashov, as he used to do at the end of his walk in the yard. Rubashov felt his gaze as a burden; he took off his pince-nez, rubbed it on his sleeve, and averted his eyes.

When Hare-lip was gone, he nearly envied him. Gletkin's voice grated in his ear, precise and with brutal freshness:

"Do you now admit that Kieffer's confession accords with the facts in the essential points?"

Rubashov had again to turn to the lamp. There was a humming in his ears and the light flamed hot and red through the thin skin of his lids. Yet the phrase "in the essential points" did not escape him. With this phrase Gletkin bridged over the rent in the accusation and gave himself the possibility of changing "instigation to murder by poison" into "instigation to murder" simply.

"In the essential points—yes," said Rubashov.

Gletkin's cuffs creaked, and even the stenographer moved in her chair. Rubashov became aware that he had now spoken the decisive sentence and sealed his confession of guilt. How could these Neanderthalers ever understand what he, Rubashov, regarded as guilt—what he, by his own standards, called the truth?

"Does the light disturb you?" asked Gletkin suddenly.

Rubashov smiled. Gletkin paid cash. That was the mentality of the Neanderthaler. And yet, when the blinding light of the lamp became a degree milder, Rubashov felt relief and even something kindred to gratefulness.

Though only blinkingly, he could now look Gletkin in the face. He saw again the broad red scar on the clean-shaven skull.

". . . excepting only one point which I consider essential," said Rubashov.

"Namely?" asked Gletkin, again become stiff and correct.

Now, of course, he thinks I mean the *tête-à-tête* with the boy, which never took place, thought Rubashov. That is what matters to *him:* to put the dots on the i's—even if the dots look more like smudges. But, from his point of view, he may be right. . . .

"The point which matters to me," he said aloud, "is this. It is true that according to the convictions I held at the time, I spoke of the necessity of acting by violence. But by this I meant political action, and not individual terrorism."

"So you preferred civil war?" said Gletkin.

"No. Mass action," said Rubashov.

"Which, as you know yourself, would inevitably have led to civil war. Is that the distinction on which you place so much value?"

Rubashov did not answer. That was indeed the point which, a moment ago, had seemed so important—now it also had become indifferent to him. In fact, if the opposition could attain victory against the Party bureaucracy and its immense apparatus only by means of a civil war—why was this alternative better than to smuggle poison into the cold snack of No. 1, whose disappearance would perhaps cause the régime to collapse quicker and less bloodily? In what way was political murder less honourable than political mass killing? That unfortunate boy had evidently mistaken his meaning—but was there not more consistency in the boy's mistake than in his own behaviour during the last few years?

He who opposes a dictatorship must accept civil war as a means. He who recoils from civil war must give up opposition and accept the dictatorship.

These simple sentences, which he had written nearly a lifetime ago, in a polemic against the "moderates", contained his own condemnation. He felt in no state to continue the argument with Gletkin. The consciousness of his complete defeat filled him with a kind of relief; the obligation to continue the fight, the burden of responsibility were taken from him; the drowsiness of before returned. He felt the hammering in his head only as a faint echo, and for a few seconds it seemed to him that behind the desk sat, not Gletkin, but No. 1, with that look of strangely understanding irony he had given Rubashov as they shook hands at their last leave-taking. An inscription came into his mind which he had read on the gateway of the cemetery at Errancis where Saint-Just, Robespierre and their sixteen beheaded comrades lay buried. It consisted of one word:

Dormir—to sleep.

From that moment onwards, Rubashov's recollection again became hazy. He had probably fallen asleep for the second time—for a few minutes or seconds; but this time he did not remember having dreamed. He must have been woken by Gletkin to sign the statement. Gletkin passed him his fountain pen which, Rubashov noticed with slight disgust, was still warm from his pocket. The stenographer had ceased writing; there was complete silence in the room. The lamp had also stopped humming and spread a normal, rather faded light, for dawn appeared already at the window.

Rubashov signed.

The feeling of relief and irresponsibility remained, though he had forgotten the reason for it; then, drunk with sleep, he read through the statement in which he confessed to having incited young Kieffer to murder the leader of the Party. For a few seconds he had the feeling that it was all a grotesque misunderstanding; he had an impulse to cross out his signature and to tear up the document; then everything came back to him again, he rubbed his pince-nez on his sleeve and handed the paper over the desk to Gletkin.

The next thing he could remember was, that he was walking through the corridor again, escorted by the uniformed giant who had conducted him to Gletkin's room an immeasurable time ago. Half asleep, he passed the barber's room and the cellar steps; his fears on the way there occurred to him; he wondered a little at himself and smiled vaguely into the distance. Then he heard the cell door bang behind him and sank down on his bunk with a feeling of physical bliss; he saw the grey morning light on the window-panes with the familiar piece of newspaper stuck to the frame, and fell asleep at once.

When his cell door opened again, it was not yet quite daylight; he could hardly have slept an hour. He thought at first that the breakfast was being brought; but outside stood, instead of the old warder, again the giant in uniform. And Rubashov understood that he had to return to Gletkin and that the cross-examination would go on.

He rubbed cold water on forehead and neck at the washbasin, put on his pince-nez, and again started the march through the corridors, past barber's room and cellar stairs, with steps which swayed slightly without his knowing it.

4

From then onwards the veil of mist over Rubashov's memory became thicker. Later, he could only remember separate fragments of his dialogue with Gletkin, which extended over several days and nights, with short intervals of an hour or two. He could not even say exactly how many days and nights it had been; they must have spread over a week. Rubashov had heard of this method of complete physical crushing of the accused, in which usually two or three examining magistrates relieved each other in turn in a continuous cross-examination. But the difference with Gletkin's method was that he never had himself relieved, and exacted as much from himself as from Rubashov. Thus he deprived Rubashov of his last psychological resort: the pathos of the mal-treated, the moral superiority of the victim.

After forty-eight hours, Rubashov had lost the sense of day and night. When, after an hour's sleep, the giant shook him awake, he was no longer able to decide whether the grey light at the window was that of dawn or of evening. The corridor, with the barber's shop, cellar steps and barred door, was always lit by the same stale light of the electric bulbs. If, during the hearing, it gradually grew lighter at the window, until Gletkin finally turned out the lamp, it was morning. If it got darker, and Gletkin turned the lamp on, it was evening.

If Rubashov got hungry during the examination, Gletkin let tea and sandwiches be fetched for him. But he seldom had any appetite; that is to say, he had fits of ravenous hunger, but when the bread stood before him, he was overcome by nausea. Gletkin never ate in his presence, and Rubashov for some inexplicable reason found it humiliating to ask for food. Anything which touched on physical functions was humiliating to Rubashov in the presence of Gletkin, who never showed signs of fatigue, never yawned, never smoked, seemed neither to eat nor to drink, and always sat behind his desk in the same correct position, in the same stiff uniform with creaking cuffs. The worst degradation for Rubashov was when he had to ask permission to relieve himself. Gletkin would let him be conducted to the lavatory by the warder on duty, usually the giant, who then waited for him outside. Once Rubashov fell asleep behind the closed door. From then onwards the door always remained ajar.

His condition during the hearing alternated between apathy and an unnatural, glassy wakefulness. Only once did he actually become unconscious; he often felt on the brink of it, but a feeling of pride always saved him at the last minute. He would light a cigarette, blink, and the hearing would go on.

At times he was surprised that he was able to stand it. But he knew that lay opinion set far too narrow limits to men's capacity of physical resistance; that it had no idea of their astonishing elasticity. He had heard of cases of prisoners who had been kept from sleeping for fifteen to twenty days, and who had stood it.

At his first hearing by Gletkin, when he had signed his deposition, he had thought that the whole thing was over. At the second hearing it became clear to him, that it was only the beginning of it. The accusation consisted of seven points, and he had as yet confessed to only one.

He had believed that he had drunk the cup of humiliation to the dregs. Now he was to find that powerlessness had as many grades as power; that defeat could become as vertiginous as victory, and that its depths were bottomless. And, step by step, Gletkin forced him down the ladder.

He could, of course, have made it simpler for himself. He had only to sign everything, lock, stock and barrel, or to deny everything in a lump—and he would have peace. A queer, complicated sense of duty prevented him giving in to this temptation. Rubashov's life had been so filled by one absolute idea that he had known the phenomenon "temptation" only theoretically. Now temptation accompanied him through the indistinguishable days and nights, on his swaying walk through the corridor, in the white light of Gletkin's lamp: the temptation, which consisted of the single word written on the cemetery of the defeated: Sleep.

It was difficult to withstand, for it was a quiet and peaceful temptation; without gaudy paint, and not carnal. It was dumb; it did not use arguments. All the arguments were on Gletkin's side; it merely repeated the words which had been written on the barber's message: "Die in silence."

Occasionally, in the moments of apathy which alternated with transparent wakefulness, Rubashov's lips moved, but Gletkin could not hear the words. Then Gletkin would clear his voice and shove his cuffs into place; and Rubashov would rub his pince-nez on his sleeve and nod bewilderedly and drowsily; for he had identified the tempter with that dumb partner whom he had believed already forgotten, and who had no business in this room, of all places: the grammatical fiction. . . .

"So you deny having negotiated with representatives of a foreign Power on behalf of the opposition, in order to overthrow the present regime with their help? You contest the charge that you were ready to pay direct or indirect support of your plans with territorial concessions —that is, by the sacrifice of certain provinces of our country?"

Yes, Rubashov did contest this; and Gletkin repeated to him the day and occasion of his conversation with the foreign diplomat in question—and Rubashov again remembered that little, unimportant scene, which had bobbed up in his memory while Gletkin had been reading the accusation. Sleepy and confused, he looked at Gletkin and knew it was hopeless to try to explain that scene to him. It had taken place after a diplomatic lunch in the legation in B. Rubashov sat next to corpulent Herr von Z., Second Councillor to the Embassy of the very same State where, a few months ago, Rubashov had had his teeth knocked out—and pursued a most entertaining conversation with him about a certain rare variety of guinea-pig, which had been bred both on Herr von Z.'s estate and on that of Rubashov's father; in all probability, Rubashov's and von Z.'s respective fathers had even exchanged specimens with each other in their time.

"What has now become of your father's guinea-pigs?" asked Herr von Z.

"They were slaughtered during the Revolution and eaten," said Rubashov.

"Ours are now made into *ersatz* fat," said Herr von Z. with melancholy. He made no effort to hide his contempt for the new régime in his country, which presumably had only by accident omitted to kick him out of his post so far.

"You and I are really in a similar situation," he said comfortably and emptied his liqueur glass. "We both have outlived our time. Guinea-pig breeding is finished with; we live in the century of the Plebeian."

"But don't forget I am on the side of the Plebeian," Rubashov said smilingly.

"That is not what I meant," said Herr von Z. "If it comes to the point, I also agree with the programme of our manikin with the black mustache—if he only wouldn't shriek so. After all, one can only be crucified in the name of one's own faith." They sat a while longer, drinking coffee, and at the second cup Herr von Z. said: "If you should once again make a revolution in your country, Mr. Rubashov, and depose your No. 1, then take better care of the guinea-pigs."

"That is most unlikely to happen," said Rubashov, and after a pause, added: ". . . although one seems to count with this possibility amongst your friends?"

"Most certainly," Herr von Z. had replied in the same easy tone of voice. "After what your last trials gave us to hear, something rather funny must be going on in your country."

"Then, amongst your friends, there must also be some idea of what steps would be taken on your part in this very unlikely eventuality?" Rubashov had asked.

Whereupon Herr von Z. answered very precisely, almost as though he had been expecting this question: "Lie low. But there is a price."

They were standing beside the table, with their coffee cups in their hands. "And has the price, too, been decided upon already?" Rubashov asked, feeling himself that his light tone sounded rather artificial.

"Certainly," answered Herr von Z.; and he named a certain wheat-growing province inhabited by a national minority. Then they had taken leave of each other. . . .

Rubashov had not thought of this scene for years—or at least had not consciously recalled it. Idle chatter over black coffee and brandy—how could one explain to Gletkin its complete insignificance? Rubashov looked sleepily at Gletkin sitting opposite him, as stony and expressionless as ever. No, it was impossible to start talking to him about guinea-pigs. This Gletkin understood nothing of guinea-pigs. He had never drunk coffee with Herren von Z.'s. It occurred to Rubashov how haltingly Gletkin had read, how often with the wrong intonation. He was of proletarian origin, and had learnt to read and write when already grown-up. He would never understand that a conversation beginning with guinea-pigs could end God knew where.

"So you admit the conversation took place," Gletkin said.

"It was completely harmless," Rubashov said tiredly,

and knew that Gletkin had pushed him a step further
down the ladder.

"As harmless," said Gletkin, "as your purely theoretic
dissertations to young Kieffer on the necessity of the removal of the leader by violence?"

Rubashov rubbed his spectacles on his sleeve. Had the
conversation been really so harmless as he tried to make
himself believe? Certainly he had neither "negotiated"
nor come to any agreement; and comfortable Herr von
Z. had had no kind of official authority to do so. The
whole thing could at most be considered as what was
known in diplomatic language as "taking soundings". But
this kind of sounding had been a link in the logical chain
of his ideas of that time; besides, it fitted in with certain
Party traditions. Had not the old leader, shortly before
the Revolution, used the services of the General Staff of
that same country in order to be able to return from
exile and lead the Revolution to victory? Had he not
later, in the first peace treaty, abandoned certain ter-
ritories as a price for being left in peace? "The old man
sacrifices space to gain time," a witty friend of Rubashov's had remarked. The forgotten, "harmless" conversation fitted into the chain so well that it was now
difficult for Rubashov to see it otherwise than through
Gletkin's eyes. This same Gletkin, who read clumsily,
whose brain worked just as clumsily and arrived at simple,
graspable results—perhaps precisely because he understood nothing of guinea-pigs. . . . How, by the way, did
Gletkin know of this conversation? Either it had been
overheard, which in the circumstances was rather unlikely; or else the comfortable Herr von Z. had been
acting as *agent provocateur*—God only knew for what
complicated reasons. Such things had happened often
enough before. A trap had been laid for Rubashov—a
trap planned according to the primitive mentality of
Gletkin and No. 1; and he, Rubashov, had promptly
walked into it. . . .

"Being so well informed of my conversation with Herr
von Z.," Rubashov said, "you must also know that it
had no consequences."

"Certainly," said Gletkin. "Thanks to the fact that we arrested you in time, and destroyed the opposition throughout the country. The results of the attempted treason would have appeared if we had not."

What could he answer to that? That it would not in any case have led to serious results, if only for the reason that he, Rubashov, was too old and worn-out to act as consequentially as the Party traditions required, and as Gletkin would have done in his place? That the whole activity of the so-called opposition had been senile chatter, because the whole generation of the old guard was just as worn-out as he himself? Worn by the years of illegal struggle, eaten by the damp of the prison walls, between which they had spent half their youth; spiritually sucked dry by the permanent nervous strain of holding down the physical fear, of which one never spoke, which each had to deal with alone—for years, for tens of years. Worn by the years of exile, the acid sharpness of factions within the Party, the unscrupulousness with which they were fought out; worn out by the endless defeats, and the demoralization of the final victory? Should he say that an active, organized opposition to No. 1's dictatorship had never really existed; that it had all only been talk, impotent playing with fire, because this generation of the old guard had given all it had, had been squeezed out to the last drop, to the last spiritual calorie; and like the dead in the graveyard at Errancis, had only one thing left to hope for: to sleep and to wait until posterity did them justice.

What could he answer this immovable Neanderthal man? That he was right in everything, but had made one fundamental mistake: to believe that it was still the old Rubashov sitting opposite him, whilst it was only his shadow? That the whole thing came to this—to punish him, not for deeds he had committed, but for those he had neglected to commit? "One can only be crucified in the name of one's own faith," had said comfortable Herr von Z. . . .

Before Rubashov had signed the statement and was conducted back to his cell, to lie unconscious on his bunk until the torment started anew, he put a question to Gletkin. It had nothing to do with the point under discussion, but Rubashov knew that each time a new deposition was to be signed, Gletkin became a shade more tractable—Gletkin paid cash. The question Rubashov asked—concerned the fate of Ivanov.

"Citizen Ivanov is under arrest," said Gletkin.

"May one know the reason?" asked Rubashov.

"Citizen Ivanov conducted the examination of your case negligently, and in private conversation expressed cynical doubts as to the well-foundedness of the accusation."

"What if he really could not believe in it?" asked Rubashov. "He had perhaps too good an opinion of me?"

"In that case," said Gletkin, "he should have suspended the enquiry and should have officially informed the competent authorities that in his opinion you were innocent."

Was Gletkin mocking him? He looked as correct and expressionless as ever.

The next time that Rubashov again stood bowed over the day's record, with Gletkin's warm fountain pen in his hand—the stenographer had already left the room—he said:

"May I ask you another question?"

While speaking, he looked at the broad scar on Gletkin's skull.

"I was told that you were a partisan of certain drastic methods—the so-called 'hard method'. Why have you never used direct physical pressure on me?"

"You mean physical torture," said Gletkin in a matter-of-fact tone. "As you know, that is forbidden by our criminal code."

He paused. Rubashov had just finished signing the protocol.

"Besides," Gletkin continued, "there is a certain type of accused who confess under pressure, but recant at the public trial. You belong to that tenacious kind. The political utility of your confession at the trial will lie in its voluntary character."

It was the first time that Gletkin had spoken of a public trial. But on the way back along the corridor, walking behind the giant, with short tired steps, it was not this perspective which occupied Rubashov, but the sentence "you belong to that tenacious kind". Against his will, this sentence filled him with a pleasant self-satisfaction.

I am becoming senile and childish, he thought as he lay down on his bunk. Yet the pleasant feeling lasted until he fell asleep.

Each time he had, after tenacious argument, signed a new confession and lain down on his bunk, exhausted and yet in a strange way satisfied, with the knowledge that he would be wakened in an hour or at most two— each time Rubashov had but one wish: that Gletkin would just once let him sleep and come to his senses. He knew that this desire would not be fulfilled until the fight was fought to the bitter end, and the last dot put on the last "i"—and he knew, too, that each new duel would end in a new defeat and that there could be no possible doubt about the final result. Why, then, did he go on tormenting himself and letting himself be tormented, instead of giving up the lost battle, so as not to be wakened any more? The idea of death had a long time ago lost any metaphysical character; it had a warm, tempting, bodily meaning—that of sleep. And yet a peculiar, twisted sense of duty forced him to remain awake and continue the lost battle to the end—even though it were only a battle with windmills. To continue until the hour when Gletkin would have forced him down the last rung of the ladder, and in his blinking eyes, the last clumsy smudge of the accusation had been turned into a logically dotted "i". He had to follow the road until the end. Then only, when he entered the darkness with open eyes, had he conquered the right to sleep and not to be wakened any more.

In Gletkin, too, a certain change occurred during this

unbroken chain of days and nights. It was not much, but Rubashov's feverish eyes did not miss it. Until the end Gletkin sat stiffly with unmoved face and creaking cuffs in the shadow of his lamp behind the desk; but gradually, bit by bit, the brutality faded from his voice, in the same way as, bit by bit, he had turned down the shrill light of the lamp, until it had become nearly normal. He never smiled, and Rubashov wondered whether the Neanderthalers were capable of smiling at all; neither was his voice supple enough to express any shades of feeling. But once, when Rubashov's cigarettes ran out after a dialogue of several hours, Gletkin, who did not smoke himself, took a packet out of his pocket and passed it over the desk to Rubashov.

In one point Rubashov even managed to achieve a victory; that was the point in the accusation concerning his alleged sabotage in the aluminum trust. It was a charge which did not weigh much in the sum total of the crimes to which he had already confessed, but Rubashov fought it with the same obstinacy as on the decisive points. They sat opposite each other nearly the whole night. Rubashov had refuted point for point all incriminating evidence and one-sided statistics; in a voice thick with tiredness, he had cited figures and dates, which as by miracle came up at the right moment in his numbed head; and all the time Gletkin had not been able to find the starting point from which he could unroll the logical chain. For at their second or third meeting already, as it were, an unspoken agreement had come into existence between them: if Gletkin could prove that the root of charge was right—even when this root was only of a logical, abstract nature—he had a free hand to insert the missing details; "to dot the i's", as Rubashov called it. Without becoming aware of it, they had got accustomed to these rules for their game, and neither of them distinguished any longer between actions which Rubashov had committed in fact and those which he merely should have committed as a consequence of his opinions; they had gradually lost the sense of appearance and reality, logical fiction and fact. Rubashov would occasionally become conscious of this in his rare moments of clearheadedness, and he would then have the sensation of awakening from a strange state of intoxication; Gletkin, on the other hand, seemed never to be aware of it.

Towards morning, when Rubashov still had not given in over the question of sabotage in the aluminum trust, Gletkin's voice acquired an undertone of nervousness —just as in the beginning, when Hare-lip had brought out the wrong answer. He turned the lamp on more sharply, which had not happened for a long time; but he turned it down again when he saw Rubashov's ironic smile. He put a few more questions, which had no effect, and said conclusively:

"So you definitely deny having committed any wrecking or subversive acts in the industry entrusted to you —or to have even planned such acts?"

Rubashov nodded—with a sleepy curiosity as to what would happen. Gletkin turned to the stenographer:

"Write: the examining magistrate recommends that this charge be dropped for lack of evidence."

Rubashov quickly lit a cigarette to conceal the movement of childish triumph which overcame him. For the first time he had won a victory over Gletkin. Certainly it was a pathetic little local victory in a lost battle, but yet a victory; and it had been so many months, even years, since he had last known this feeling. . . . Gletkin took the day's record from the secretary and dismissed her, according to the ritual which had latterly developed between them.

When they were alone, and Rubashov had stood up to sign the protocol, Gletkin said, passing him his fountain pen:

"Industrial sabotage is, according to experience, the most effective means for the opposition to create difficulties for the Government, and to produce discontent amongst the workers. Why do you so stubbornly maintain that you did not use—or intend to use—just this method?"

"Because it is a technical absurdity," said Rubashov.

"And this perpetual harping on the *saboteur* as a bogyman produces an epidemic of denunciation which revolts me."

The long-missed sensation of triumph caused Rubashov to feel fresher and speak louder than usual.

"If you hold sabotage for a mere fiction, what, in your opinion, are the real causes of the unsatisfactory state of our industries?"

"Too low piece-work tariffs, slave-driving and barbaric disciplinary measures," said Rubashov. "I know of several cases in my Trust in which workers were shot as *saboteurs* because of some trifling negligence caused by over-tiredness. If a man is two minutes late at clocking-in, he is fired, and a stamp is put in his identity-papers which makes it impossible for him to find work elsewhere."

Gletkin looked at Rubashov with his usual expressionless gaze, and asked him, in his usual expressionless voice:

"Were you given a watch as a boy?"

Rubashov looked at him in astonishment. The most conspicuous trait of the Neanderthal character was its absolute humourlessness or, more exactly, its lack of frivolity.

"Don't you want to answer my question?" asked Gletkin.

"Certainly," said Rubashov, more and more astonished.

"How old were you when the watch was given you?"

"I don't quite know," said Rubashov; "eight or nine probably."

"I," said Gletkin in his usual correct voice, "was sixteen years old when I learnt that the hour was divided into minutes. In my village, when the peasants had to travel to town, they would go to the railway station at sunrise and lie down to sleep in the waiting-room until the train came, which was usually at about midday; sometimes it only came in the evening or next morning. These are the peasants who now work in our factories. For example, in my village is now the biggest steel-rail factory in the world. In the first year, the foremen would lie down to sleep between two emptyings of the blast furnace, until they were shot. In all other countries, the peasants had one or two hundred years to develop the habit of industrial precision and of the handling of machines. Here they only had ten years. If we didn't sack them and shoot them for every trifle, the whole country would come to a standstill, and the peasants would lie down to sleep in the factory yards until grass grew out of the chimneys and everything became as it was before. Last year a women's delegation came to us from Manchester in England. They were shown everything, and afterwards they wrote indignant articles, saying that the textile workers in Manchester would never stand such treatment. I have read that the cotton industry in Manchester is two hundred years old. I have also read, what the treatment of the workers there was like two hundred years ago, when it started. You, Comrade Rubashov, have just used the same arguments as this women's delegation from Manchester. You, of course, know better than these women. So one may wonder at your using the same arguments. But then, you have something in common with them: you were given a watch as a child. . . ."

Rubashov said nothing and looked at Gletkin with a new interest. What was this? Was the Neanderthaler coming out of his shell? But Gletkin sat stiffly on his chair, as expressionless as ever.

"You may be right in some ways," Rubashov said finally. "But it was you who started me off on this question. What use is it to invent scapegoats for difficulties, the natural causes of which you have just so convincingly described?"

"Experience teaches," said Gletkin, "that the masses must be given for all difficult and complicated processes a simple, easily grasped explanation. According to what I know of history, I see that mankind could never do without scapegoats. I believe it was at all times an indispensable institution; your friend Ivanov taught me that it was of religious origin. As far as I remember, he explained that the word itself came from a custom of the Hebrews, who once a year sacrificed to their god a

goat, laden with all their · sins." Gletkin paused and
shoved his cuffs into place. "Besides, there are also examples in history of voluntary scapegoats. At the age
when you were given a watch, I was being taught by
the village priest that Jesus Christ called himself a lamb,
which had taken on itself all sin. I have never understood in what way it could help mankind if someone declares he is being sacrificed for its sake. But for two
thousand years people have apparently found it quite
natural."

Rubashov looked at Gletkin. What was he aiming at?
What was the object of this conversation? In what labyrinth was the Neanderthaler straying?

"However that may be," said Rubashov, "it would be
more in accordance with our ideas to tell the people
the truth, instead of populating the world with *saboteurs*
and devils."

"If one told the people in my village," said Gletkin,
"that they were still slow and backward in spite of the
Revolution and the factories, it would have no effect
on them. If one tells them that they are heroes of work,
more efficient than the Americans, and that all evil only
comes from devils and *saboteurs*, it has at least some
effect. Truth is what is useful to humanity, falsehood
what is harmful. In the outline of history published by
the Party for the evening classes for adults, it is emphasized that during the first few centuries the Christian
religion realized an objective progress for mankind.
Whether Jesus spoke the truth or not, when he asserted
he was the son of God and of a virgin, is of no interest to any sensible person. It is said to be sym-
bolical, but the peasants take it literally. We have the
same right to invent useful symbols which the peasants
take literally."

"Your reasoning," said Rubashov, "sometimes reminds
me of Ivanov's."

"Citizen Ivanov," said Gletkin, "belonged, as you do,
to the old intelligentsia; by conversing with him, one
could acquire some of that historical knowledge which
one had missed through insufficient schooling. The differ-

ence is that I try to use that knowledge in the service of the Party; but Citizen Ivanov was a cynic."

"Was . . . ?" asked Rubashov, taking off his pince-nez.

"Citizen Ivanov," said Gletkin, looking at him with expressionless eyes, "was shot last night, in execution of an administrative decision."

After this conversation, Gletkin let Rubashov sleep for two full hours. On the way back to his cell, Rubashov wondered why the news of Ivanov's death had not made a deeper impression on him. It had merely caused the cheering effect of his little victory to vanish and made him tired and drowsy again. Apparently he had reached a state which precluded any deeper emotion. Anyhow, even before he had learnt of Ivanov's death, he had been ashamed of that idle feeling of triumph. Gletkin's personality had gained such power over him that even his triumphs were turned into defeats. Massive and expressionless, he sat there, the brutal embodiment of the State which owed its very existence to the Rubashovs and Ivanovs. Flesh of their flesh, grown independent and become insensible. Had not Gletkin acknowledged himself to be the spiritual heir of Ivanov and the old intelligentsia? Rubashov repeated to himself for the hundredth time that Gletkin and the new Neanderthalers were merely completing the work of the generation with the numbered heads. That the same doctrine became so inhuman in their mouths, had, as it were, merely climactic reasons. When Ivanov had used the same arguments, there was yet an undertone in his voice left by the past by the remembrance of a world which had vanished. One can deny one's childhood, but not erase it. Ivanov had trailed his past after him to the end; that was what gave everything he said that undertone of frivolous melancholy; that was why Gletkin had called him a cynic. The Gletkins had nothing to erase; they need not deny their past, because they had none. They were born without umbilical cord, without frivolity, without melancholy.

5

Fragment of the Diary of N. S. Rubashov

"*. . . With what right do we who are quitting the
scene look down with such superiority on the Gletkins?
There must have been laughter amidst the apes when the
Neanderthaler first appeared on earth. The highly
civilized apes swung gracefully from bough to bough;
the Neanderthaler was uncouth and bound to the earth.
The apes, saturated and peaceful, lived in sophisticated
playfulness, or caught fleas in philosophic contemplation; the Neanderthaler trampled gloomily through the
world, banging around with clubs. The apes looked down
on him amusedly from their tree tops and threw nuts at
him. Sometimes horror seized them; they ate fruits and
tender plants with delicate refinement; the Neanderthaler
devoured raw meat, he slaughtered animals and his fellows. He cut down trees which had always stood, moved
rocks from their time-hallowed place, transgressed against
every law and tradition of the jungle. He was uncouth,
cruel, without animal dignity—from the point of view of
the highly cultivated apes, a barbaric relapse of history.
The last surviving chimpanzees still turn up their noses
at the sight of a human being. . . .*"

6

After five or six days an incident occurred: Rubashov
fainted during the examination. They had just arrived at
the concluding point in the accusation: the question of
the motive for Rubashov's actions. The accusation defined the motive simply as "counter-revolutionary mentality", and mentioned casually, as if it were self-evident,
that he had been in the service of a hostile foreign Power.
Rubashov fought his last battle against that formulation.
The discussion had lasted from dawn to the middle of the
morning, when Rubashov, at a quite undramatic moment, slid sideways from his chair and remained lying on
the ground.

When he came to a few minutes later, he saw the little

fluff-covered skull of the doctor over him, pouring water on his face out of a bottle, and rubbing his temples. Rubashov felt the doctor's breath, which smelt of peppermint and bread-and-dripping, and was sick. The doctor scolded in his shrill voice, and advised that Rubashov should be taken into the fresh air for a minute. Gletkin had watched the scene with his expressionless eyes. He rang and ordered the carpet to be cleaned; then he let Rubashov be conducted back to his cell. A few minutes later, he was taken by the old warder into the yard for exercise.

For the first few minutes Rubashov was as if intoxicated by the biting fresh air. He discovered that he had lungs which drank in oxygen, as the palate a sweet refreshing drink. The sun shone pale and clear; it was just eleven in the morning—the hour at which he always used to be taken for his walk an immeasurable time ago, before this long, hazy row of days and nights had started. What a fool he had been not to appreciate this blessing. Why could one not just live and breathe and walk through the snow and feel the pale warmth of the sun on one's face? Shake off the nightmare of Gletkin's room, the glaring light of the lamp, that whole ghostly *mise en scène*—and live as other people do?

As it was the usual hour for his exercise, he again had the thin peasant with the bast-shoes as neighbour in the roundabout. He watched sideways as Rubashov walked along beside him with slightly swaying steps, cleared his throat once or twice, and said, with a glance at the warders:

"I have not seen you for a long time, your honour. You look ill, as though you won't last much longer. They say there will be a war."

Rubashov said nothing. He resisted the temptation to pick up a handful of snow and press it to a ball in his hand. The circle moved slowly round the yard. Twenty paces ahead the next pair stamped along between the low banks of snow—two men of about the same height in grey coats, with little clouds of steam in front of their mouths.

be sowing time," said the peasant. "After
of the snows the sheep go into the hills. It
days until they are up there. Before, all the
n the district sent their sheep on the journey the
sa. .day. At sunrise it started, sheep everywhere, on all
paths and fields, the whole village accompanied the herds
during the first day. You have perhaps in all your life
never seen so many sheep, your honour, and so many
dogs and so much dust and such barking and bleating.
. . . Mother of God, what merriment it was. . . ."

Rubashov held his face lifted to the sun; the sun was
still pale, but already it lent the air a tepid softness. He
watched the gliding, swerving play of the birds, high
above the machine-gun turret.

The peasant's whining voice went on:

"A day like to-day, when one smells the melting of the
snow in the air, takes hold of me. We will neither of us
last much longer, your honour. They have crushed us
because we are reactionaries, and because the old days
when we were happy must not come back. . . ."

"Were you really so happy in those days?" asked Rubashov; but the peasant only murmured something unintel-
ligible, while his Adam's apple slid up and down his
throat several times. Rubashov watched him from the
side; after a time he said:

"Do you remember the part in the Bible where the
tribes in the desert begin to cry: Let us make a captain,
and let us return into Egypt"?

The peasant nodded eagerly and uncomprehendingly.
. . . Then they were conducted back into the building.

The effect of the fresh air vanished, the leaden drowsiness, the giddiness and nausea returned. At the entrance
Rubashov bent down, picked up a handful of snow,
and rubbed it on his forehead and burning eyes.

He was not taken back to his cell as he had hoped,
but straight to Gletkin's room. Gletkin was sitting at his
desk, in the same position as Rubashov had left him
in—how long ago? He looked as though he had not moved
during Rubashov's absence. The curtains were drawn,

the lamp burning; time stood still in this room, as in a putrefying pond. While sitting down again opposite Gletkin, Rubashov's glance fell on a damp patch on the carpet. He remembered his sickness. So it was, after all, but an hour since he had left the room.

"I take it that you feel better now," said Gletkin. "We left off at the concluding question of the motive for your counter-revolutionary activities."

He stared in slight surprise at Rubashov's right hand, resting on the arm of the chair and still clenching a tiny lump of snow. Rubashov followed his glance; he smiled and lifted his hand to the lamp. They both watched the little lump melting on his hand in the warmth of the bulb.

"The question of motive is the last," said Gletkin. "When you have signed that, we will have finished with one another."

The lamp radiated a sharper light than it had for a long time. Rubashov was forced to blink.

". . . And then you will be able to rest," said Gletkin.

Rubashov passed his hand over his temples, but the coolness of the snow was gone. The word "rest", with which Gletkin had ended his sentence, remained suspended in the silence. Rest and sleep. Let us choose a captain and return into the land of Egypt. . . . He blinked sharply through his pince-nez at Gletkin:

"You know my motives as well as I do," he said. "You know that I acted neither out of a 'counter-revolutionary mentality', nor was I in the service of a foreign Power. What I thought and what I did, I thought and did according to my own conviction and conscience."

Gletkin had pulled a dossier out of his drawer. He went through it, pulled out a sheet and read in his monotonous voice:

"'. . . For us the question of subjective good faith is of no interest. He who is in the wrong must pay; he who is in the right will be absolved. That was our law. . . .' You wrote that in your diary shortly after your arrest."

Rubashov felt behind his eye-lids the familiar flickering of the light. In Gletkin's mouth the sentence he had thought and written acquired a peculiarly naked sound —as though a confession, intended only for the anonymous priest, had been registered on a gramophone record, which now was repeating it in its cracked voice.

Gletkin had taken another page out of the dossier, but read only one sentence from it, with his expressionless gaze fixed on Rubashov:

" 'Honour is: to serve without vanity, and unto the last consequence.' "

Rubashov tried to withstand his gaze.

"I don't see," he said, "how it can serve the Party that her members have to grovel in the dust before all the world. I have signed everything you wanted me to sign. I have pleaded guilty to having pursued a false and objectively harmful policy. Isn't that enough for you?"

He put on his pince-nez, blinked helplessly past the lamp, and ended in a tired, hoarse voice:

"After all, the name N. S. Rubashov is itself a piece of Party history. By dragging it in dirt, you besmirch the history of the Revolution."

"To that I can also reply with a citation from your own writings. You wrote:

" 'It is necessary to hammer every sentence into the masses by repetition and simplification. What is presented as right must shine like gold; what is presented as wrong must be black as pitch. For consumption by the masses, the political processes must be coloured like ginger-bread figures at a fair.' "

Rubashov was silent. Then he said:

"So that is what you are aiming at: I am to play the Devil in your Punch and Judy show—howl, grind my teeth and put out my tongue—and voluntarily, too. Danton and his friends were spared that, at least."

Gletkin shut the cover of the dossier. He bent forward a bit and settled his cuffs:

"Your testimony at the trial will be the last service you can do the Party."

Rubashov did not answer. He kept his eyes shut and relaxed under the rays of the lamp like a tired sleeper in the sun; but there was no escape from Gletkin's voice.

"Your Danton and the Convention," said the voice, "were just a gallant play compared to what is at stake here. I have read books about it: those people wore powdered pigtails and declaimed about their personal honour. To them, it only mattered to die with a noble gesture, regardless of whether this gesture did good or harm."

Rubashov said nothing. There was a buzzing and humming in his ears; Gletkin's voice was above him; it came from every side of him; it hammered mercilessly on his aching skull.

"You know what is at stake here," Gletkin went on. "For the first time in history, a revolution has not only conquered power, but also kept it. We have made our country a bastion of the new era. It covers a sixth of the world and contains a tenth of the world's population."

Gletkin's voice now sounded at Rubashov's back. He had risen and was walking up and down the room. It was the first time this had happened. His boots creaked at every step, his starched uniform crackled and a sourish smell of sweat and leather became noticeable.

"When our Revolution had succeeded in our country, we believed that the rest of the earth would follow suit. Instead, came a wave of reaction, which threatened to swamp us. There were two currents in the Party. One consisted of adventurers, who wanted to risk what we had won to promote the revolution abroad. You belonged to them. We recognized this current to be dangerous, and have liquidated it."

Rubashov wanted to raise his head and say something. Gletkin's steps resounded in his skull. He was too tired. He let himself fall back, and kept his eyes shut.

"The leader of the Party," Gletkin's voice went on, "had the wider perspective and the more tenacious tactics. He realized that everything depended on surviving the period of world reaction and keeping the bastion. He had realized that it might last ten, perhaps twenty, perhaps fifty years, until the world was ripe for a fresh wave of revolution. Until then we stand alone. Until then we have only one duty: not to perish."

A sentence swam vaguely in Rubashov's memory: "It is the Revolutionary's duty to preserve his own life." Who had said that? He, himself? Ivanov? It was in the name of that principle that he had sacrificed Arlova. And where had it led him?

". . . Not to perish," sounded Gletkin's voice. "The bulwark must be held, at any price and with any sacrifice. The leader of the Party recognized this principle with unrivalled clearsightedness, and has consistently applied it. The policy of the International had to be subordinated to our national policy. Whoever did not understand this necessity had to be destroyed. Whole sets of our best functionaries in Europe had to be physically liquidated. We did not recoil from crushing our own organizations abroad when the interests of the Bastion required it. We did not recoil from co-operation with the police of reactionary countries in order to suppress revolutionary movements which came at the wrong moment. We did not recoil from betraying our friends and compromising with our enemies, in order to preserve the Bastion. That was the task which history had given us, the representative of the first victorious revolution. The shortsighted, the aesthetes, the moralists did not understand. But the leader of the Revolution understood that all depended on one thing: to be the better stayer."

Gletkin interrupted his pacing through the room. He stopped behind Rubashov's chair. The scar on his shaven skull shone sweatily. He panted, wiped his skull with his handkerchief, and seemed embarrassed at having broken his customary reserve. He sat down again behind the desk and settled his cuffs. He turned down the light a little, and continued in his usual expressionless voice:

"The Party's line was sharply defined. Its tactics were determined by the principle that the end justifies the means—all means, without exception. In the spirit of this principle, the Public Prosecutor will demand your life, Citizen Rubashov.

"Your faction, Citizen Rubashov, is beaten and destroyed. You wanted to split the Party, although you must have known that a split in the Party meant civil war. You know of the dissatisfaction amongst the peasantry, which has not yet learnt to understand the sense of the sacrifices imposed on it. In a war which may be only a few months away, such currents can lead to a catastrophe. Hence the imperious necessity for the Party to be united. It must be as if cast from one mould —filled with blind discipline and absolute trust. You and your friends, Citizen Rubashov, have made a rent in the Party. If your repentance is real, then you must help us to heal this rent. I have told you, it is the last service the Party will ask of you.

"Your task is simple. You have set it yourself: to gild the Right, to blacken the Wrong. The policy of the opposition is wrong. Your task is therefore to make the opposition contemptible; to make the masses understand that opposition is a crime and that the leaders of the opposition are criminals. That is the simple language which the masses understand. If you begin to talk of your complicated motives, you will only create confusion amongst them. Your task, Citizen Rubashov, is to avoid awakening sympathy and pity. Sympathy and pity for the opposition are a danger to the country.

"Comrade Rubashov, I hope that you have understood the task which the Party has set you."

It was the first time since their acquaintance that Gletkin called Rubashov "Comrade". Rubashov raised his head quickly. He felt a hot wave rising in him, against which he was helpless. His chin shook slightly while he was putting on his pince-nez.

"I understand."

"Observe," Gletkin went on, "that the Party holds out to you no prospect of reward. Some of the accused have been made amenable by physical pressure. Others, by the promise to save their heads—or the heads of their relatives who had fallen into our hands as hostages. To you, Comrade Rubashov, we propose no bargain and we promise nothing."

"I understand," Rubashov repeated.

Gletkin glanced at the dossier.

"There is a passage in your journal which impressed

me," he went on. "You wrote: 'I have thought and acted as I had to. If I was right, I have nothing to repent of; if wrong, I shall pay.' "

He looked up from the dossier and looked Rubashov fully in the face:

"You were wrong, and you will pay, Comrade Rubashov. The Party promises only one thing: after the victory, one day when it can do no more harm, the material of the secret archives will be published. Then the world will learn what was in the background of this Punch and Judy show—as you called it—which we had to act to them according to history's text-book. . . ."

He hesitated a few seconds, settled his cuffs and ended rather awkwardly, while the scar on his skull reddened:

"And then you, and some of your friends of the older generation, will be given the sympathy and pity which are denied to you to-day."

While he was speaking, he had pushed the prepared statement over to Rubashov, and laid his fountain-pen beside it. Rubashov stood up and said with a strained smile:

"I have always wondered what it was like when the Neanderthalers became sentimental. Now I know."

"I do not understand," said Gletkin, who had also stood up.

Rubashov signed the statement, in which he confessed to having committed his crimes through counter-revolutionary motives and in the service of a foreign Power. As he raised his head, his gaze fell on the portrait of No. 1 hanging on the wall, and once again he recognized the expression of knowing irony with which years ago No. 1 had taken leave of him—that melancholy cynicism which stared down on humanity from the omnipresent portrait.

"It does not matter if you don't understand," said Rubashov. "There are things which only that older generation, the Ivanovs, Rubashovs and Kieffers have understood. That is over now."

"I will give order that you are not to be troubled until the trial," said Gletkin after a short pause, again stiff and precise. Rubashov's smiling irritated him. "Have you any other particular wish?"

"To sleep," said Rubashov. He stood in the open door, beside the giant warder, small, elderly and insignificant with his pince-nez and beard.

"I will give orders that your sleep must not be disturbed," said Gletkin.

When the door had shut behind Rubashov, he went back to his desk. For a few seconds he sat still. Then he rang for his secretary.

She sat down in her usual place in the corner. "I congratulate you on your success, Comrade Gletkin," she said.

Gletkin turned the lamp down to normal.

"That," he said with a glance at the lamp, "plus lack of sleep and physical exhaustion. It is all a matter of constitution."

The Grammatical Fiction

> *Show us not the aim without the way.*
> *For ends and means on earth are so en-*
> *tangled*
> *That changing one, you change the other*
> *too;*
> *Each different path brings other ends in*
> *view.*
>
> FERDINAND LASSALLE:
> *Franz von Sickingen*

1

"ASKED WHETHER HE PLEADED GUILTY, the accused Rubashov answered 'Yes' in a clear voice. To a further question of the Public Prosecutor as to whether the accused had acted as an agent of the counter-revolution, he again answered 'Yes' in a lower voice. . . ."

The porter Wassilij's daughter read slowly, each syllable separately. She had spread the newspaper on the table and followed the lines with her finger; from time to time she smoothed her flowered head-kerchief.

". . . Asked whether he wanted an advocate for his defence, the accused declared he would forgo that right. The court then proceeded to the reading of the accusation. . . ."

The porter Wassilij was lying on the bed with his face turned to the wall. Vera Wassiljovna never quite knew whether the old man listened to her reading or slept. Sometimes he mumbled to himself. She had learnt not to pay any attention to that, and had made a habit of reading the paper aloud every evening, "for educational reasons" even when after work at the factory she had to go to a meeting of her cell and returned home late.

". . . The Definition of the Charge states that the accused Rubashov is proved guilty on all points contained in the accusation, by documentary evidence and his own confession in the preliminary investigation. In answer to a question of the President of the Court as to whether he had any complaint to make against the conduct of the preliminary investigation, the accused answered in the negative, and added that he had made his confession of his own free will, in sincere repentance of his counter-revolutionary crimes. . . ."

The porter Wassilij did not move. Above the bed, directly over his head, hung the portrait of No. 1. Next to it a rusty nail stuck out of the wall: until a short time ago the photograph of Rubashov as Partisan-commander had hung there. Wassilij's hand felt automatically for the hole in his mattress in which he used to hide his greasy Bible from the daughter; but shortly after Rubashov's arrest the daughter had found it and thrown it away, for educational reasons.

". . . At the Prosecutor's request, the accused Rubashov now proceeded to describe his evolution from an opponent of the Party line to a counter-revolutionary and traitor to the Fatherland. In the presence of a tense audience, the accused began his statement as follows: 'Citizen Judges, I will explain what led me to capitulate before the investigating magistrate and before you, the representatives of justice in our country. My story will demonstrate to you how the slightest deflection from the line of the Party must inevitably end in counter-revolutionary banditry. The necessary result of our oppositional struggle was that we were pushed further and further down into the morass. I will describe to you my fall, that it may be a warning to those who in this decisive hour still waver, and have hidden doubts in the leadership of the Party and the rightness of the Party line. Covered with shame, trampled in the dust, about to die, I will describe to you the sad progress of a traitor, that it may serve as a lesson and terrifying example to the millions of our country. . . .' "

The porter Wassilij had turned round on the bed and pressed his face into the mattress. Before his eyes was the picture of the bearded Partisan-commander Rubashov, who in the worst sort of mess knew how to swear in such a pleasant way that it was a joy to God and man. "Trampled in the dust, about to die. . . ." Wassilij groaned. The Bible was gone, but he knew many passages by heart.

". . . At this point the Public Prosecutor interrupted the accused's narrative to ask a few questions concerning the fate of Rubashov's former secretary, Citizen Arlova, who had been executed on the charge of treasonable activities. From the answers of the accused Rubashov, it appears that the latter, driven into a corner at that time by the watchfulness of the Party, had laid the responsibility of his own crimes to Arlova's charge, so as to save his head and be able to continue his disgraceful activities. N. S. Rubashov confesses to this monstrous crime with un-ashamed and cynical openness. To the Citizen Prosecutor's remark: 'You are apparently quite without any moral sense,' the accused answers with a sarcastic smile: 'Apparently.' His behaviour provoked the audience to repeated spontaneous demonstrations of anger and contempt, which were, however, quickly suppressed by the Citizen President of the Court. On one occasion these expressions of the revolutionary sense of justice gave place to a wave of merriment—namely, when the accused interrupted the description of his crimes with the request that the proceedings might be suspended for a few minutes, as he was suffering from 'intolerable toothache'. It is typical of the correct procedure of revolutionary justice that the President immediately granted this wish and, with a shrug of contempt, gave the order for the hearing to be interrupted for five minutes."

The porter Wassilij lay on his back and thought of the time when Rubashov had been conducted in triumph through the meetings, after his rescue from the foreigners; and of how he had stood leaning on his crutches up on the platform under the red flags and decorations, and, smiling, had rubbed his glasses on his sleeve, while the cheerings and shoutings never ceased.

"And the soldiers led him away, into the hall called Prætorium; and they called together the whole band.

*And they clothed him with purple and they smote him on
the head with a reed and did spit upon him; and bowing
their knees worshipped him."*

"What are you mumbling to yourself?" asked the
daughter.

"Never mind," said old Wassilij, and turned to the
wall. He felt with his hand in the hole in the mattress,
but it was empty. The hook hanging over his head was
also empty. When the daughter had taken the portrait
of Rubashov from the wall and thrown it in the dust-bin,
he had not protested—he was now too old to stand the
shame of prison.

The daughter had interrupted her reading and put the
Primus stove on the table to prepare tea. A sharp smell
of petrol spread over the porter's lodge. "Were you listening to my reading?" asked the daughter.

Wassilij obediently turned his head towards her. "I
heard it all," he said.

"So now you see," said Vera Wassiljovna, pumping
petrol into the hissing apparatus. "He says himself that
he is a traitor. If it weren't true, he wouldn't say so himself. In the meeting at our factory we have already carried a resolution which all have to sign."

"A lot you understand about it," sighed Wassilij.

Vera Wassiljovna threw him a quick glance which had
the effect of making him turn his head to the wall again.
Each time she gave him that peculiar glance, Wassilij
was reminded that he was in Vera Wassiljovna's way,
who wanted to have the porter's lodge for herself. Three
weeks ago, she and a junior mechanic at her factory
had put their names down together in the marriage re-
gister, but the pair had no home; the boy shared a room
with two colleagues and nowadays it often was many
years before one was assigned a flat by the housing trust.

The Primus was at last alight. Vera Wassiljovna put
the kettle on it.

"The cell secretary read us the resolution. In it is
written that we demand that the traitors be mercilessly
exterminated. Whoever shows pity to them is himself a
traitor and must be denounced," she explained in a pur-

posely matter-of-fact voice. "The workers must be watch-ful. We have each received a copy of the resolution in order to collect signatures for it."

Vera Wassiljovna took a slightly crushed sheet of paper out of her blouse and flattened it out on the table. Wassilij now lay on his back; the rusty nail stuck out of the wall straight above his head. He squinted over to the paper, which lay spread next to the Primus stove. Then he turned his head away quickly.

"And he said: I tell thee, Peter, the cock shall not crow this day before that thou shalt thrice deny that thou knowest me. . . ."

The water in the kettle began to hum. Old Wassilij put on a cunning expression:

"Must also those sign who were in the Civil War?"

The daughter stood bent over the kettle, in her flowered head-kerchief. "Nobody has to," she said with the same peculiar glance as before. "In the factory they know, of course, that he lived in this house. The cell secretary asked me after the meeting whether you were friends until the end, and whether you had spoken much to-gether."

Old Wassilij sat up on the mattress with a jump. The effort made him cough, and the veins swelled on his thin, scrofulous neck.

The daughter put two glasses on the edge of the table and scattered some tea-leaf dust into each out of a paper bag. "What are you mumbling again?" she asked.

"Give me that damned paper," said old Wassilij.

The daughter passed it to him. "Shall I read it to you, so that you know exactly what is in it?"

"No," said the old man, writing his name on it. "I don't want to know. Now give me some tea."

The daughter passed him the glass. Wassilij's lips were moving; he mumbled to himself while drinking the pale yellow liquid in small sips.

After they had drunk their tea, the daughter went on reading from the newspaper. The trial of the accused Rubashov and Kieffer was nearing its end. The debate on the charge of the planned assassination of the leader of the Party had released storms of indignation amongst the audience; shouts of "Shoot the mad dogs!" were heard repeatedly. To the Public Prosecutor's concluding question, concerning the motive of his actions, the accused Rubashov, who seemed to have broken down, answered in a tired, dragging voice:

"I can only say that we, the opposition, having once made it our criminal aim to remove the Government of the Fatherland of the Revolution, used methods which seemed proper to our purpose, and which were just as low and vile as that purpose."

Vera Wassiljovna pushed back her chair. "That is disgusting," she said. "It makes you sick the way he crawls on his belly."

She put aside the newspaper and began noisily to clear away Primus and glasses. Wassilij watched her. The hot tea had given him courage. He sat up in bed.

"Don't you imagine that you understand," he said. "God knows what was in his mind when he said that. The Party has taught you all to be cunning, and whoever becomes too cunning loses all decency. It's no good shrugging your shoulders," he went on angrily. "It's come to this in the world now that cleverness and decency are at loggerheads, and whoever sides with one must do without the other. It's not good for a man to work things out too much. That's why it is written: 'Let your communication be, Yea, yea; Nay, nay; for whatever is more than these cometh of evil.' "

He let himself sink back on the mattress and turned away his head, so as not to see the face his daughter would make. He had not contradicted her so bravely for a long time. Anything might come of it, once she had it in her mind that she wanted the room for herself and her husband. One had to be cunning in this life, after all —else one might in one's old age go to prison or have to sleep under the bridges in the cold. There one had it: either one behaved cleverly or one behaved decently: the two did not go together.

"I will now read you the end," announced the daughter.

The Public Prosecutor had finished his cross-examination of Rubashov. Following it, the accused Kieffer was examined once more; he repeated his preceding statement on the attempted assassination in full detail. ". . . Asked by the President whether he desired to put any questions to Kieffer, which he would be entitled to do, the accused Rubashov answered that he would forgo this right. This concluded the hearing of evidence and the Court was adjourned. After the re-opening of the sitting, the Citizen Public Prosecutor begins his summing-up. . . ."

Old Wassilij was not listening to the Prosecutor's speech. He had turned to the wall and gone to sleep. He did not know afterwards how long he had slept, how often the daughter had refilled the lamp with oil, nor how often her forefinger had reached the bottom of the page and started on a new column. He only woke up when the Public Prosecutor, summing up his speech, demanded the death sentence. Perhaps the daughter had changed her tone of voice towards the end, perhaps she had made a pause; in any case, Wassilij was awake again when she came to the last sentence of the Public Prosecutor's speech, printed in heavy black type:

"I demand that all these mad dogs be shot."

Then the accused were allowed to say their last words. ". . . The accused Kieffer turned to the judges and begged that, in consideration of his youth, his life be spared. He admitted once again the baseness of his crime and tried to attribute the whole responsibility for it to the instigator Rubashov. In so doing, he started to stammer agitatedly, thus provoking the mirth of the spectators, which was, however, rapidly suppressed by the Citizen President. Then Rubashov was allowed to speak. . . ."

The newspaper reporter here vividly depicted how the accused Rubashov "examined the audience with eager eyes and, finding not a single sympathetic face, let his head sink despairingly".

Rubashov's final speech was short. It intensified the

unpleasant impression which his behaviour in court had already made.

"Citizen President," the accused Rubashov declared, "I speak here for the last time in my life. The opposition is beaten and destroyed. If I ask myself to-day, 'For what am I dying?' I am confronted by absolute nothingness. There is nothing for which one could die, if one died without having repented and unreconciled with the Party and the Movement. Therefore, on the threshold of my last hour, I bend my knees to the country, to the masses and to the whole people. The political masquerade, the mummery of discussions and conspiracy are over. We were politically dead long before the Citizen Prosecutor demanded our heads. Woe unto the defeated, whom history treads into the dust. I have only one justification before you, Citizen Judges: that I did not make it easy for myself. Vanity and the last remains of pride whispered to me: Die in silence, say nothing; or die with a noble gesture, with a moving swan-song on your lips; pour out your heart and challenge your accusers. That would have been easier for an old rebel, but I overcame the temptation. With that my task is ended. I have paid; my account with history is settled. To ask you for mercy would be derision. I have nothing more to say."

". . . After a short deliberation, the President read the sentence. The Council of the Supreme Revolutionary Court of Justice sentenced the accused in every case to the maximum penalty: death by shooting and the confiscation of all their personal property."

The old man Wassilij stared at the rusty hook above his head. He murmured:

"Thy will be done. Amen,"
and turned to the wall.

2

So now it was all over. Rubashov knew that before midnight he would have ceased to exist.

He wandered through his cell, to which he had returned after the uproar of the trial; six and a half steps to the window, six and a half steps back. When he stood still, listening, on the third black tile from the window, the silence between the whitewashed walls came to meet him, as from the depth of a well. He still did not understand why it had become so quiet, within and without. But he knew that now nothing could disturb this peace any more.

Looking back, he could even remember the moment when this blessed quietness had sunk over him. It had been at the trial, before he had started his last speech. He had believed that he had burnt out the last vestiges of egotism and vanity from his consciousness, but in that moment, when his eyes had searched the faces of the audience and found only indifference and derision, he had been for a last time carried away by his hunger for a bone of pity; freezing, he had wanted to warm himself by his own words. The temptation had gripped him to talk of his past, to rear up just once and tear the net in which Ivanov and Gletkin had entangled him, to shout at his accusers like Danton: "You have laid hands on my whole life. May it rise and challenge you. . . ." Oh, how well he knew Danton's speech before the Revolutionary Tribunal. He could repeat it word for word. He had as a boy learnt it by heart: "You want to stifle the Republic in blood. How long must the footsteps of freedom be gravestones? Tyranny is afoot; she has torn her veil, she carries her head high, she strides over our dead bodies."

The words had burnt on his tongue. But the temptation had only lasted a moment; then, when he started to pronounce his final speech, the bell of silence had sunk down over him. He had recognized that it was too late.

Too late to go back again the same way, to step once more in the graves of his own footprints. Words could undo nothing.

Too late for all of them. When the hour came to make their last appearance before the world, none of them could turn the dock into a rostrum, none of them could unveil the truth to the world and hurl back the accusation at his judges, like Danton.

Some were silenced by physical fear, like Hare-lip; some hoped to save their heads; others at least to save their wives or sons from the clutches of the Gletkins. The best of them kept silent in order to do a last service to the Party, by letting themselves be sacrificed as scape-goats—and, besides, even the best had each an Arlova on his conscience. They were too deeply entangled in their own past, caught in the web they had spun them-selves, according to the laws of their own twisted ethics and twisted logic; they were all guilty, although not of those deeds of which they accused themselves. There was no way back for them. Their exit from the stage happened strictly according to the rules of their strange game. The public expected no swan-songs of them. They had to act according to the text-book, and their part was the howling of wolves in the night. . . .

So now it was over. He had nothing more to do with it. He no longer had to howl with the wolves. He had paid, his account was settled. He was a man who had lost his shadow, released from every bond. He had fol-lowed every thought to its last conclusion and acted in accordance with it to the very end; the hours which re-mained to him belonged to that silent partner, whose realm started just where logical thought ended. He had christened it the "grammatical fiction" with that shame-facedness about the first person singular which the Party had inculcated in its disciples.

Rubashov stopped by the wall which separated him from No. 406. The cell was empty since the departure of Rip Van Winkle. He took off his pince-nez, looked round furtively and tapped:

2—4 . . .

He listened with a feeling of childlike shame and then knocked again:

2—4 . . .

He listened, and again repeated the same sequence of signs. The wall remained mute. He had never yet con-sciously tapped the word "I". Probably never at all. He listened. The knocking died without resonance.

He continued pacing through his cell. Since the bell

of silence had sunk over him, he was puzzling over certain questions to which he would have like to find an
answer before it was too late. They were rather naïve
questions; they concerned the meaning of suffering, or,
more exactly, the difference between suffering which made
sense and senseless suffering. Obviously only such suffering made sense as was inevitable; that is, as was
rooted in biological fatality. On the other hand, all suffering with a social origin was accidental, hence point-
less and senseless. The sole object of revolution was the
abolition of senseless suffering. But it had turned out
that the removal of this second kind of suffering was
only possible at the price of a temporary enormous increase in the sum total of the first. So the question now
ran: Was such an operation justified? Obviously it was,
if one spoke in the abstract of "mankind"; but, applied
to "man" in the singular, to the cipher 2—4, the real
human being of bone and flesh and blood and skin,
the principle led to absurdity. As a boy, he had believed
that in working for the Party he would find an answer to
all questions of this sort. The work had lasted forty
years, and right at the start he had forgotten the question for whose sake he had embarked on it. Now the
forty years were over, and he returned to the boy's
original perplexity. The Party had taken all he had to
give and never supplied him with the answer. And neither
did the silent partner, whose magic name he had tapped
on the wall of the empty cell. He was deaf to direct
questions, however urgent and desperate they might be.

    And yet there were ways of approach to him. Some-
times he would respond unexpectedly to a tune, or even
the memory of a tune, or of the folded hands of the
Pietà, or of certain scenes of his childhood. As if a
tuning-fork had been struck, there would be answering
vibrations, and once this had started a state would be
produced which the mystics called "ecstasy" and saints
"contemplation"; the greatest and soberest of modern
psychologists had recognized this state as a fact and
called it the "oceanic sense". And, indeed, one's personality dissolved as a grain of salt in the sea; but at

the same time the infinite sea seemed to be contained in the grain of salt. The grain could no longer be localized in time and space. It was a state in which thought lost its direction and started to circle, like the compass needle at the magnetic pole; until finally it cut loose from its axis and travelled freely in space, like a bunch of light in the night; and until it seemed that all thoughts and all sensations, even pain and joy itself, were only the spectrum lines of the same ray of light, disintegrating in the prisma of consciousness.

Rubashov wandered through his cell. In old days he would have shamefacedly denied himself this sort of childish musing. Now he was not ashamed. In death the metaphysical became real. He stopped at the window and leaned his forehead against the pane. Over the machine-gun tower one could see a patch of blue. It was pale, and reminded him of that particular blue which he had seen overhead when as a boy he lay on the grass in his father's park, watching the poplar branches slowly moving against the sky. Apparently even a patch of blue sky was enough to cause the "oceanic state'". He had read that, according to the latest discoveries of astrophysics, the volume of the world was finite—though space had no boundaries, it was self-contained, like the surface of a sphere. He had never been able to understand that; but now he felt an urgent desire to understand. He now also remembered where he had read about it: during his first arrest in Germany, comrades had smuggled a sheet of the illegally printed Party organ into the cell; at the top were three columns about a strike in a spinning-mill; at the bottom of a column, as a stop-gap, was printed in tiny letters the discovery that the universe was finite, and halfway through it the page was torn off. He had never found out what had been in the torn-off part.

Rubashov stood by the window and tapped on the empty wall with his pince-nez. As a boy he had really meant to study astronomy, and now for forty years he had been doing something else. Why had not the Public Prosecutor asked him: "Defendant Rubashov, what about

the infinite?" He would not have been able to answer—
and there, there lay the real source of his guilt. . . .
Could there be a greater?

When he had read that newspaper notice, then also
alone in his cell, with joints still sore from the last bout
of torturing, he had fallen into a queer state of exaltation
—the "oceanic sense" had swept him away. Afterwards
he had been ashamed of himself. The Party disapproved
of such states. It called them *petit-bourgeois* mysticism,
refuge in the ivory tower. It called them "escape from
the task", "desertion of the class struggle". The "oceanic
sense" was counter-revolutionary.

For in a struggle one must have both legs firmly
planted on the earth. The Party taught one how to do
it. The infinite was a politically suspect quantity, the "I"
a suspect quality. The Party did not recognize its
existence. The definition of the individual was: a multi-
tude of one million divided by one million.

The Party denied the free will of the individual—and
at the same time it exacted his willing self-sacrifice. It
denied his capacity to choose between two alternatives
—and at the same time it demanded that he should constantly choose the right one. It denied his power to distinguish good and evil—and at the same time it spoke
pathetically of guilt and treachery. The individual stood
under the sign of economic fatality, a wheel in a clockwork which had been wound up for all eternity and
could not be stopped or influenced—and the Party demanded that the wheel should revolt against the clockwork and change its course. There was somewhere an
error in the calculation; the equation did not work out.

For forty years he had fought against economic
fatality. It was the central ill of humanity, the cancer
which was eating into its entrails. It was there that one
must operate; the rest of the healing process would follow. All else was dilettantism, romanticism, charlatanism.
One cannot heal a person mortally ill by pious exhorta-
tions. The only solution was the surgeon's knife and his
cool calculation. But wherever the knife had been applied,

a new sore had appeared in place of the old. And again the equation did not work out.

For forty years he had lived strictly in accordance with the vows of his order, the Party. He had held to the rules of logical calculation. He had burnt the remains of the old, illogical morality from his consciousness with the acid of reason. He had turned away from the temptations of the silent partner, and had fought against the "oceanic sense" with all his might. And where had it landed him? Premises of unimpeachable truth had led to a result which was completely absurd; Ivanov's and Gletkin's irrefutable deductions had taken him straight into the weird and ghostly game of the public trial. Perhaps it was not suitable for a man to think every thought to its logical conclusion.

Rubashov stared through the bars of the window at the patch of blue above the machine-gun tower. Looking back over his past, it seemed to him now that for forty years he had been running amuck—the running-amuck of pure reason. Perhaps it did not suit man to be completely freed from old bonds, from the steadying brakes of "Thou shalt not" and "Thou mayst not", and to be allowed to tear along straight towards the goal.

The blue had begun to turn pink, dusk was falling; round the tower a flock of dark birds was circling with slow, deliberate wing-beats. No, the equation did not work out. It was obviously not enough to direct man's eyes towards a goal and put a knife in his hand; it was unsuitable for him to experiment with a knife. Perhaps later, one day. For the moment he was still too young and awkward. How he had raged in the great field of experiment, the Fatherland of the Revolution, the Bastion of Freedom! Gletkin justified everything that happened with the principle that the bastion must be preserved. But what did it look like inside? No, one cannot build Paradise with concrete. The bastion would be preserved, but it no longer had a message, nor an example to give the world. No 1's régime had besmirched the ideal of the Social state even as some Mediæval Popes had besmirched the ideal of a Christian Empire. The flag of the Revolution was at half-mast.

Rubashov wandered through his cell. It was quiet and nearly dark. It could not be long before they came to fetch him. There was an error somewhere in the equation—no, in the whole mathematical system of thought. He had had an inkling of it for a long time already, since the story of Richard and the *Pietà*, but had never dared to admit it to himself fully. Perhaps the Revolution had come too early, an abortion with monstrous, deformed limbs. Perhaps the whole thing had been a bad mistake in timing. The Roman civilization, too, had seemed to be doomed as early as the first century B.C.; had seemed as rotten to the marrow as our own; then, too, the best had believed that the time was ripe for a great change; and yet the old worn-out world had held out for another five hundred years. History had a slow pulse; man counted in years, history in generations. Perhaps it was still only the second day of creation. How he would have liked to live and build up the theory of the relative maturity of the masses! . . .

It was quiet in the cell. Rubashov heard only the creaking of his steps on the tiles. Six and a half steps to the door, whence they must come to fetch him, six and a half steps to the window, behind which night was falling. Soon it would be over. But when he asked himself, For what actually are you dying? he found no answer.

It was a mistake in the system; perhaps it lay in the precept which until now he had held to be uncontestable, in whose name he had sacrificed others and was himself being sacrificed: in the precept, that the end justifies the means. It was this sentence which had killed the great fraternity of the Revolution and made them all run amuck. What had he once written in his diary? "We have thrown overboard all conventions, our sole guiding principle is that of consequent logic; we are sailing without ethical ballast."

Perhaps the heart of the evil lay there. Perhaps it did not suit mankind to sail without ballast. And perhaps reason alone was a defective compass, which led one on such a winding, twisted course that the goal finally disappeared in the mist.

Perhaps now would come the time of great darkness.

Perhaps later, much later, the new movement would arise—with new flags, a new spirit knowing of both: of economic fatality *and* the "oceanic sense". Perhaps the members of the new party will wear monks' cowls, and preach that only purity of means can justify the ends. Perhaps they will teach that the tenet is wrong which says that a man is the quotient of one million divided by one million, and will introduce a new kind of arithmetic based on multiplication: on the joining of a million individuals to form a new entity which, no longer an amorphous mass, will develop a consciousness and an individuality of its own, with an "oceanic feeling" increased a millionfold, in unlimited yet self-contained space.

Rubashov broke off his pacing and listened. The sound of muffled drumming came down the corridor.

3

The drumming sounded as though it were brought from the distance by the wind; it was still far, it was coming closer. Rubashov did not stir. His legs on the tiles were no longer subject to his will; he felt the earth's force of gravity slowly mounting in them. He took three steps backwards to the window, without taking his eye off the spy-hole. He breathed deeply and lit a cigarette. He heard a ticking in the wall next to the bunk:

THEY ARE FETCHING HARE-LIP. HE SENDS YOU HIS GREETINGS.

The heaviness vanished from his legs. He went to the door and started to beat against the metal quickly and rhythmically with the flat of both hands. To pass the news on to No. 406 was no use now. The cell stood empty; the chain broke off there. He drummed and pressed his eye to the spy-hole.

In the corridor the dim electric light was burning as always. He saw the iron doors of No. 401 to No. 407, as always. The drumming swelled. Steps approached,

slow and dragging, one heard them distinctly on the tiles.
Suddenly Hare-lip was standing in the spy-hole's range
of vision. He stood there, with trembling lips, as he had
stood in the light of the reflector in Gletkin's room; his
hands in handcuffs hung down behind his back in a
peculiarly twisted position. He could not see Rubashov's eye behind the judas and looked at the door with
blind, searching pupils, as though the last hope of salvation lay behind it. Then an order was spoken, and Hare-
lip obediently turned to go. Behind him came the giant
in uniform with his revolver-belt. They disappeared from
Rubashov's field of vision, one behind the other.

The drumming faded; all was quiet again. From the
wall next to the bunk came the sound of ticking:

HE BEHAVED QUITE WELL. . . .

Since the day when Rubashov had informed No. 402
of his capitulation, they had not spoken to each other.
No. 402 went on:

YOU STILL HAVE ABOUT TEN MINUTES. HOW
DO YOU FEEL?

Rubashov understood that No. 402 had started the
conversation in order to make waiting easier for him.
He was grateful for it. He sat down on the bunk and
tapped back:

I WISH IT WERE OVER ALREADY. . . .

YOU WON'T SHOW THE WHITE FEATHER,
tapped No. 402. WE KNOW YOU'RE THE DEVIL OF
A FELLOW. . . . He paused, then, quickly, repeated
his last words: THE DEVIL OF A FELLOW . . . . He
was obviously anxious to prevent the conversation coming
to a standstill. DO YOU STILL REMEMBER
'BREASTS LIKE CHAMPAGNE GLASSES'? HA-HA!
THE DEVIL OF A FELLOW. . . .

Rubashov listened for a sound in the corridor. One
heard nothing. No. 402 seemed to guess his thoughts, for
he at once tapped again:

DON'T LISTEN. I WILL TELL YOU IN TIME
WHEN THEY ARE COMING. . . . WHAT WOULD
YOU DO IF YOU WERE PARDONED?

Rubashov thought it over. Then he tapped:

STUDY ASTRONOMY.

HA-HA! expressed No. 402. I, TOO, PERHAPS.
PEOPLE SAY OTHER STARS ARE PERHAPS ALSO
INHABITED. PERMIT ME TO GIVE YOU SOME
ADVICE.

CERTAINLY, answered Rubashov, surprised.

BUT DON'T TAKE IT ILL. TECHNICAL SUG-
GESTION OF A SOLDIER. EMPTY YOUR BLAD-
DER. IS ALWAYS BETTER IN SUCH CASES. THE
SPIRIT IS WILLING BUT THE FLESH IS WEAK.
HA-HA!

Rubashov smiled and went obediently to the bucket.
Then he sat down again on the bunk and tapped:

THANKS. EXCELLENT IDEA. AND WHAT ARE
YOUR PROSPECTS?

No. 402 was silent for a few seconds. Then he tapped,
rather slower than he had before:

EIGHTEEN YEARS MORE. NOT QUITE, ONLY
6,530 DAYS. . . . He paused. Then he added:

I ENVY YOU REALLY. And then, after another
pause: THINK OF IT—ANOTHER 6,530 NIGHTS
WITHOUT A WOMAN.

Rubashov said nothing. Then he tapped:

BUT YOU CAN READ, STUDY. . . .

HAVEN'T GOT THE HEAD FOR IT, tapped No.
402. And then, loud and hurriedly: THEY'RE COMING.
. . .

He stopped, but a few seconds later, added:

A PITY. WE WERE JUST HAVING SUCH A
PLEASANT CHAT. . . .

Rubashov stood up from the bunk. He thought a
moment and then tapped:

YOU HELPED ME A LOT. THANKS.

The key ground in the lock. The door flew open. Outside stood the giant in uniform and a civilian. The civilian
called Rubashov by name and reeled off a text from a
document. While they twisted his arms behind his back
and put on the handcuffs, he heard No. 402 hastily tapping:

I ENVY YOU. I ENVY YOU. FAREWELL.

In the corridor outside, the drumming had started again. It accompanied them till they reached the barber's room. Rubashov knew that from behind each iron door an eye was looking at him through the spy-hole, but he turned his head neither to the left nor to the right. The handcuffs grazed his wrists; the giant had screwed them too tightly and had strained his arms while twisting them behind his back; they were hurting.

The cellar steps came in sight. Rubashov slowed down his pace. The civilian stopped at the top of the steps. He was small and had slightly protuberant eyes. He asked:

"Have you another wish?"

"None," said Rubashov, and started to climb down the cellar steps. The civilian remained standing above and looked down at him with his protuberant eyes.

The stairs were narrow and badly lit. Rubashov had to be careful not to stumble, as he could not hold on to the stair rail. The drumming had ceased. He heard the man in uniform descending three steps behind him.

The stairs turned in a spiral. Rubashov bent forward to see better; his pince-nez detached itself from his face and fell to the ground two steps below him; splintering, it rebounded lower down and remained lying on the bottom step. Rubashov stopped a second, hesitatingly; then he felt his way down the rest of the steps. He heard the man behind him bend down and put the broken pince-nez in his pocket, but did not turn his head.

He was now nearly blind, but he had solid ground under his feet again. A long corridor received him; its walls were blurred and he could not see the end of it. The man in uniform kept always three steps behind him. Rubashov felt his gaze in the back of his neck, but did not turn his head. Cautiously he put one foot before the other.

It seemed to him that they had been walking along this corridor for several minutes already. Still nothing happened. Probably he would hear when the man in uniform took the revolver out of its case. So until then there was time, he was still in safety. Or did the man behind him proceed like the dentist, who hid his instruments in his sleeve while bending over his patient? Rubashov tried to think of something else, but had to concentrate his whole attention to prevent himself from turning his head.

Strange that his toothache had ceased in the minute when that blessed silence had closed round him, during the trial. Perhaps the abscess had opened just in that minute. What had he said to them? "I bow my knees before the country, before the masses, before the whole people. . . ." And what then? What happened to these masses, to this people? For forty years it had been driven through the desert, with threats and promises, with imaginary terrors and imaginary rewards. But where was the Promised Land?

Did there really exist any such goal for this wandering mankind? That was a question to which he would have liked an answer before it was too late. Moses had not been allowed to enter the land of promise either. But he had been allowed to see it, from the top of the mountain, spread at his feet. Thus, it was easy to die, with the visible certainty of one's goal before one's eyes. He, Nicolas Salmanovitch Rubashov, had not been taken to the top of a mountain; and wherever his eye looked, he saw nothing but desert and the darkness of night.

A dull blow struck the back of his head. He had long expected it and yet it took him unawares. He felt, wondering, his knees give way and his body whirl round in a half-turn. How theatrical, he thought as he fell, and yet I feel nothing. He lay crumpled up on the ground, with his cheek on the cool flagstones. It got dark, the sea carried him rocking on its nocturnal surface. Memories passed through him, like streaks of mist over the water.

Outside, someone was knocking on the front door, he dreamed that they were coming to arrest him; but in what country was he?

He made an effort to slip his arm into his dressing-gown sleeve. But whose colour-print portrait was hanging over his bed and looking at him?

Was it No. 1 or was it the other—he with the ironic smile or he with the glassy gaze?

A shapeless figure bent over him, he smelt the fresh leather of the revolver belt; but what insignia did the figure wear on the sleeves and shoulder-straps of its uniform—and in whose name did it raise the dark pistol barrel?

A second, smashing blow hit him on the ear. Then all became quiet. There was the sea again with its sounds. A wave slowly lifted him up. It came from afar and travelled sedately on, a shrug of eternity.